COMMUNITY DAY

Andy Smarick

For Kathie, Will, Eddie, and Maisie— the greatest family a husband and dad could ever wish to have.

The world will someday get me on some ludicrous pretext; I simply await the day that they drag me to some air-conditioned dungeon and leave me there beneath the fluorescent lights and soundproofed ceiling to pay the price for scorning all that they hold dear within their little latex hearts.

—IGNATIUS J. REILLY, A CONFEDERACY OF DUNCES

CONTENTS

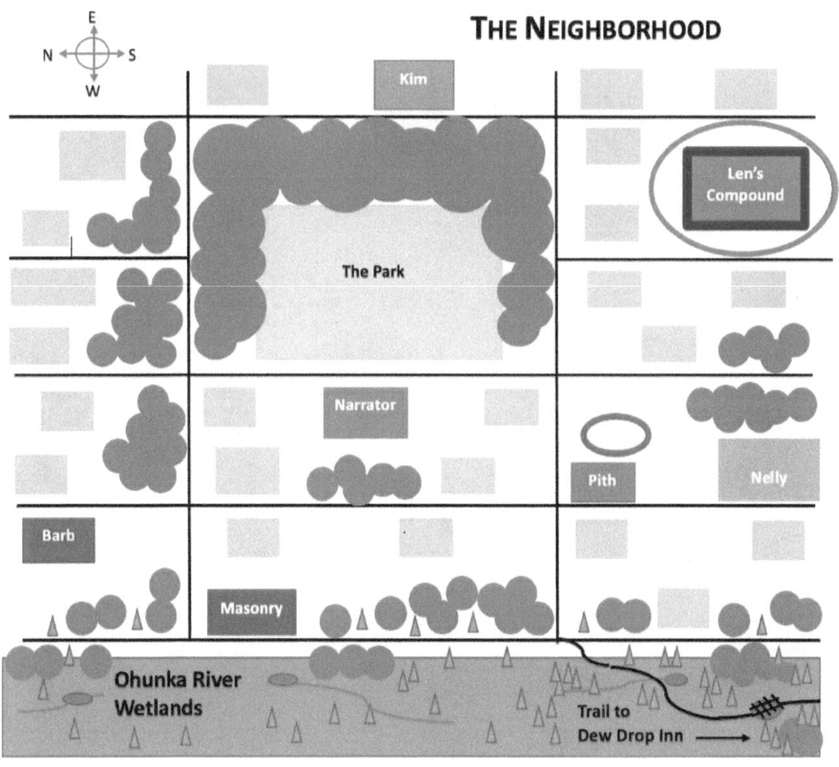
THE NEIGHBORHOOD
E
N
S
W
Kim
Len's Compound
The Park
Narrator
Pith
Nelly
Barb
Masonry
Ohunka River Wetlands
Trail to Dew Drop Inn

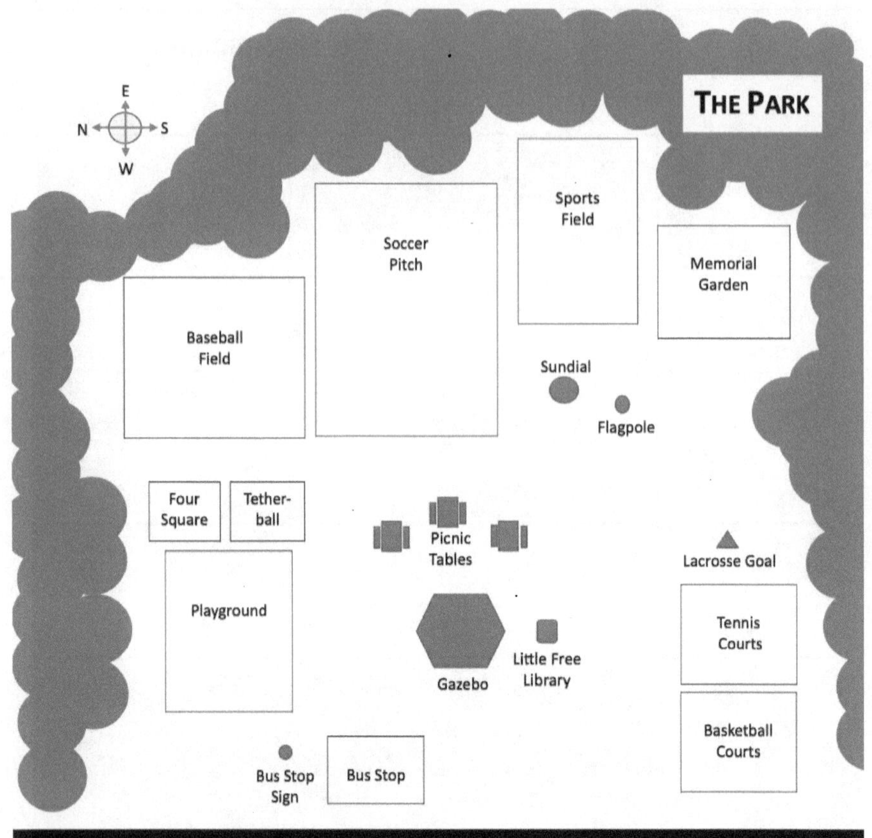
E
N
S
W
THE PARK
Sports Field
Soccer Pitch
Memorial Garden
Baseball Field
Sundial
Flagpole
Four Square
Tether-ball
Picnic Tables
Lacrosse Goal
Playground
Tennis Courts
Gazebo
Little Free Library
Basketball Courts
Bus Stop Sign
Bus Stop
Narrator's House

PROLOGUE

From: Executive Office [INTERNAL]
Date: December 30, 2020 at 2:12 PM
Subject: Assignment
To: Elizabeth Jones [INTERNAL]

Lizzy: You wanted more opportunities. Be careful what you wish for. I'm assigning you to the guy from the mass casualty event at the neighborhood park. Get on it. Initial folders are in the front office. You need to get him to explain. Just make it happen.

Also, you need to contact Jennifer Davis yesterday. Her info is on top with the memo from the judge.

Now listen. Everyone wants this done fast. Everyone. Figure out what in God's name happened. Serve your client. Roll credits. Welcome to the big league.
-M

Office of the State Public Defender
Fiat justitia ruat caelum

Part 1:

The Park

Chapter 1: Initiation

START: 12:25pm
Saturday, January 2, 2021
C.C.S.H.

I would've bet every dollar I had and every cent I could've borrowed that Nelly's RV-and-camper dealership was nothing but a money-laundering operation. I had no proof yet, but I felt it in my bones.

I first came across Nelly maybe six or seven years ago, not all that long after we moved into that spacious neighborhood in that rural county. Her house was a block and a half from ours, about a half mile to our southwest. Each night, while taking my walk, I'd see her jogging—well, more like scurrying—with her amiable, simple-minded golden retriever.

Nelly, on the younger side of middle-aged, is 4 feet and 11 ¾ inches of frayed nerves. Even while running, her pupils are dilated, her head always on a swivel, her bouncing, tightly pulled, coffee-black ponytail hiding behind one shoulder then taking cover behind the other. Though she always wears gray running tights and a white headband, she has a variety of blaze-orange t-shirts and pullovers so all dangers—hunters, approaching cars, falling leaves—can spot her from a country mile off. I remember thinking back then that her skittishness was especially odd because we lived in the most uneventful community. I had much to learn.

I asked around, and just about everyone said that Nelly had been on edge for as long as they could remember. Word was, though, that she had started listening to meditation podcasts to practice mindfulness and universal love. Good on her.

But it didn't take. Not long after that I saw her slam her headphones to the ground and swear like a scurvy sailor: She'd been startled by an artless squirrel engaged in completely standard squirrel behavior. Her grievances not yet fully aired, she then dressed down her oblivious dog for not protecting her. To his credit he handled the scolding with grace—eyes straight ahead, tongue dangling. I'm sure, though, that deep down he felt ashamed for lacking his owner's ability to see danger where none exists.

As far as I could tell, Nelly's dealership hadn't sold a vehicle in eons. Prior to Covid, I'd drop by out of neighborliness and to snoop around. I sensed that all the "customers" milling about were props paid to camouflage her grift. If I'm being honest, part of me found it hard to believe that Nelly's anxiety would allow for a life of crime: Eventually the IRS or some other busybody government agency would start looking into how she came to own a three-story Victorian on nearly two acres when her entire inventory was collecting dust. Heck, if harmless wildlife sent her into a panic, she'd fold fast under interrogation.

You know, I shouldn't be so glib about Nelly. That was an unfair introduction. Of all the characters you're about to meet, I'm not sure if anyone is more admirable than Nelly. And that's the truth. Yes, she was part of the problem with the old community. No doubt about that. But so were most of us. Myself included, I confess. The difference is that she admitted it. She repented and changed before anyone else. She's the model. We owe her. She's going to keep doing great things for that place. I just know it.

But back then, before I understood everything, I couldn't muster much compassion for her. She projected. Constantly. She imagined the unseemliest things about our neighbors. In Nelly's uneasy mind, the loveliest, boringest person harbored impure thoughts or was neck-deep in some illicit side-hustle. She had at least 10 distinct facial expressions—raised eyebrow, pursed lips, Edvard-Munch scream, Macauley-Culkin-*Home-Alone* scream, and so on—that she could pair with her groundless-innuendo catch phrase, "You have to wonder what's going on there..."

In particular, she had it out for two neighbors I rather liked. The first is Masonry Brown. He's easily the grouchiest non-rabid mammal I've ever come across. Yikes, that guy. It's like he's fueled by bile. I guess I found him entertaining at that point. Certainly an original. Antagonized for sport. Short fuse. Unkempt bowl cut. Patchy facial hair. His protruding forehead and wild, bushy eyebrows made his permanent glower almost cartoonish. Almost. A barrel of monkeys he ain't. Sure, it was odd that he spent 10-15 hours each weekend moving bricks around his yard for no apparent reason. But I found that quirky, not as evidence that he was building a crypt, *Nelly*.

The other is Pith-Helmet Smith (Nelly's next-door neighbor). He's as affable and generous as the day is long. No ego, no vanity. T-shirts and jeans. Shaves his head ever since his hairline beat a retreat. Crazy-tall and wiry. All arms and legs. Slouched shoulders and head tilted down like he's charting the terrain. I think he works in a pawn shop that specializes in wigs. Seriously, I couldn't make that up. He's forever belly-laughing and giving bear hugs—well, before fist bumps replaced hugs—that inevitably spill the contents of his ever-present red-plastic party cup. Good dude. I simply stay away from him after 6pm and when he gets into his golf cart.

* * *

Not long before the pandemic took hold, I mentioned to my wife that Nelly probably got the world's most lovable and uncomplicated dog so she could have one thing in her life unworthy of a conspiracy theory. My wife, not wanting my head to swell over this latest brilliant insight, said I was being "utterly irrational again." The way she paused ever so slightly before the "again" was expert. She claimed Nelly was "entirely normal—she knits and does jigsaw puzzles for goodness sakes!"—and that, despite the tough things she'd been through, Nelly had remained "loyal, tender, and conscientious."

My wife must've intuited that I was unpersuaded after I said, "You're nuts—Nelly's paranoid." Without missing a beat, she replied, correctly as it turns out, that the world could use more Nellies. But she also said, incorrectly, that the world could use fewer "delusional middle-aged guys prattling on about advanced basketball analytics and Star Wars fanfic." My wife and I have different hobbies.

She also said that instead of "concocting poppycock" about Nelly, I should spend some time getting to know her better at the upcoming spring Community Day at the park—yes, yes, *that* Community Day. I declined. With utmost sensitivity, I explained to my wife that Nelly would have a massive stroke if an Adonis-like figure talked to her out of the blue and that I'd prefer not to have that on my conscience. My wife kissed me on the forehead and replied that she didn't realize Adonis ate so many Buffalo wings or showed signs of male-pattern baldness. Obviously, I refused to dignify that unfounded personal attack with a response. My build is stout; my hairline distinguished.

I quietly calculated: If I were to prove that Nelly side-eyes even the gracious and pure, I'd need a better Exhibit A than Masonry. He's an acquired taste. So I asked my wife if it was "conscientiousness" that caused Nelly to scorn the ever-charming Pith, who serves up cheer wherever he goes. My wife sighed and said that there was more to the Nelly-Pith story. She also said that I knew full well that Pith had crashed his golf cart into Nelly's rhododendrons twice in the last week. I grudgingly conceded that my wife might have the makings of a point there.

Then she followed up, without provocation I might add, "I love you, but, dear God, you need to stop this 'Pith' business! His name is Bob. *Bob*! You know that. He wore a pith helmet once, and that was on Halloween years ago! Stop it."

My wife had become unreasonable because she saw I was winning this argument in a landslide. So, in the spirit of marital harmony, I aggressively pressed my advantage. I asked if it was "conscientiousness" that caused Nelly to freak out anytime she saw that old scamp Blowtorch Len McGregor or even heard his name. My wife gave me her exasperated look, one I'd gotten to know reasonably well during our 13 years of marriage, and said, "That ancient man is an unhinged, dangerous kook. And from what I hear there's *way* more to the Len-Nelly story."

I was sure she'd fabricated that mysterious tidbit in a desperate attempt to recover in our debate. She completely ignored my celebratory dance, and said, "Unless you're careful, Blowtorch Len is your future."

It takes a great deal of humility to make a marriage work, and I have that in spades. So I said to my loving wife, "I've again drubbed you in an argument. I'm the greatest of all time." Over the years, I've learned that laughing, rolling her eyes, and walking away is her style of surrender.

* * *

When we met, my wife had just graduated college, and I was only a few years out. The first time I saw her...I'm telling you... it was a bolt of lightning. I knew in that moment...I'll never forget—under the foggy fluorescent ceiling light above the vending machine with the Pop Tarts and Rice Krispie Treats —I knew that we'd be together forever. It sounds made-up... schmaltzy movie stuff. I can't explain it. But I knew for certain.

To be honest, it took her a good deal longer to acquire that knowledge. She's the measure-twice-cut-once type. But eventually she came to the same conclusion. Or a similar one, at least.

It wasn't just that she was gorgeous. I could tell—maybe intuition or a lucky guess... wishful thinking? —but I could tell that she was generous and affectionate. Understanding. Steady. I knew all that in an instant. Unbelievable when you think about it.

We were both working in the capital for the state legislature. This was back in 2003. I was running the leadership office of the state Senate, and she was an analyst in the finance office. We were both fueling up with snacks before an appropriations meeting. Second level of the statehouse, late on a Wednesday afternoon. She had on a black, gray, and burgundy plaid skirt, a burgundy turtleneck sweater, black tights, chunky shoes, and a thin gold necklace with a cross. It was August, but she had on a turtleneck sweater and tights!

She was a wisp of a slip of a thing. Dark pixie-ish hair—short in the back and on the sides, a little longer on top. When she was thinking hard, she'd unconsciously move her index finger along her forehead, guiding her bangs toward her right ear. She had hazel eyes and phalanx-thick eyelashes.

She quickly became a fixture at important meetings. She had all but memorized the state's budget during her three months on the job and could do insanely hard calculations in her head. The older men called her Rain Man; the older women detested her. While others were talking, she kept her head down and doodled minuscule, adjoining circles on a small white notepad. But she was always listening, always prepared when asked a question. Her responses were succinct. The haters whispered about her. Said she was haughty. But I knew better: She just didn't like the spotlight.

When she got nervous, she'd squint and pull her lips backward over her teeth, like she wanted to cushion all the words she was preventing from escaping her mouth. She had the fullest lips I'd ever seen. But she'd never, ever wear red lipstick. She would've thought it gaudy. Or needy.

My boss—she was still the newly elected Senate president at this point—somehow figured out I was smitten. One afternoon, she called me into her office, scowling. She told me to close the door. I girded myself. She's a straight shooter; once, a cranky, old editorial writer called her "brassy," and she framed the column and put it on her office wall.

I had no idea why she wanted to talk in private. I assumed it was a state emergency, like a tornado or budget crisis. I brought a notepad, sat at her conference table, and pulled out a chair for her. But she stood in the middle of the office in her navy pinstripe power suit, exhaled in aggravation and said—I'll never forget this—"Boy, you could be at ease talking to a farmer, a thief, or the Queen of England! But that cute numbers girl ties you in knots! Enough already. Cowboy up!"

I'm sure I turned beet-red. But I composed myself and came clean. I needed that push. I'd never gotten that kind of advice... my dad hadn't...let's just say I needed that push. Anyway, I made a plan. I started jotting down topics we might talk about.

You know, various levels of familiarity so I'd have material regardless of the situation. Municipal bonds, news events, magazines, favorite restaurants and movies. Books.

True story: Sometimes when I was alone in my apartment, I'd practice what I might say to her. So embarrassing. Eventually, we progressed from pleasantries and pregnant eye contact to work talk and television chatter to jokes about my low-budget dress shirts and her collection of summer winterwear.

She'd transform when she smiled. Her body—forehead, shoulders, tapping left foot—would settle. Her mind and tongue, too. For that moment, a circuit breaker would stop the electricity coursing through her. Soon, I'd do anything to make her laugh. I gave people nicknames and imitated voices and mannerisms. Told her outlandish stories. I could get her to smile. And blush. But blush in a way that caused her to lift her eyes instead of dropping them—if that makes sense? It took months, but when it was just the two of us together, her diffidence-as-self-protection turned into reservation-with-the-door-ajar, if you know what I mean?

I found out when it was her birthday. I wanted to do something special for her. I went to the best department store at the mall. I bought her a burgundy lipstick—I still remember: The shade was called "Confident Claret." God, it was so expensive for what I was making. I waited until she left for lunch, and then I put the box on her desk with a note: "I know that beige nudes are more your style, but I saw this and thought it would match your August turtleneck. Happy birthday."

She never mentioned it. But from that point on, she would look at me for an extra moment when I talked in a meeting. When I said hello to her, she'd raise her chin a pinch higher than would be natural and straighten her back as though she'd prepared in front of a mirror. She'd offhandedly say something about the basketball team I liked. And when we talked, she wouldn't hide her lips. I felt like she was surrendering. No, that's not right.

More like willing herself vulnerable. Like she had accepted a fate with me and was now rehearsing the part.

On my birthday, a full four months later, I was working late. The building was dead. She walked into my office. She was wearing the skirt and the sweater from the day I first saw her. And she had on the lipstick I gave her. She took my breath away. She handed me a wrapped box; inside was an expensive blue-gray dress shirt—far better than any I'd ever owned. She raised her chin and said, "You deserve it. And it matches your eyes."

Before I could ruin the moment with some defense-mechanism joke, she reached her left arm over my right shoulder and placed her hand on the back of my head. She put her right hand on my left cheek and brushed my lips with her thumb. Her perfume smelled like lilacs. Her nail polish was rouge noir. She stared at me, thick eyelashes peaceful and still. Serene. She said quietly, "You know I will never give up on this. Promise me you won't ever take advantage of that." I promised, and then she raised up on her tiptoes and kissed me.

Chapter 2: Orientation

OK, enough of that sap. Back to business. If I'm going to tell you about Community Day 2020, you need to understand our area. And you must understand the park and its defunct bus stop. Only then can you truly appreciate the fall and rise of Nelly, the wit and wisdom of Pith, the ridiculousness and sublimity of Blowtorch Len McGregor, and the comedy and tragedy of Matty. You're in for a ride.

Our neighborhood is just outside of Grangerford, a lightly populated town that's nevertheless the largest in the county. Most folks there believe in law and order, faith and family, tradition and morals, big trucks and small government. Some of that started to change in 2016 with the fluke election of that vile county executive. He only squeaked in because he ran a filthy campaign. Anyway, most families have been in the area for generations. The locals now generally work for the prison, the school system, or what's left of farms in the Ohunka Valley and a few industries extracting what's remaining in the hills to the south.

To find our house, you leave the strip-mall sprawl of any given suburb; cross a bridge or drive to where the speed limit jumps to 75; pass four seasonal farmers' markets, three vape shops, or two tattoo parlors; turn left at the Elks or Moose Lodge that hosts book-release parties for retired men who self-publish tendentious histories of forgotten naval vessels; and then turn right at the American Legion or VFW that hosts poker "fund-raisers" that are legal because the sheriff likes kick-backs.

From our door, it's about 17 miles to the closest library, which is next to the sprawling consignment shop that settled in the space Best Buy abandoned a few years after taking over the lease of the shuttered Ames. A bad traffic day on that stretch of road means getting stuck behind a harvester. There are no office parks or even big shopping centers around, and the nearest major city is 90 minutes away, assuming no harvester has other plans for your schedule. You can see why it was a complete mystery to me how a hinterland neighborhood in a hinterland county came to have its own public bus stop.

But every time I looked down our driveway and across the street to the park, I'd see that forsaken bus-stop sign and wonder.

* * *

The park is carved into a six-acre clearing in the otherwise undeveloped wooded area in the center of our neighborhood. It has the standard amenities: fields, basketball hoops, deer ticks. On most early-spring and late-autumn mornings, the park's north end is covered by a dense mist that burns off as the sun rises above the trees to the east.

On the park's west side, not far from the street, is an octagonal gazebo. It has bench seating along the sides and a circular oak table in the center. It can hold 16 people during non-pandemic times; six when viral loads are on the mind. Every spring, it gets a new coat of white paint whether it needs it or not, compliments of our Homeowners Association dues. Its roof was also recently re-shingled; some other time I'll tell you about the three teenage boys with the ladder and fireworks who necessitated that project.

In the early 1980s, the HOA built a small memorial garden in the southeast corner of the park for residents' family members who gave the ultimate sacrifice in our nation's conflicts. A local craftsman donated a series of bespoke trellises that became the backbone of an expansive arbor shading two benches and a fountain. The midmorning sun illuminates the plaque bearing the names of the departed. Closer to the center of the park, next to the flagpole and near the soccer field, stood the limestone sundial donated by the community's founders.

I met Pith—my lanky, unpretentious, well lubricated pal—at the park during the first Community Day after we'd arrived in 2013. He was wearing a Screaming Trees concert t-shirt, jeans faded and torn by time rather than a stylist, and busted-up original 1985 Jordans that collectors consider "vintage" but he calls "near about broken in." He pointed to a bowl of coleslaw on the gazebo table, leaned down, and whispered to me like we were partners in crime, "Bro, lemme give you some investment advice real quick: Buy all the cabbage you can. Pronto." I surmised he was not a professional wealth manager. But I wasn't sure if he was dense or deranged. I smiled politely.

"Them rich folks will pay triple the price for shredded cabbage," he continued with raised eyebrows, "if you tell 'em it's bok choy." I think I blinked rapidly. I know I was speechless. He concluded his seminar: "I believe the *er-u-dite* call that 'arbitrage.' I call it 'capitalizin' on conspicuous consumption.' Take it to the bank, my man. Cabbage. Real talk."

That's Pith. Simple? No. Genius? Possibly. Distinctive? Thoroughly.

It's hard to place Pith's accent. It has elements of southern Appalachia, Toledo, and Baltimore. My wife once called it "Rust

Belt Cockney;" I think of it as "American cosmopolitan." He and I got closer over the years. When I was still new to the area, he'd introduce me to his infinite acquaintances with, "Meet my bud. He's a come-here but he's alright. Used to be a fancy-pants muckety-muck, but now he's just ordinary folk. My kind of odd duck, I'll tell you what."

I prefer "maverick" to "odd duck," but six of one, half dozen of the other, I guess.

* * *

I learned early on that although the park is meant to be a place for camaraderie, it also plays host to the pettiest conflicts. The American public square with monkey bars. A place for child's play employed by adults. Teens gather there on summer nights and engage in the mildest mischief yet suffer lectures from hectoring grownups that invariably begin, "You should stop and think about what you're doing" or "I've already called the police." It's where those same peevish adults gossip about neighbors while pushing toddlers on swings and drink too much on the 4th of July and then seamlessly segue into, "This ain't gonna be popular, but let me tell you my thoughts on immigration..." Not long after we moved in, two old men got into a fistfight over there while playing euchre.

I also met Masonry (my weasel-mean, brick-moving dear friend) at the park. It was the summer of 2019. He was taking part in a protest just a couple weeks after his family moved into the neighborhood. You see, a group of civic-minded neighbors had taken it upon themselves to build, place, and stock a Little Free Library next to the gazebo so neighbors could share books without the long drive. A different group of civic-minded neighbors assembled to strenuously object to the Little Free Library because it posed a financial and emotional threat to the public library and was probably an anarchist plot to allow book-swapping without proper government-issued library cards.

I strolled over to the park because I saw marching and picket signs and because I like to watch wastes of energy and blossoming intergenerational feuds. Except for the new guy, I recognized all the demonstrators from previous low-stakes, high-intensity community skirmishes (you know, the speed bump on Elm, the wildflowers on Maple). Though he didn't appear to be a man who takes part in regular physical exertion, Masonry was chanting and tramping about with verve. I introduced myself and tried to get his story. I wanted to understand why he'd launch his neighborhood brand by taking sides in a meaningless quarrel.

After rolling his eyes at me and insisting that I must be "a champion-level ignoramus," he explained that he had absolutely no dog in this fight over a "useless and chintzy do-gooder book box." I deduced, accurately as time would tell, that I was in the presence of that special type of man who refused to let an opportunity to make enemies pass him by.

I asked why, if he didn't care about the issue in dispute, he decided to side so passionately with the anti-Little Free Library forces. He said he had flipped a coin, and—then motioning to his protestor colleagues— "these oafs won." He must've sensed that I was confused by his answer because he said, "You seem confused by my answer, numbskull." Exasperated, he explained that in the case of heated disputes, he always supports "the side with the most non-morons. These two groups of dunderheads tied at zero. A coin toss was obviously required." It was hard to argue with his logic.

Before long, Masonry grew bored with or exhausted by the mild exercise and realized there would be plenty of other opportunities to alienate neighbors, so I walked him home. He lives in a gray Cape Cod two blocks to our west, on the fringe of the neighborhood on the last stretch of buildable land before the vast swampy wastelands of the nymph-departed Ohunka river. (For the record, I saw zero evidence that he was building a crypt, *Nelly.*)

I learned of Masonry's great bad luck, which seemed to have infected his children. At their previous school, his son and daughter repeatedly got suspended—unfairly!—from the bus for stealing the driver's wallet and throwing items from their lunchboxes at passing cars. Masonry said the principal and entire school board "deserve to be covered in ravenous leeches."

He told me he must have done wrong in a past life because everywhere he moves, he ends up with neighbors who are "feebleminded and morally degenerate." He said this directly. To me. His neighbor. And he held eye contact. I'd describe Masonry's frank demeanor as "bracing." My wife uses a different word.

Unfortunate incidents like the Little Free Library Dust-Up were the calling card of the park. Its playground equipment caused a melee over the powers of the neighborhood's Procurement Committee. It was the scene of an unconscionable property crime early in the pandemic and the setting for the Wildlife Day-Camp Fiasco of 2004.

And, of course, it's where the unbelievable events of Community Day 2020 took place.

Chapter 3: Gathering

I can see you're getting antsy. I should probably move us along to the infamous smoked-meats-and-a-cappella party.

At the time, I thought it was just a campy gathering. Eccentric characters, silly interactions. But now, after everything that's happened, I realize that I was learning that the park has the most bizarre history and that, in our neighborhood, what's past is prologue. That's from *The Tempest*. Very fitting.

OK, the timing of the party is key. For two reasons now that I think of it. First, it was during the last week of February 2020. Little did anyone know that this would be the neighborhood's last social event before the pandemic. The governor—good woman all in all, she was in a tough position—declared a state of emergency the following week and then a full lockdown the week after that.

Obviously tough times were ahead, but on the day of the party, I was in a great mood. A few days later I was scheduled to meet with a recruiter from a search firm: A major publishing house was looking for a founding editor of its new historical-fiction imprint. They said I was their top candidate. I was genuinely excited.

I'm getting off track, huh? Well, you did say you wanted to know more about my career. Maybe a short detour makes sense. We'll just call this the scenic route to Community Day.

When the recruiter called in early 2020, I was still working at Swift College. Oh, it's just on the other side of the county line up north. On the lake, by the reservation. I'd been there since 2013, writing for and editing *The Ironist*. I never thought I'd work at a college, but fate, you know? We plan; God laughs.

For 50 years, the school's English department had run a sleepy journal of literary criticism. It lost money every year. The school's bean-counters wanted to pull the plug, but the college president wanted to give the journal one last chance. She and I had studied together in England after college. She sought me out and begged me to come aboard and try to revive that dying publication. By sheer coincidence, she made the offer just as my wife and I were thinking about leaving the city. I'd gotten tired of working for the government—that's all I'd done since grad school. I wanted to try something new. That's why we left the city. And at the time, the college job did seem ideal.

Before getting waylaid into public service, I had studied literature as an undergrad and in my graduate program. I even wrote a book back when I was 24. It's my only real youthful indiscretion. It compares the inner lives of two dozen fictional characters. What drives them, what haunts them, how they understand their purposes. Interesting subject. Anyway, the college president did a good job of selling the journal job: I'd be in complete control of the publication, and since it was already on life support, I was free to take chances. I'd get to work at a respected liberal arts college in a quaint, rural town; and I'd have the opportunity to publish other talented storytellers.

I took the gig, and my wife and I found a neighborhood we liked and house we loved 37 miles from campus. And, honestly, the job was great for a while. I turned it from a boring quarterly academic journal into a monthly magazine of popular fiction. In two years, I doubled subscriptions. We won some awards. We even turned a profit.

Also, on the side, as a kind of personal public-service project, I was doing local-history research for Grangerford's upcoming 300th anniversary celebration. The county wanted to tell the twisting tale of the town. They were hoping to put together an exhibit for the state's history museum. Maybe produce a coffee-table book. They needed someone to do the grunt work, someone who knew the state archives. I guess I drew the short straw.

Anyway, you can see why I was being recruited for the historical-fiction editorship: I had experience with history, literature, publications, management. And since things had taken a bad turn at the college by that time, I was open to talk when the search firm called. The college president just wasn't the same woman I knew back in grad school. She'd gotten stiff and paranoid. Power-hungry. And some professors and administrators were jealous of my success. They were making my life miserable. So even before the virus took hold, I felt like big life changes were imminent.

Alright, back to the party. The second reason its timing is important is that on the following Sunday, the neighborhood was scheduled to host Community Day at the park.

Every year, Community Day marks the beginning of spring. Even though it's just a neighborhood-wide picnic with a food truck, folks circle it on their calendars. Come out of hibernation and get reacquainted. And in 2020, as you can imagine, it came to take on far greater meaning. People desperately needed to leave their caves.

As the virus spread, the recruiter and I changed our lunch to a video call; that was easy. Rescheduling Community Day was more complicated. It was initially postponed until the first week in April...then early May...then the middle of June...

The pandemic unraveled so many people. Some of our isolated, apprehensive neighbors saw each new date as something to latch onto, as a sign that life was about to return to normal. For them, each postponement was a life-preserver floating away. But I didn't pay much mind to all that scheduling drama. I didn't need Community Day like others did. Thanks to the lockdown, I had more time to dedicate to my personal research and writing projects. So I was good to go.

* * *

The party was a few blocks away, just a 15-minute circuitous stroll by sidewalk. But a straight line through the sundial and the woods on the park's east side would've connected our mailbox to the host's back door. We arrived unfashionably punctual at the cedar, two-story colonial with powder blue shutters. Everything about the house and yard—manicured lawn, impeccably trimmed shrubs, eight tidy "Keep Off the Grass" signs—was perfectly symmetrical, as though a mirror bisected the property.

Behind this religiously tended façade was a deteriorating detached two-car garage with one car inside, rotting shingles on top, and a handful of furtively smoking partygoers around the edges. Embarrassed and mostly forgotten, the garage seemed to be attempting to slink off into the tree line bordering the back yard. The tasteful front yard would've welcomed that: The garage was an insult to its geometry and theology.

As for the party itself, I think it was meant to celebrate a marital engagement or Shark Week or someone's release from prison. Who knows. The home was owned by someone named Margot or Fran or Kim. Again, how was I supposed to keep up with all of this? I went with Fran.

I've never liked big groups of people, so parties aren't exactly my thing. We moved out to the country to get away from the congestion and rat-race mentality. But as soon as we settled in, my wife "encouraged" me to join the Knights of Columbus at our parish. She also whatever-is-more-forceful-than-encouraged me to accompany her to events whenever she thought I was "on the verge of qualifying for recluse status." So I was pressed into service for this party. And I was told I had to wear a polo shirt. The uniform of the capitulant bourgeois male.

When we walked in, I heard my good pal Masonry regaling a neighbor with his latest hard-luck story: The delivery guy brought the wrong pizza the night before. Masonry demanded $100 cash and a free calzone to compensate for his pain and suffering. But the lousy restaurant refused, the useless chamber of commerce wouldn't fine the restaurant, and the lazy 911 dispatcher wouldn't send any officers to rough up the delivery guy. "Feebleminded moral degenerates as far as the eye can see," editorialized the non-capitulant Masonry.

I have good manners, so I decided to stroll around the house and eat something before inventing a reason to leave. I was leaning toward spring allergies or a migraine, but I'd let fate decide. No reason to commit prematurely and steal serendipity's thunder. As I made my way toward the serving table, fibbing politely along the way ("I was hoping to see you here!" "I'm going to text you about those tickets!"), I overheard riveting conversations about property-tax assessments, the travel costs for cheerleading teams, and what a mild winter it had been.

It seemed as though everyone was at the party other than Barb, which was odd. Barb's our neighbor likeliest to attend gatherings, give unsolicited advice, and inform strangers that she has a master's degree in public health. Maybe she was previously booked to lecture a local couple about how they're raising their kids.

Sweet, skittish Nelly, however, was in attendance. I saw a Class B motorcoach parked on the street as we walked up to the party, so I knew she had to be on the scene. Since her dealership is moribund, she drives her inventory on rotation, presumably to shake off the dust. And sure enough, when we walked in, I saw Nelly camped behind a curtain, hiding from the imminent peril. She had opened the window in case she needed an emergency egress.

Pith was there, too. But he and I had had an unfortunate encounter recently, so I kept my distance.

After some chit-chat with strangers about mulch, the paleo diet, and insurance copays, I whispered to my wife that I needed to roll: The universe had selected "migraine," and it was my duty to respect that choice. She rolled her eyes and said, "I'd think Mr. Tough Guy would at least say hello to the host before getting laid low by an ouchy head." She nodded toward a woman emerging from the kitchen carrying a silver platter stacked with high-end charcuterie and cheeses. I'm so fortunate to have a wife that encourages my social grace, so I smiled at my bride tenderly and said, "Your wish is my command, my love." Her eyes got big, and she mouthed, "Please, no."

I turned to the host and shouted with wonderment and glee, "Holy Christ, Fran! Look at you and your assortment of gourmet sausage! Good godamighty, you could've laid out some rotgut appetizers and no one would've been the wiser!"

My wife, who was, for some reason, trying to slink away, looked like she was about to have an embolism. It was the same look she had after she told me to say hello to her book club and I explained to them, at length, my theories about Stonehenge, the pyramids, and ancient aliens. But it could have been the look she'd give me if she were really pleased by my behavior. I had less experience with that look, so I couldn't be sure. Given the uncertainty, I pressed on.

"Honey, over here! Honey, look at this!" I wanted to make sure I had my wife's attention. "You told me Fran was a high-class lady, but you didn't say a word about any Abe-Froman, haute-cuisine, luxe-sausage operation! For real, Franny, feel free to start bringing out the swill because I'm about to get sausage-drunk on this Gucci product!"

Long story short, my wife's look was *not* an indication of her being pleased with me, so I hushed up. But the host, who had a majestic air about her, was touched by my compliment (even though it turned out her name was "Kim" not "Fran." Oops.). Apparently, not a single other person at the party had loudly celebrated her hors d'oeuvres. Cretins. She took their insult regally; she explained to me quietly that she was accustomed to such impudence, and it only made her stronger.

Kim was tall and sinewy. Narrow shoulders, drawn cheeks. Unusually wrinkly knuckles. She wore a naturally-blonde-*ahem* pageboy haircut. Her flat-front slacks and high-neck blouse were complementary earth tones. She accented the ensemble with a vivid-by-comparison taupe sweater, a buttonless tunic cardigan that she repetitively closed by hugging the front together and crossing her arms tight just above her hips. Eventually, she'd need to use her hands for something, so she'd release the sweater temporarily, realize her torso was unprotected, and then restart the cycle.

My first impression was that Kim was trying to disappear inside of a wearable security blanket. But she also wore the glitteriest, jangliest crystal bib necklace as though she were guarding against being misplaced and forgotten. The ambivalence of attention, I supposed.

As a reward for my good manners, Lady Kim gave me a tour of her exurban Crate-&-Barrel castle. She spoke in clipped, certain sentences like she was charged by the word and had to pay double for commas or adjectives: "Built in 1978;" "Quartz not granite;" "My neighbor has a mistress."

But she let loose, peacocking like you couldn't imagine, as she showed off her clock collection—dozens upon dozens of mantel, shelf, grandfather, cuckoo, pendulum, pocket, hourglass, and alarm clocks. "Weirdest flex ever," I thought to myself while marveling aloud that each was in perfect working order and synced precisely with the others.

She gave me a closed-lip smile and replied proudly, "Timeliness is best in all matters."

Kim and I were now thick as thieves. I could tell this was a by-the-book, keep-it-together kind of woman.

Every square inch of non-clock wall space was taken up by photographs of the fairest, jolliest little boy on God's green earth. Whether playing chess, shooting skeet, or dressed as a ninja for Halloween, he radiated goodness. I pointed to one photo with the cherub holding a rifle bigger than he was, but before I could make a witty joke about Chekhov's gun, she said—abandoning her verbal parsimony—"I am positively certain that you would absolutely love to meet my most precious prince! He's glowed up!" Then whispering, "*Glowed up*? Did I use that right?"

When my wife and I arrived at the party, I spotted a peculiar young man by the "Bon Mardi Gras" banner. He had a gloomy aspect, slight build, rectangular eyeglasses, product-spiked sandy-blonde hair, and what looked to be French sneakers. His tight salmon shorts, which left too little to the imagination, were cinched with a white belt. Subsequently, every time I looked his way, he was scowling or rolling his eyes at someone or something. This, it turned out, was Kim's only child, the overcast "after" of the luminous "before" in the photos. His name was Matt, and, as Kim told me several times, I was very lucky to meet him.

* * *

Today's Matt, I quickly learned, was moody and cerebral. And moody. He did his best during the first part of our encounter to show complete indifference to me and my polo shirt. Kim was certain he could do no wrong. I asked if she was also his publicist.

I attempted to engage Matt in small talk, but he only responded in disinterested two-word sentences and kept looking over my shoulder toward the door like he was eager to trade up from my off-brand companionship. I tried to read him. But his face refused to give anything away—well, apart from his peach fuzz, which turned snitch about his failing attempts to grow a beard.

When his mom brought him a plate of vegetables and tzatziki, he rolled his eyes, muttered something about her "internalized misogyny," and acted put upon as he munched on the red peppers that she had sliced specially for him. When I told him he had a stylish, practical backpack, he exhaled, "I know. My drip is fire," and then looked at his watch.

After a few minutes of such delights, I figured I should stop hogging up Matt's charms. Share and share alike. But a vibrating Kim could no longer contain herself. She made the big reveal. She pulled back her shoulders, clapped her hands, and beamed, "In one week, my Matty and his team are competing in the South Region Semifinal of the national college a cappella championships! *Laissez les bons temps rouler*!"

Matty coolly sipped his drink (sparkling water with a slice of avocado and a dash of pea protein, I think). He was unembarrassed by his mom's doting. He gave the impression that it was proper for the proles to know of his high standing.

"My group slaps. Another 'W' for me," Matty sighed. I quickly assessed that the right thing for me to do, according to polite society, was feign interest in his pseudo-triumphs.

"Blech!" I blurted out, failing the test. "A cappella? That rubbish is still around? I thought that scourge had run its course, Matty."

He went owl-eyed for a split-second then composed himself. "Nah, this art form will never die. No cap," he replied frostily. "It's inevitable."

He stared me down and rattled the ice in his tumbler. He probably thought his scowl was menacing, but it came across more like the hiss of a kitten about to dart behind a couch.

I felt badly. I shouldn't act like that. So I let my eyes go soft and smiled warmly. "Oh, I'm sorry, Matty. No offense intended." I put my right hand on his left elbow and cocked my head remorsefully. "I just thought that you ironic college kids do a cappella as a gag. What do you call it? 'Camp'? I'm finna get your slang eventually!"

He smirked to dismiss me, but I caught that he shifted the weight between his feet and momentarily dropped his gaze. His trembling fingers fished the avocado slice from the glass. "You're a clown, bruh," he retorted. "Only someone ignorant would say something that stupid. You must be really stupid."

Repeating "stupid" seemed to have given him a jolt of testosterone. He lifted his eyes and glared. I bet he could feel his beard finally coming in. But I saw that he still couldn't square his shoulders to me. He put his glass down on a nearby table—purposely not using the coaster three inches away—and fidgeted with a napkin.

Kim stammered. "Uh...did I mention Matty's group is auditioning for *America's Got Talent...*"

"Mom! I am *not* doing that stupid show. I'm not going corporate. I have artistic *in-te-gri-ty*"—he clapped his hands on each syllable since nothing proves artistic integrity like accenting the downbeats to your mother—"I told you that like a hundred times!"

Kim was crestfallen. Her precious prince's rebuke was more than a momager could withstand. She pleaded with him, "You would look so good on television, Matty. I've said that since you were so little. Remember how I said that when you were little? 'He's made for television,' I'd say. You had the longest eyelashes —I wish you wouldn't hide them with those oversized glasses. Remember the sassy outfits I'd put together for you? You loved those vests..."

"I'm sure you were adorable in those sassy vests, Matty," I added ever-so sincerely. "But just remember, if you're going to take your mouth-music show to the next level, you better not let those sopranos get tinny or overplay the tritone substitutes," I offered, obviously ignorant.

Matty lost his marbles. "O. M. G! This basic Gen Xer is going to chirp at me? Go listen to some grunge and talk radio! I don't need you and your Boomer polo shirt and your cringe khaki shorts to tell me about vocal arrangements!" He lifted his head and jutted out his chin. "Why do I put myself through this! I knew there would be feebleminded degenerates at this stupid party!"

Masonry yelled out from the living room, "Everywhere you turn, kid! Get accustomed to it! The world's an endless supply of halfwits and heathens!"

Kim was livid. She said I'd gone too far. She was right. What was I thinking? I tried to deescalate the situation. When Matty finally stopped stamping his feet, I took all the blame. I expressed heartfelt contrition for causing a scene. His breath slowed, and Kim stopped wringing her hands. I gently placed my left hand on his stiff right shoulder, stooped down to make eye contact, smiled, and said, "You know, when you screamed at me just then, I realized the strength of your voice and the unusual nature of its timbre. Both were unmistakable."

Touched by my fatherly encouragement, he wiped his eyes and almost smiled. We all relaxed.

"With some practice and a whole lot of luck, Matty," I added with maximum sunshine, "you might eventually be good enough to sing in a county-fair barbershop quartet. You could even wear one of your sassy vests."

Matty fainted.

Chapter 4: Spectacle

The first time my wife heard me telling a friend about this story of Matty and the party, she sighed, shook her head, and said my version was entertaining but bore little resemblance to what actually took place that afternoon. Ha! It has far more truth than she'd like to admit.

But I do love telling stories. Always have. There's a method to it. My mom would sometimes have to tell my teachers to take me "seriously not literally." She was right. Absolutely right. Literal only gets you so far. My wife used to call my storytelling my "powers of hogwash." She said I had my superpowers working with this particular story. Funny, huh?

She also said I should be more sympathetic to Matty. "Whatever," I thought at the time, "he's a problem." But she was right. Just like she was right about Nelly. I had a lot to learn. But in this case, I gotta say, I was right, too. Matty had issues. You know, I haven't talked to my wife about Matty since Community Day. Well, water under the bridge.

Back to the story. So Matty was totally incapacitated, and Kim had caught the vapors. Worse, a grouchy throng had formed around me. Based on the murmurs I heard, a consensus had developed that I had done Matty wrong.

Nelly, as you might imagine, was unnerved by the growing tension in the room. Given the terrifying non-terrifying environment, she dropped into athletic position—hips back, knees bent, shoulders over toes. She needed a full field of vision and full range of motion to attend to the make-believe peril. As the forces mustered against me, her meditation training finally kicked in. All those podcasts were paying off. Nelly sat crossed-legged on the floor and attempted to center herself. She exhaled and touched her thumbs to her middle fingers. She closed her eyes, focused on her breath, and tried to stay in the moment. Nelly was facing down her imagination. She had prepared for this moment. The battle was joined.

Alas, no plan survives contact with the enemy. As soon as she heard me yell at my prosecutors, "Don't crowd me, people! I watch mixed martial arts on my phone!" Nelly sounded the retreat, shouting, "I'm too young to die!" Her advance planning came to good use: She leapt out the open window and sprinted away. I could hear her screaming, "Jesus, give me the wheel!" Somewhere, I imagined, her golden retriever was silently ruing that once again his owner had sensed imaginary danger before he could.

But maybe Nelly had had the right idea: I was still in a pickle. This mob wanted justice for my ruining the party. Based on their body language and "Let's learn him a lesson!" talk, this seemed to have all the makings of an old-timey tar-and-feathering.

I quickly devised a strategy: Show a little remorse, negotiate down to a lesser charge—from "willful destruction of a pointless party" to, say, "involuntary instigation of a most precious prince"—and accept a plea deal that would evict me from the party but otherwise save my hide. I had been planning an Irish exit, but forced exile would serve the same purposes. My wife, silently admiring a cuckoo clock and desperately pretending not to know me, certainly wouldn't object to that deal.

But then, who comes to my rescue but good ol' Pith! He zigzagged my way, ducking to avoid hitting his head on chandeliers and streamers, with a red-plastic party cup (naturally) and the biggest smile on his face. He shouted, "Yessir! Let's go! Get you some!"

I had no idea why he was so happy. Maybe he thought we were playing charades? Maybe he just liked that a boring party suddenly turned chaotic? Impossible to know. But his inexplicable glee made me chuckle. Before long we were both laughing like madmen. You gotta love Pith.

"Dang, son! Let's go! I love it. I can't get enough of that. Yessir! Get some, boy!"

You could describe Pith's voice as raspy. It's as if his vocal cords were stretched to their limits with the rest of him when he went through his epic growth spurt. His voice seems to stay in the back of his throat a beat too long. It sounds like he's gargling his words before spitting them out.

He stood next to me, straddling Matt's prone body, and started clapping and pounding my shoulders like I'd just leveled a running back. His head was freshly shaved, and he was sporting his black-rimmed glasses, which he didn't need but wore occasionally, as he once told me while twirling the ends of an imaginary mustache, "So nobody doubts my *sophissstication*." He also had on a "Salt Life" t-shirt even though I'm pretty certain he'd never seen an ocean and even though I was led to believe polo shirts were required at this establishment.

When he finished his hootin' and hollerin', he, of course, bear-hugged me. That caused the tension in the room to subside; people trust Pith's judgment. I seemed to be out of the woods, mob justice-wise. But that was a mixed blessing. I was glad to avoid being ridden out on a rail, but, frankly, I had been looking forward to banishment. More's the pity, the gods of justice ruled that my punishment would be more small talk about recycling pick-up schedules and septic systems.

I was flattered—surprised, actually—by Pith's support. Though we were pretty close, we'd had a strange falling out a week or so earlier. He lives a block and a half to our southwest on a corner lot in a brick California ranch with forest-green rectangular porch columns and shutters. He has a four-year old daughter who rides a motorcycle clockwise around a giant loop in their huge back yard. Not a bicycle. Not a scooter. A preschooler on a wake-the-dead loud, gas-powered motorcycle. Obviously, Pith is super-proud of her skill.

One evening, probably around 8pm, he saw me on my evening walk and called me over. He pointed to his pint-size daredevil. She was speeding around the dirt track with reckless abandon, negotiating jumps with the skill of a professional and the obliviousness-to-risk of a toddler. Pith beamed, "My little lady is straight negligent!"

He was looking for positive feedback, and I didn't have the heart to say, "Jesus, Pith, I'm pretty sure that madness right there is textbook child endangerment." So I said, "She sure can turn right like a sunavabich."

I guess this wasn't what he had wanted because he started to cry and said, "I hope your dog runs away again."

This caught me by surprise and hurt my feelings, mostly because we don't have a dog. Pith was so upset that he took a gigantic gulp from his red-plastic sedative and promptly fell asleep on his lawn. We hadn't talked since.

I guess he was willing to let bygones be bygones, because, in the middle of our bear hug above Matty, I said, "Sorry about our argument last week," and he looked at me blankly—almost like he had no recollection of it—took a long pull from his drink, and replied, "What're ya talking about, bud?"

Pith is such a considerate, conscientious man that our tiff was completely erased from his memory banks. What a gem. He's always willing to forgive and forget his post-6pm scuffles.

* * *

It turned out that, from the point of my introduction to Matty until his fainting spell, Pith had watched the entire "spectacle" (as the neighborhood newsletter took to calling the day's events) from the wet bar. He later explained appreciatively that Matty was due for some comeuppance and that I had done my part. "The universe had delayed settlin' accounts out of mercy, but in time them books gotta be squared!"

I obviously didn't know Matty had karmic debt, and I told Pith that I had no role in cosmic justice.

"Nah, my guy," Pith explained seriously, "The Man Upstairs uses all tools in the box to set things right, and that's real talk right there."

When Kim came to her senses, she lit into Pith and me something fierce. She accused us of "barbarism of the Huns" and "war crimes against decorum and Protestant rectitude" and said that we could expect "Matty's Hollywood attorney" to serve us papers before sundown.

Pith was having none of that nonsense. He snickered, looked down at Matty who was still playing a cadaver, and exclaimed, "Cool out, Kimmy! Your boy had this comin' for years. Justice was gunning for him ever since he put all them doggone aluminum pinwheels across the park! He don't get to declare himself neighborhood fox guardian! Them lawyers had worked out a deal!"

Before I could process any of that dazzling madness, Kim swore at the two of us in ways so inventive and vulgar that I almost caught feelings.

Pith, somehow, was impervious and sturdy as rebarred concrete. "Don't fire me up, now, Kimmy! I've been itching for years now to say a few things about that home-brew animal camp you put together at the park!"

In that instant, I was certain it was my destiny to decrypt that beautiful lunacy. But I didn't have the chance, at least not in the moment, to collect more intel. You see, Pith's reply crossed a line with Kim. She quivered and puckered her burnt-sienna lips. She gained control of the situation by closing her eyes and using her left hand to quiet her clattering necklace. Then she turned on her heels, picked up the platter with the sausage and, with the noblest carriage imaginable, strode out of her own home. I marked the moment, thinking—so very wrongly thanks to Community Day 2020—that I would never see a more dramatic exit involving smoked meats.

Everyone went dead silent apart from Matty who was stirring from his stupor on the floor and now muttering about "polo-shirted bourgeois savages."

Noticing Matty's resurrection, Pith looked to the heavens and shouted, "He is risen! Halleluiah! Indeed, He is risen!"

My wife claimed this conclusion to the story was "one part fact, three parts fantasyland." We had to agree to disagree about that. In my defense, she wasn't standing next to Pith as this episode was drawing to a close. So she can't deny that, as he calmly surveyed the situation, Pith grinned ever so slightly, took a healthy draw from his red-plastic celebration, and said to no one in particular, "This has got some serious Blowtorch-Len energy, I'll tell you what."

* * *

Sure. That's a natural breaking point. Tomorrow about the same time? I know exactly where we can pick up.

And, seriously, thanks for listening. I know this is hard. We just met; you want the punch line. You want to me to get to Community Day. I get it. We'll get there. Trust me. We have time. We'll get there. But there's a lot you must understand first.

And let's get this out of the way now: You and I know how this story ends. It's awful. Gut-wrenching. Truly. I know how hard some of this will be to hear.

But you need to know that I'm fine. All good. Believe me: I have zero regrets. I'm entirely at peace. Honestly, I wouldn't change a thing. He deserved it. God, that bastard deserved it. Every single little bit of it. Believe me. You'll see.

RECORDING CONCLUDED: 4:06pm
Saturday, January 2, 2021
Uncorrected transcript
Interview by Elizabeth Jones

Chapter 5: Reexamine

From: Dr. Jennifer Davis, MERCY STATE, COMS
Date: January 2, 2021 at 5:52 PM
Subject: RE: Client information
To: Elizabeth Jones, Esq. OFFICE OF THE PUBLIC DEFENDER

Ms. Jones:

Thank you for following up again today. I regret that it has taken several days to respond to your request.

As you may know, in this matter, Mercy State must adhere to strict state regulations. Before sharing the medical records of your client (DEFENDANT in INDICTMENT #20-11-486), your office must confirm that you are now counsel of record for this case, and Judge Thomas must certify that your client's wife has waived their privacy rights to those documents.

I am told that Mercy did receive your assignment paperwork today. However, we have not yet received documentation from the judge. Once it arrives, we will transmit to you all materials shared with his two previous attorneys.

I am also told that you began interviewing your client today at

Capital City State Hospital (C.C.S.H.). This administrative delay should not meaningfully affect your understanding of his condition or the events of November 1, 2020, his neighborhood's "Community Day." That process will take substantial time regardless of the paperwork.

Lastly, I have known your client professionally for a decade, and I agree with the C.C.S.H. assessment that there is no reason to believe he poses any threat to you.

You need not call again. I will notify you as soon as Judge Thomas certifies the privacy waiver.

Jennifer K. Davis, M.D., J.D.
Chief of Medical Staff
Mercy State Psychiatric Hospital

Chapter 6: Indications

START: 12:58pm
Sunday, January 3, 2021
C.C.S.H.

Good to see you. I bet you want to know more about Blowtorch Len McGregor.

On the park's west side, maybe 30 paces from the gazebo, is a faded bus-stop sign. It is the most unusual shrine attracting the most unusual pilgrim. When we first moved into the neighborhood, I noticed that every weekday at 7:12am, every Saturday at 8:55am, and every Sunday at 5:53am an old man —he looked 75 years old if a day—would arrive on foot at the sign. And stare at it. His timing was atomic-clock precise.

Now, this sign is legit—like, Antiques Roadshow-verified legit. Its rusted, erector-set-style metal post is sturdy, sunk deep in the earth. The rectangular sign on top is weathered but leaves no doubt that a county bus, the Blue Line, used to stop there. You can even make out the county seal in the bottom left corner if you squint and know, for whatever reason, what the county seal looks like.

To the south side of the sign is a 10-foot by 8-foot clearing with the remnants of gravel suggesting a designated standing spot for whomever would ride this bus to wherever it went. Separating this waiting area from the rest of the park are four bollards—short, thick wooden posts—that look eerily like nameless headstones marking the eternal resting spot of this deceased and forgotten county initiative.

From my dining room window, I can see this entire ghostly tableau, like a decrepit ride at an abandoned amusement park. And every single morning of the week, I would see ancient Blowtorch Len standing shiva by that sign.

* * *

When he's not venerating the bus stop, Blowtorch walks the neighborhood like it's his beat. His loop circumnavigates the community; he stays at the edges, peering in. His dress might suggest it's exercise, but he's definitely patrolling— "prowling" may be more like it. Though his eyesight must be shot, and though he moves glacially, he is continuously gathering intel and testing weak spots in the community's defenses. Like a velociraptor in winter.

My wife thinks he's "an unbalanced codger deserving around-the-clock monitoring." Pith seemed to admire Blowtorch; at minimum, they appeared to have some history. Our neighbor Barb—did I mention she has a master's degree in public health? —tried to steer clear of him, and Nelly behaved as though he were an ogre. My personal encounters with him had been relatively few, but I'd heard chatter. Up to that point, I'd done only the most basic digging on his life and exploits, via online message boards and such.

People agreed that he'd had a career in television news, primarily in behind-the-camera roles, and maybe some time in print journalism. Evidently, he'd been a strait-laced, just-the-facts-ma'am type, absolutely committed to the profession; loved its rigor and independence. I've heard it said that he covered everything from the McCarthy hearings and the Gary-Powers U-2 incident through the Cuban Missile Crisis and the JFK assassination to the Moon landing and Vietnam.

But nowadays, folks treated him like a neighborhood novelty or a mysterious community institution, like a haunted house or a long-deserted Ford Edsel deteriorating in the woods. I'd heard there'd been a weird happening at his compound back in 1987. But folks didn't talk about that much, so I hadn't researched it fully—not until we got well into the lockdown. Frankly, up until the pandemic, I had concluded he was just a crank who liked madcap adventures.

Blowtorch Len stands about 5'6", and he appears relatively fit—physically at least—given his propinquity to the grave. He shuffles, his feet never losing contact with the ground. But he has a bit of a hitch in his get along, like his left leg is forever finding potholes. You'd think rigor mortis had already set in because his torso and neck seem ossified. Or petrified. He keeps his gaze straight ahead and moves in straight lines, deviating course only perpendicularly by pivoting on the ball of his right foot. At first glance, he's a standard-issue doddering old man.

Before long, though, you realize you've been duped. Without warning, he'll snap his head to study a cloud or stare someone down, crouch into a fighter's stance or dance a little jig. I once told my wife that he's like a cunning predator that reels in its prey by pretending to be wounded. She offered to start a community collection to cover his relocation costs to the African savanna. I told her that wasn't very neighborly. She said that she would miss me terribly but would understand if I felt the neighborly need to accompany him. Ha, ha, ha, wifey.

When Len is pursuing a specific mission—you know, partaking in some of his signature antics—he'll wear one of his inscrutable costumes. Don't get me started. But while doing his daily rounds, he always wears the same uniform: the smallest pastel running shorts, three-stripe tube socks pulled to his knees, all-white Reeboks, and a Nike half-shirt. In the summer, he wears a tri-color athletic headband; otherwise, it's a bedazzled Kangol bucket hat. To shoo away birds or children, he'll rattle the hat's assorted flair. If it's cold, he'll sometimes put the shorts over gray sweatpants and insulate his torso with a Member's Only jacket. It's as though he landed on a sartorial style in the mid-1980s and locked it in amber.

I had a hard time knowing if Len was being serious. His getups and bizarre routine—I didn't know which parts to believe and which parts were just for effect. But one thing was for sure: From the jump, Len seemed to take an interest in me. Maybe he could sense I was a level-headed guy. Maybe he just wanted to know more about the homeowner adjacent to his bus-stop Mecca.

But occasionally, I'd be driving through the neighborhood, and he'd show up in the middle of the road right in front of me. I'd honk, smile, and wave, and he'd eventually adjust his fanny pack and then move to the side. After one such event, I was so unsettled that I sent a letter to the HOA asking that they remove the useless bus stop sign from the park. Maybe, I thought, if he didn't have a reason to pass by our house each day, his interest in me would fade. The HOA promised to keep my "suggestion on file." Sigh. The sign remained.

Often Len seemed more fey than freakish. Several times, while I was out on a walk, I saw him standing in some kid's treehouse or sitting on a recycling bin. Since he was up to no good, he'd, of course, be wearing something crazy: An eyepatch or 15th century pantaloons or a toga or clown shoes. Maybe all the above. He'd just point at me and wink.

Once, I was raking leaves in our front yard when I heard rustling in the woods on the north end of the park; it was Len wearing a kilt and a powdered wig. He was looking at me through opera glasses and laughing. I think he was sizing me up because a couple months before the modern bubonic arrived, he orchestrated our first formal-ish encounter.

In those days before everything closed down, I'd leave the house around 7:15am and drive to my office in the annex building off-campus where the college's administration had "relocated" me. They overreacted about everything, and at this point they were out to get me, eager to turn any little complaint into a capital offense. Whatever.

Blowtorch Len was on the side of the road, just outside our neighborhood, standing next to a red Camaro with its hood up. I got chills when I noticed he was wearing one of his special outfits. Something was cooking. He had on teal Crocs and a bomber jacket over what appeared to be a polka-dot unitard. I assumed his Elvis-style black mutton chops were glued on for this performance. He flagged me down. I pulled over to lend him a hand and—better safe than sorry—administered myself the Last Rites and quickly scrawled a will.

He came to my window and announced in a hoarse staccato. "Listen *heah*. I'll tell *ya* just once. I like the cut of *ya* jib. Always have." His rat-a-tat cadence was from a 1940s gangster film. His accent was mid-century Northeast, like Boston-by-way-of-Hell's-Kitchen.

"But, Mr. Secretary," he continued, narrowing his eyes and indicating he knew more about me than I thought. "Y*a caih* about this *neighbahood* or *yaself*?" He showed me both palms with fingers pointed down, then moved his hands in tandem from left to right, then right to left, like a salesman emphasizing two options.

I had no idea what to say.

"I know *ya* retreated *heah*. Saw this place as a refuge. But *weah* more than that, *ya folla* me? Supposed to be a community. Can't accept any *moah* selfish types. Won't do it." He moved his palms-down hands from side to side like he was cutting off a drunk.

I said I understood, though I most certainly did not. I motioned to his car and asked if he needed help.

He smiled. "That's the right question, *ma* boy."

I think I said thank you.

He patted the hood of my car twice, and said, "Now skedaddle b*efah* the streetlights come on."

I needed to process this incident out loud with someone wise, especially since the streetlights wouldn't come on for another 12 hours. Pith took it all in, finished whatever was in his cup, burped, and said, "Blowtorch Len's got eyes for you, I'll tell you what."

Chapter 7: Lore

"I couldn't help but notice that you watch Mr. McGregor from your window when he pines at the bus stop." The wonderful thing about our neighbor Barb is that she has no compunction about revealing that she's been spying on you.

In one sense, Barb lives with her family about a block and half from us in a crimson farmhouse with a wraparound porch. In another sense, Barb is everywhere, always.

When we moved into the neighborhood, Barb didn't take any special interest in me. Just the normal stuff—offering advice on our landscaping, reminding us where our trash bins should be stored, checking my credit score. At some point, though, she must've consulted Google. She started telling everyone that she and I were very close friends and explaining to me that state leaders should know how perfect she'd be for all high-level public-health positions. When I apologetically told her that wasn't my life anymore, she gave me an exaggerated wink and said she understood. She then proceeded to send me an updated résumé every 10 days.

I had run into Barb at the giant consignment store the day after the Matty-Kim-bourgeois-savages party. My wife had sent me to look for a wicker stool that we just *had* to have in our glassed-in porch. You know, the kind of inexplicable, time-consuming request that would only go unscrutinized in a happy marriage. As soon as I walked in, I saw-heard-felt Barb. Her aura is sprawling.

She was holding a gargantuan, half-eaten cinnamon roll and explaining to the clerk that the aisles seemed too narrow to meet the county fire code. He could borrow her tape measure to check, she offered. "It's just in my purse, you should have your own at the ready of course, but that's fine, why don't you use mine, and you really should dust the merchandise and check the water spot on that ceiling tile while you're at it."

He politely agreed to look into these matters as soon as feasible. His unruffled-ness ruffled Barb. She responded with her famous "Hmmp!"—a quick, high-pitched vocal emission that conveyed, depending on the context, one or more of the many types of irritation she is wont to feel. She coolly replied that, fine, whatever, I guess these tasks don't matter that much but then emphasized that, given her expertise, they probably ought to be his top priority. After all, she explained, she did have a master's degree in public health.

I just couldn't with Barb that morning, so I decided to sneak out. But as she was looking around—naturally—for the manager, Barb saw me. She beelined my way.

For half a second, I allowed myself to imagine that she hadn't heard about my unfortunate role in the "spectacle" at Kim's house. But this was Barb we're talking about. She'd spent years cultivating sources and developing phone trees and group texts for this exact purpose. I wouldn't be surprised if she prays nightly for the mailman to accidentally leave others' mail at her house.

I decided to preempt whatever conversation she had prepared for me. When she started with, "*Sooooo*, Mr. Secretary, a little birdie told me about...," I laughingly interrupted her with a snide joke about Kim's pride and necklace and Matty's awkwardness and fainting. I knew Barb would lunge at this tasty bait. But she demurred. She even seemed to wince a bit.

"Hmmp?" I thought.

See, this was odd. Barb lives for discovering and discussing others' flaws. Every Sunday morning, while the county heads off to church, Barb visits the consignment store and six local thrift shops. Nosing around is her religion; a second-hand retailer is her temple.

She likes to track what people are getting rid of so she can speculate about the state of their finances and relationships. I guess I should appreciate that she at least takes care to conduct slapdash research at pawn shops and such prior to wildly conjecturing about others' intimate lives. When she reports on her findings to her old friend Nelly during their early-morning chats at the diner, the combination of context-free intel and uncharitable guesswork can fuel hours of specious dot-connecting:

> *Did you see that Don and Doris are painting their fence, again? They just did that six or seven years ago...*
>
> *Hmmp! By the by, I couldn't help but notice they're also trying to sell an antique floor lamp at the consignment shop...*
>
> *You have to wonder what's going on there...*

I once told my wife that Barb and Nelly should be more judicious: Half-baked stories that come out of slipshod reasoning can be a public menace. My wife said that self-awareness is one of my areas for personal growth.

* * *

For whatever reason, Barb wanted to gossip about Blowtorch and the bus stop instead of Matty and Kim. I acquiesced.

"Yes, I have noticed McGregor's silent ceremonies," I replied to

Barb. "Thank you for noticing and bringing up in public what I do inside the privacy of my house."

She grinned from ear to ear. Barb loves compliments.

"It seems strange to me," I moved past my passive-aggression, "that, like clockwork, Len pays his respects to an extinct bus line."

Barb is above average in height, likewise in mass. Pith once said she was "half a biscuit away from trouble." Her face is puffy, her eyes wideset, her voice reedy; her timbre lacks her body's heft. Always wears shimmery pink lipstick; her fluorescent faux nails are squared at the ends. And let's just say that there are some empty seats at her fan club's events.

But I always suspected that there was something sturdy, maybe even endearing behind her garish façade. She did seem to have a small group of very loyal friends. She was on the steering committee of every local charity event. As my wife would say, I probably should've gotten to know more about her sooner.

But I did know that her two now-young-adult kids are adored by the community. They used to babysit and mow lawns for free. Lemonade stands. Walking dogs. The daughter, I know for a fact, donated her long ponytail every few years to an organization that makes wigs for pediatric cancer patients. And Barb's husband was considered a living saint.

About 5'8", short chestnut brown hair parted on his right, tortoise-shell glasses. Big into sweater vests. The first time I saw him, I thought, "That's the type of man whose solid upbringing and middle age have provided the composure and dull back pain necessary for wearing sneakers with dress pants." He greeted everyone with a smile, volunteered his truck when a couch needed moving, took Pith home in a wheelbarrow, and genially helped his wife do things for him that he didn't want done.

[...EXTENDED PAUSE...]

God, that family deserved better.

Truly.

* * *

Anyway, over the years, Barb has cut her hair shorter and shorter, but her false eyelashes keep getting longer and longer. They were starting to look like awnings for her cheekbones. That day, she was wearing a leopard-print kaftan and black leggings and carrying a handbag the size of a parachute. It said something about "wine o'clock."

"Len adored that bus stop," she said somewhat sadly as I haggled with the manager over the price of the useless wicker stool. "But you know...Matty's pinwheels, the lawsuits, rabies shots...everything kind of fell apart."

She said it so matter-of-factly. As though those things go together. But I had zero idea what any of it meant. It was like Mad Libs on meth. It did, however, jibe with Pith's inscrutable speech to Kim at the party. Beautiful lunacy.

I tried to disengage from Barb—laughing and walking away; saying things like, "OK, then..." and "I don't want to take up any more of your time..."—but she assured me that she wasn't in a rush and that she'd be happy to join me on my day's errands. She nattered amiably as she followed me around the store.

Barb's toes point at 10 and 2 as she walks. In others, this would lead to a heels-heavy waddle. But Barb was destined to have a more confident gait. So she tilts her torso backward and sort of gallops ahead, leading with her bladder. It looks like a horse is tugging her forward by an invisible rope tied around her pelvis.

Since Barb had committed to being my chatty shadow, I thought I'd at least press her for more intel. "Honestly, what's the deal with McGregor?" I asked. "He tries to make like he's a riddle wrapped in an enigma dressed like a mid-1980s jogger. And God knows he's scared the living bejesus out of poor Nelly. The lady's bound to have a conniption if she picks up his scent on the breeze. For a while I thought he was a harmless scallywag, but now I'm starting to wonder what he's got buried in his basement. That dude's straight creepy."

You would've thought I'd walked under a ladder, broken a mirror, and chanted "Bloody Mary" in the dark. Barb shrieked—more of an "Aaack!" than a "Hmmp!"—turned white, grabbed my forearm, and whispered fiercely, "I have four things to say to you, mister, and you *better* listen close. First, don't you ever let it be known that you called Len McGregor 'creepy.' Second, never, *ever* talk to him about Nelly. Third, I have a bad feeling that Len has eyes for you. Fourth, did you know I have a master's degree in public health?"

At this point, I was captivated by the lore of Blowtorch Len. I just couldn't figure out what the lore was. I'm a sensible guy, so all this ominous business about a sketchy dude pushing triple digits had finally peeved me. I was standing in the middle of the consignment shop, holding a wicker stool I didn't want and an antique floor lamp I didn't need, and I vented.

"Barb, let's stop behaving like this gimpy artifact is a brainteaser! Plain and simple: He's a fossil who appointed himself neighborhood nightwatchman out of boredom or bossiness. As far as I can tell, his core competency is senility. He's probably an inch away from telling the mailman to place the lotion in the basket. Everyone needs to stop giving him a wide berth and instead give him a good kick square in his pants!"

Barb discharged an involuntary "Gahhh!" and then collapsed with the poetry of a giraffe struck by lightning. For the next 20 minutes she was prostrate. The clerk and manager took turns stroking her hair and keeping her cool with a vintage hand fan (that, until recently, had been owned by a couple working through a seven-year itch). The decanter and sandwich bag of pills that Barb discreetly pulled from her cavernous sack helped settle her, too.

When she was finally able to get herself together, she looked up at a shelf of fox figurines, let out a long, hoarse moan, and monotoned like an oracle, "What misery to be wise."

"Word," I replied with utmost sincerity and absolute bewilderment. "Word."

I expected her to elaborate, but she merely stared into the void. I was torn. This was my big chance to get away and avoid having Barb as my sidekick for the day. But I might never have a better chance to get more neighborhood information out of her. A semi-delirious Barb was bound to spill precious tea.

It was worth the risk.

"Barb, just level with me," I said softly, as I joined the hair-stroking effort. "What is it with you and Len and Nelly and that park? What's the mystery here? And more importantly, why do people keep saying Len has eyes for me?"

She sat bolt upright, eyes glassy but index finger pointed to the sky, and pronounced, "Best that thou should bear thy burden and I mine! My voice will never reveal my miseries or thine!" And then she passed out, cold.

As the old saying goes, "When a fevered gossip starts speaking in rhyming couplets in a consignment shop, that's your cue to scram." I decided to parse her prophesy on the go.

* * *

I see that look on your face! OK, maybe I'm embellishing a little, connecting some dots, adding some spackling to fill in the holes. But all in service of the story's underlying truth.

You know, my mom loved my storytelling more than anyone. They say she had the same gift. That's probably why she appreciated my ability so much. She'd always laugh at the right parts and then tell me at the end which lines she liked best. "Seriously not literally," you know? Once I heard her tell another mom that my tales were "always located in the vicinity of the truth, though sometimes on the outskirts."

My dad didn't have the same gift. He was "the practical one," he'd say. He was focused on dates and things. And numbers. He was great with numbers. Thought about money a lot. At night, he'd sit in his chair. He had a yellow pad. Adding, subtracting. Scratching things out. Sometimes he'd seem sad. Angry.

One time I tried to tell him a story. To get his mind off things. I made it up. I was probably eight or nine. It was about a knight who was protecting a town. Protecting innocent people from an evil wizard. A good guy fighting the bad guy. I remember that. My dad said it didn't matter. "Make-believe garbage," he called it. He flung his pad. It hit the wall near this brown lamp with an eagle. I'd never seen him like that. But it didn't bother me. I was fine.

He came to my room that night. He woke me up. He hugged me. Told me how sorry he was. He said how much he loved me. He said he was sorry about everything that was going on. He said we deserved better. That made me feel so good. It's weird seeing your dad cry. He didn't like stories as much as my mom.

There was this one time in Sunday school. I think I was seven. We read a Bible story about Moses. He was protecting his people from Pharaoh. I told the priest I liked the story. But I said I would've written it differently. I didn't like that God hardened Pharaoh's heart. God softens hearts, I said. The priest screamed at me. In front of the whole class. Said I was criticizing the Holy Word. First time I heard the word "sinful." He made me stay after class. He yelled at my mom in front of me. Said my mom was "paving the child's road to Hell."

My mom kept her head down. She said, "Yes, Father," "You're right, Father." I thought I was in so much trouble. I was shaking. From my chest and shoulders. I hated that feeling. I couldn't control it. In the parking lot, my mom hugged me tight. She kissed my forehead. She said God gave me my special brain. If people didn't like it, that's their problem. That made me feel so good. Warm. Tingly. The shaking stopped. My mom was the only one to understand me.

She was in the hospital a while. She couldn't always control her thoughts. Her brain was a little under the weather, she'd say. They were going to help her. That's what she said. She was in the hospital a while. She wrote me letters. Told me to keep daydreaming and inventing. She told me to never lose my spark. My dad once said it was good that we were so young. A blessing, he said. We were too young to understand what was happening with my mom. Maybe he was right. But I could tell she was affecting my mind.

Chapter 8: Incident

Anyway, after my encounter with Len by the Camaro, Kim's party, and Barb's cryptic musings at the consignment shop, I became engrossed by the park. I had to learn its story.

Once the Covid lockdown started, I had more time for my personal research. I didn't sit around worrying about the virus or moaning about isolation. I made the best of the situation. I was very productive. You probably know that my political writing was becoming popular at this point.

Anyway, when I was researching the park, I learned about an event back in March 2004. It's so hilarious and bizarre you can easily miss how portentous it was. I don't want to exaggerate, but apart from the circus at Len's compound back in 1987, no event better explains, or at least foreshadows, Community Day 2020: A young mom relatively new to the neighborhood enjoying a lovely day at the park briefly thought she'd become embroiled in an international scandal involving a secret agent/martial artist. But, in truth, this was simply Barb's first time dealing with Blowtorch Len McGregor acting a fool.

You're going to love this.

* * *

OK, the year's 2004. Reagan died and *Friends* ended. The launch of Facebook and the Battles of Fallujah. Barb's kids were very young, so she wasn't on much of a social circuit. She'd gotten to know another neighborhood mom, Kim, whose son Matty was a little older than her own tykes. Barb and Kim didn't hit it off perfectly; they were both competitive and strong-willed. They weren't close enough to be chums or antagonistic enough to be foes. Their mutual feelings on both dimensions were more muted. So maybe less "frenemies" than "acquaint-opponents."

Diapers and sleep-deprivation kept Barb from caring much about local scuttlebutt, but she'd heard some peculiar stories about an older guy named Len. There was some chatter about a long-ago, completely bonkers occurrence at his compound—you know, his house surrounded by a giant wall and moat—but folks didn't seem eager to relive that. It was pretty hush-hush. By the time Barb moved to the neighborhood, Len mostly kept to himself apart from his regular walkabouts. If she crossed paths with him, Barb would politely wave and then move along. She didn't have the energy to think much about the local eccentric; just enough to decide that keeping some distance from him was probably wise.

One day, Barb was scheduled to meet a new friend, Nelly, for coffee at the park. These two jelled from the start, complementing each other perfectly. Thelma and Louise. Elle and Paulette. Nelly, who'd been in the neighborhood for about five years, didn't have kids. She married early and divorced quickly. Her philandering ex-husband's exploits (e.g., nun, motel) were too much to bear. But Nelly had rebounded and directed her energy into starting her "dealership"—actually, I shouldn't put that in air quotes; maybe it was more than a money-laundering operation at first.

On that day, Nelly wanted to talk to Barb about the neighborhood's (then still active) bus stop. Nelly had big plans of some sort, something related to her RVs and campers, and she'd been floating an idea to a few neighbors. Barb had always liked a fair share of intrigue, but with little ones at home she hadn't really been able to dedicate much time to it recently. But now that her kids were a bit older and she'd have some extra mental bandwidth, she had committed to involving herself more in local gossip. Getting up to speed on Nelly's plot was the perfect way to make good on that New Year's resolution.

But Nelly never showed that day. She later told Barb she'd gotten a call from someone with a British accent claiming to be from the gas company. He said Nelly *had* to stay home because an inspector would be coming by to check on a possible leak. But no inspector materialized. When Nelly followed up with the gas company later, they said they knew nothing about a leak or a phone call to her house. *Somebody*, it seems, did not want Nelly and Barb conspiring about the bus stop. Hmmp.

Back at the park, Barb passed the time by allowing her two young children to dig in the sand (where the polarizing playground equipment would later stand) while she discreetly indulged in her guilty pleasure: reading Amish erotica. As she turned a page, eager to see if the strapping farmhand would remove his broadbrimmed hat while painting the silo, she noticed that an older gentleman had seated himself across from her at the picnic table.

Mortified, she threw the randy book into her purse. Realizing this betrayed guilt, she composed herself, flipped her hair (which was still shoulder-length at this point) and said sternly, "Hmmp! May I help you?"

The old man introduced himself with a cartoonish Russian accent, "I am top-*syecret* Soviet spy and karate yellow *byelt*."

Before she could convey her many questions, which he could read on her face, he sought to explain: "My cover story is *dat* of plumber." Barb's questions multiplied.

She was worldly enough to know top-secret spies would be

unlikely to introduce themselves as such. Moreover, the Soviet Union had collapsed more than a decade earlier. Her skepticism grew as she noticed this "plumber" was wearing capri pants, a raspberry beret, and a three-quarter sleeve t-shirt that read "Soviet Agent" on the front.

Barb was speechless. She had always struggled to find the right words when confronted by elderly yellow belt-plumber-spies.

The nattily clad, unusually forthcoming secret agent broke the silence. He stood and announced, "Enough of *ze* diplomacy! I have claimed *zis* park for *ze Moderland* and my dojo! By *trespyassing* on *zis* sovereign *tyerritory*, you have broken long, successful Peace of Westphalia, violated *eenternational* law, and *seenned* against Nature's God!"

Barb was shattered. She had come to the park to chat with her new friend Nelly about a bus, but she'd been stood up, and now she was being accused of sparking an international crisis and affronting a probably imaginary karate school. Moreover, the nature of these charges made it difficult to mount a defense. It was not obvious to Barb that a 350-year-old treaty authorized a deranged elderly man to expropriate a neighborhood park. But she silently conceded to herself that she couldn't say for sure: Her expertise was, after all, *not* in international affairs; it was, thanks to her master's degree program, in public health.

While she struggled to find her voice and equilibrium, her prosecutor straightened his beret and tucked his disheveled t-shirt back into his capri pants and said with great satisfaction, "My sensei and *supyeriors* at Politburo will be pleased with my *eeneetiatyive*!" He nodded at the bus-stop sign and then limped toward the woods.

Barb's daughter laughed and said, "Mommy, who is the funny man?"

He turned on a dime and stared at Barb, waiting for her answer.

Barb thought for a long time, realizing that so very much, or maybe so very little, hung on her response. Barb replied to her daughter, "A local plumber, sweetie. Just looking for customers."

He smiled in agreement, confident that he had made clear to this new resident that the park was serious business. As he was disappearing down a path into the woods, he turned around and pointed to Barb's purse. Losing the Russian accent, he said, "By the way, that one's among my favorites. The *fahm*hand never takes off that broadbrimmed hat. Makes the *bahn* scene even *steamiah*."

* * *

Oh. OK.

I can keep going if you want.

OK.

Alright. I can push us ahead tomorrow.

RECORDING CONCLUDED: 3:13pm
Sunday, January 3, 2021
Uncorrected transcript
Interview by Elizabeth Jones

Chapter 9: Retry

From: Dr. Jennifer Davis, MERCY STATE, COMS
Date: January 3, 2021 at 4:24 PM
Subject: Certification and preserved documents [CONFIDENTIAL]
To: Elizabeth Jones, Esq. OFFICE OF THE PUBLIC DEFENDER

Ms. Jones:

With the receipt of the court's privacy-waiver certification, Mercy State is now authorized to provide your client's written medical records.

As you might know, your client dismissed both of his previous (privately retained) lawyers because he believed they were not taking seriously his version of events. That turnover has repeatedly delayed the legal process.

Accordingly, the court has engaged your office and authorized me, as his attending physician a decade ago, to provide any additional medical and personal information you request. Judge Thomas—for whom I clerked many moons ago—believes that your client will be more likely to trust you (and retain you as his counsel, allowing this process to proceed) if you know his full story and listen to the full story he tells.

Your office should receive an official copy of the court's full order tomorrow, but the judge's chambers called me this afternoon to explain the outlines. Please note that 1) All medical information provided to you by Mercy is done so confidentially and may not be shared in any form without the court's approval; and 2) You must preserve all correspondence from me, including this message and yesterday's, along with your required client-interview transcripts so the court has a full written record of these conversations.

In the morning, my team will begin to transmit to you copies of all relevant medical records. Assuming you agree to the court's terms, you may also begin sending additional information requests directly to me. I will respond as quickly and fully as I can.

Dr. Davis

Part 2:

The Dew Drop

Chapter 10: Quixotic

START: 12:22pm
Monday, January 4, 2021
C.C.S.H.

"C'mon my man, what are you gonna do instead? Just sit on that doggone computer all night?" asked Pith, who was calling me regularly now. Yes, I thought, that's exactly what I have in mind. I have important research to do.

"I'll tell you what, bro, the real world's more reliable than them screens. Less drama, too."

We were a good bit into the pandemic by this point. Pith had been on me to join him for a "guys' night" ever since Community Day got postponed a fourth time. Some were lonely and needed socializing and such. Pith and others didn't understand that I wasn't so needy. I was keeping busy just fine.

He whispered like we were in cahoots, "Help me out here, big man. My reputation needs goosing. If I can get you to stop instigating everyone with your newsletters and emails for one night, the whole county will hail me as a hero." Pith was joking. My writing was respected and influential. But I appreciated the thought. I'd heard all kinds of stories about people struggling with sadness and drugs and gambling and eating.

"Besides," Pith went on, "it'll give you an excuse to shower and shave, too. Lordy bagordy, the world's comin' undone on account of some worldwide virus, and my guy's avoiding shampoo and razors like they're the plague!" Pith was kidding. I'd grown a beard. No one was really going into the office, so I was casual more often, too.

He interpreted my silence as agreement to his plan. "Alright, buddy, here's our scheme," I could imagine him looking from side to side like we were under surveillance. "We're gonna get you reacquainted with deodorant and the outside world. Just you and me—no big production. We'll blow off some steam, take the edge off, cool beans? Trust me, it's all good. I'll pick you up in my golf cart tonight at seven. Nice and chill."

Alright, I thought, this did sound like a pretty good idea. And I'm so glad I gave in. The next 24 hours proved indispensable to understanding the history of the park and, later, appreciating Community Day 2020.

* * *

Pith loves the Dew Drop Inn, a shoddy roadhouse about a mile away. It has most certainly never, according to Pith, been condemned or been credibly accused of being a brothel. The floor is always sticky, and it smells like sweaty work-out clothes forgotten in a hamper. The owner assures first-timers that the scent is caused by stagnant air and humidity from the river. But every year Barb—who, if I'm not mistaken, has a master's degree in public health—files a new complaint with the state, and inspectors confirm it's likelier the result of septic and mildew issues.

Pith is like royalty there. He tells everyone that he likes that the

Dew Drop "don't have no stuffy people." My wife said that he likes that he can get there—thanks to his golf cart and a path in the woods—without a driver's license.

Pith had doubled his pestering about a guys' night at the Dew Drop after my wife left town. She was staying at her sister's place for a little while. She needed a change in scenery after those first few weeks or months of the lockdown. I missed her, but it turned out to be a blessing in disguise.

A couple cops came to "visit" me while she was away. They "just wanted to converse" about some of my recent articles about the county executive. But I cleared that up quick. I told them the pandemic hadn't taken away my First Amendment rights and sent them on their way. It wasn't an issue, I took care of it, but my wife would've gotten worked up.

Anyway, she and her sister are very close. Strength and safety in numbers. Their dad was rotten to the core. My wife wears her hair over the right side of her forehead to cover up a scar from one of his rages. She was a bit heavy as a kid. He called her "Swine-girl" and "Piggy." She finished high school a year early to get away from him, but an eating disorder followed her to college and has stalked her since. But she never complained about how he treated her. She said her older sisters had it worse. Much worse.

While she was gone, I realized home confinement is what you make of it. Some took advantage of the time and space, broadening our minds. Others couldn't grow. Sometimes they even resented those who did.

My analysis and commentary were filling much of my time at this point. I was publishing on multiple sites multiple times a day. It can blow minds when the truth seems unbelievable. I was generating so much online interaction that I was somewhat relieved when the recruiter emailed to say that the publishing house had decided to go in a different direction for that historical-fiction editor position. She was a complete professional. She didn't let on at all about how disappointed she was about the publisher's decision.

I remember my wife was away when I got that news because she made a big deal about it when she found out later. I tried to explain corporate politics and how flighty some search firms could be. But things had changed with my wife. She started mentioning that she was considering going back to grad school to finish her MBA. A couple times she even said she regretted not finishing. Covid was brutal. Stress and uncertainty can make people irritable and anxious, you know, sad, fearful, distrustful. Covid was brutal.

* * *

Pith was a little late picking me up. He apologized and explained he'd had to pound out a dent in his golf cart's front bumper and patch one of its tires. His neighbors really need to stop parking their cars wrong, he said. "But it's all good, I ain't sore at 'em. Decent folks," he reassured me as he took a gulp from his red-plastic peacemaker.

I told him how good it was to see him and offered him a warm smile and—distancing be damned—an even warmer handshake. When he finally released his bear hug, we both looked across the park toward the memorial garden. It had been defaced a few nights earlier. The plaque had been spray painted with anti-war and anti-colonialism graffiti, and the benches had been busted up. The trellis and the entwined branches it had supported for a generation had all fallen under a vandal's axe. Countless hours of a craftsman's work and years of nature's course undone in minutes.

The HOA was concerned about future acts of destruction, so a team of workmen had already taken down from the flagpole and packed away the neighborhood's banner and the flags of the nation, the state, and the county. Now they were removing the park's sundial; it was not clear what would become of it.

I asked Pith if he'd seen the email from the county's health director about the vandalism. He chewed the inside of his cheek, pulled his cup to his chest, and said, "Yessir, read it this very afternoon—twice in fact," and then he took a drink.

County health director Scarlett Bennet's message said that it would be immoral to investigate the incident since those responsible were obviously on the side of social justice: They were confronting the celebration of nationalist aggression; they were challenging America's wars of greed and oppression. Moreover, repairing the damage to the garden would, Bennet educated us, retraumatize these unknown freedom fighters.

A half dozen or so people had evidently not gotten that email or were indifferent to trauma. I recognized the two trying to scrub paint from the plaque and repair the benches. One lost a brother in the attack on the USS Cole in 2000; the other, a son in Afghanistan in 2004. Barb was there too—her dad served in Korea. It looked like she'd purchased some second-hand outdoor furniture to stand in while the benches were mended.

Nelly was on the scene as well, handing out bottles of water and what looked to be homemade cookies with American-flag icing. She saw us watching. I waved and said, "Thank you for doing this." Nelly smiled and nervously stammered a thank you.

Pith gave her a thumbs up and said, with his singular brand of homespun moralism, "Good on you, Nelly. Unpopularity doing right is glory." She completely ignored Pith. Hmmp. More to the Nelly-Pith story, indeed. Maybe my wife was on to something.

My grumpy pal Masonry was leaning against the gazebo watching the clean-up effort. He turned around and said to

Pith and me, "If I had to choose sides between idiot vandals and nimrod do-gooders, I'd take a nap. None of them are worth the effort of a coin flip. They all deserve a root canal."

I appreciated Masonry's efficient malice; his ability to vent his spleen in so few words is unparalleled. He turned back to the garden so he could concentrate on a scene that infuriated him.

There was one older gentleman toiling in the garden who I didn't recognize. He looked like a Rotarian who'd ask for a bowl of seasonal fruit instead of the cheesecake at a finance-committee lunch. Clean shaven, probably pushing 60; his hair still more pepper than salt. He had on a crisp white button-down shirt and midnight blue chinos. He was shoring up the arbor. Given the collection of stakes, braces, wires, and tools at his feet, it sure looked like he knew what he was doing. All the while he was encouraging his co-volunteers with a song in his heart.

As though Pith could read my mind, he motioned his cup toward the stranger and said, "Jimmy Callahan, there. The prodigal-est of sons. Does the heart good to see him back here. I'd wager a king's ransom that he ain't stepped foot in this neighborhood in—doggone—must be 33 years. Yup, it was 1987, I reckon. And look at 'em now, pulling some serious *Antigone* business! Defying the authorities and honoring the dead!"

Pith quietly pondered his apt metaphors while I respectfully waited, having no idea what to say.

"I'll tell you what, bro," Pith eventually announced, preparing me for a telling of the what. "The Good Book and them ancient Greeks knew the score. Real talk."

The entire scene—the destruction and rehabilitation, the uprooting of a timepiece, Pith's literary references and peculiar specificity about this guy's homecoming—made my head spin. I said, a bit too loudly I think, "This can't be real." Shoulder-to-shoulder with Pith, I realized I hadn't been this close to anyone in quite some time.

As the workers twisted and turned the sundial, unmooring it from the earth, the shadow cast by its pointer, for years, steady as the day is long, darted erratically among the timelines on the base. Eventually the sundial was loaded into a lightless crate.

"Things have gone sideways, my man, no doubt—no doubt whatsoever," Pith said as he started up his cart. "Far as I can tell, the laws of the universe and current events are perpendicular right now. No way to stay on both tracks; one or the other. Gotta pick: One or the other. If you try to stay at that intersection..." –he slowly brought his two fists together and made the sound of an explosion as they collided.

I nodded in agreement, though I wasn't sure what I was agreeing with. Or to. We both went quiet.

In time, he cleared his throat, slapped the steering wheel with both hands, and announced, "Alright then, bro, time to do this. These bad decisions ain't gonna make themselves." Pith's moralism is limber.

We headed south down my street, too fast for my taste but perfect for Pith's palate. At the stop sign, which Pith ignored, we took a sharp right turn, skidding around the corner and nearly tipping over. Pith laughed, "Buckle up, my guy," but of course there were no seatbelts.

I relaxed as we got our equilibrium back and set a course for the Dew Drop. "We're on an adventure, bro. Good times ahead," said my Sancho. He took another sip with his left hand and patted me on the side of my knee with his right—leaving the steering wheel to its own devices—and said a bit softer, "Knights-errant, adventuring." I liked that.

When I was a kid, I'd make up adventure stories for my sister. We called ourselves the "two musketeers." When we were home alone for long periods, I'd be OK. But she'd get scared sometimes. I'd be completely fine. She would never cry, though, when I made up stories. I'd come up with a crazy scenario. Then we'd pretend we were on an important mission. Or investigating a mystery. The two musketeers. She loved my hero stories. Battling invading aliens or defeating zombies. The strong taking care of the weak.

Sometimes, when we visited my mom in the hospital, we'd pretend the lobby was a castle. Or enemy headquarters. My dad always said it was better that the two of us stayed down there near the reception desk. We didn't need to see mom like that, he'd say. He'd go up to that special floor by himself.

My sister loved hiding under tables and jumping out at doctors, shouting, "*En garde*!" Then she'd lose interest and say she wanted to be alone. She'd disappear for a while. That's when I started reading the real-life dramatic stories in *Reader's Digest*. They had so many copies. Sometimes a nurse would hug me and tell me I could take one home.

I got saved by a real-life hero once. My mom was still in the hospital. My dad wanted to do something for my sister and me. We drove into the city. We were going to the dinosaur museum. He kept telling them at the door that he thought it was free. They said no but kids were half off.

He didn't have enough in his wallet. He took off his left shoe. He had extra money in there. It was folded up tight. I didn't know he did that. He was so smart. But it still wasn't enough. He told them he thought it was free. They said they have a free day a few times a year. He should check the paper for the dates, they said.

My sister was hungry. She kept saying that. I tried to get her to stop. We could eat when we got home. My dad found a cafeteria in the Goodwill store. My sister and I shared a hot dog. They cooked it in a deep fryer. My dad wasn't hungry. But he was polite and ate the three packets of Saltines the man gave him.

We drove all the way to the lake up north instead. That was still free, my dad said. My sister and I swam in our shorts. The two musketeers. It was so fun.

But a storm came in really fast. We were swimming so we didn't notice. My dad said it came in so fast. The waves were too much for me. I couldn't get back in. I tried so hard, but I didn't go anywhere. I couldn't get in. I couldn't breathe. My dad was screaming on the beach. He didn't know how to swim. He couldn't do anything.

This tall, skinny man with a bald head swam out and got me. He told me to relax. Breathe. Breathe. He got me in. My dad hugged me so hard and kept kissing my hair. The man turned mean. Yelled at my dad. Called him names. But my dad didn't know how to swim. And the storm came in so fast.

We drove home. My dad was silent the whole way. I tried to talk to him, but he was tired. My sister pretended to be asleep. It was one of my favorite days ever. Going into the city. Eating a deep-fried hot dog. Swimming in the lake.

When we got home, I hugged my dad and told him it was my favorite day ever. He kissed my cheek. I asked him if it was his favorite day ever. He said, "No, son. But I loved being with you. But not my best day. Not my best day." Maybe his favorite was a day he had had with his dad.

RECORDING PAUSED 1:31pm
Monday, January 4, 2021

Chapter 11: Ohunka

RECORDING RESUMED 2:33pm
Monday, January 4, 2021

I can do some more context-setting. Sorry about all that reminiscing.

The Dew Drop, our neighborhood, and much of what passes for attractions in the county are within a stone's throw of the pitiful Ohunka River. It mopes through six counties and empties itself, exhausted, into the lake up north. Occasionally during the spring, the water is high and the current active enough to allow for a couple weeks of splashing and tube floating in a few spots. But generally it's so shallow and stagnant that it attracts more mosquitoes than humans.

Two centuries ago, they say, it was perfect for rafts transporting provisions among settlements; later, barges carried lumber and stone between the region's mines, mills, and towns. In the generations since, drought and irrigation projects drained its volume, and trains and trucks stole its purpose. Depressed, the river idles away the time, days melting into months melting into years, collecting fertilizer and pesticide runoff from the corporate farms that devour families' land and expel chemical waste.

I learned from my research for the 300th anniversary committee that the Ohunka had, for ages, been the connection between our otherwise landlocked region and the outside world. Grangerford became the county seat because it had been a way station for merchants, politicians, adventurers, and vagabonds. Lewis and Clark even passed through. Our county and our town may not have been polished, but they were abreast of news and culture, seasoned in interchange. Approachable, assured. The Ohunka's demise was the region's.

Isolation doesn't only lead to loneliness. It breeds insularity, then vulnerability, then suspicion. Approachable and assured no more. Locals now see the river as a jilted lover sees the ex who still lives nearby: the cause of what is and the constant reminder of what was and could've been.

Prior to the pandemic, the only souls traipsing around the river's banks were there to take pictures of the algae blooms: vibrant patches spread across the surface, preventing sunlight from reaching underwater vegetation and decimating aquatic life: Smiling observers creating a photographic record of the Ohunka's unvoiced suffering.

But at some point, after this plague arrived and everyone was locked away, some county residents descended on the river. I guess these first defiant few were just rebelling against confinement. But then their numbers grew. Organically. Dozens, then hundreds at a time. They didn't come to pick up plastic bottles or restore the shoreline. They came to walk. Just walk.

They'd arrive by car or truck and park on the edge of a nearby field or in a clearing in the woods. Everyone walked counterclockwise around the same loop. On the east side of the river, they'd proceed north, staying between the soybean field and cattails on the water's edge, past the old barge quay that had tried unsuccessfully to resurrect itself as a canoe launch, and up the incline to the tracks.

They'd cross the river, heading west, over the abandoned wood-and-iron trestle bridge built a century ago by ambitious industrialists convinced the Central Union Railroad would last. They'd turn south and walk on the sandy, willowy banks of the Ohunka's western shoreline, taking care to edge closer to the water where the crumbling Central Union Highway has its sharpest turn and, not coincidentally, two small white crosses solemnized the side of the road.

Pedestrian traffic heading back to the river's east side would get bottlenecked at the narrow footbridge: The county's Parks and Recreation Department, which built the crossing during the region's last budgetary boom time 35 years ago, projected daily use to be a few people on a casual stroll, not hordes on a pandemic-fueled circular pilgrimage.

The entire course was about a mile in total. Some would walk a single loop, others 10. It went on all day, every day, and soon all night too. They brought portable outdoor lights and maintained bonfires. These pedestrian pedestrians—let's call them the Wayfarers—walked and walked, six feet apart and in complete silence. No words, no whistling, no humming. An inaudible, mobile group-therapy session.

New arrivals seamlessly joined the queue, staring at the backs of the skulls ahead in line and ignoring the dead fish. No one jogged. No one passed another walker along the course. No one stopped to rest or admire the scenery. They walked until they were spent and then returned to their cars. It was as though medieval monks in penitential procession praying for the Black Death to end had been transported from a monastery's cloister bordering a courtyard to a makeshift track bordering a dying 21st century waterway. Our very own *via dolorosa*.

I saw the first shades of the Wayfarers on the day the governor issued the state's lockdown. The second Tuesday in March 2020. Grim-faced—maybe steely-eyed is more like it—she announced it in an early afternoon press conference. But the order didn't take effect until 8pm. I went to the grocery store while I still could even though we didn't need anything in particular. Others went too, crowds of them, for the same non-reason. Though packed to the rafters, the store was still; just a 1984 Phil Collins ballad on the speakers and buzzing from the frozen-foods cabinets and the sprayers keeping the produce moist.

From time to time someone whispered about cold cuts at the deli or told a friend what his brother's wife—you know, the doctor—had heard at a conference about this type of virus. But for the most part the shoppers were afraid to make eye contact, much less speak, worried that any type of human interaction would excite the bug. So they walked, six feet apart, up and down aisles, from the dairy section to the bakery, and back again. Everyone knew it wasn't safe to be around others; but like a diet, self-denial could start tomorrow. They had to be alone together. Once they tired, they'd return to their cars to begin the era of being alone alone. All I remember buying that afternoon was too much cereal.

That store was a sight to behold: Suffering people walking about aimlessly but giving the impression of purpose.

It made me think of Blowtorch Len McGregor silently patrolling the neighborhood.

Chapter 12: Gaslight

After leaving the scene at the park, Pith and I drove west through the neighborhood, heading to the path that would take us through the Ohunka River wetlands to the Dew Drop. And, lo and behold, we came across Blowtorch Len. He was standing in the middle of the road, looking down at a card table. Even from a distance, it was clear he was dressed up as Napoleon. Single-breasted blue coat with a red collar, white tights, black riding boots, sword with golden handle, and side-to-side two-corner hat. Of course he was holding his right hand under his waistcoat.

Once again, Len had something cooking. God only knows what. As you can imagine, I was unnerved, but Pith smiled and then said quietly, "Yessir, the adventuring knights' first encounter." As we approached, it appeared that Len was playing a military board game like Risk or Axis and Allies. Pith slowed down as we got close and said in the most nonjudgmental fashion conceivable, "What's the news, Mr. McGregor?"

Len replied angrily, "*Ferme la bouche*!"

I was dumbstruck. It wasn't a board game. Len was looking down at a map of the park. A perfectly drawn rendering: the trees, fields, gazebo, basketball courts. Everything in place and to scale. Sitting atop the map were dozens of small objects that he was moving around while writing notes on a small pad and mumbling in French ("*Zut alors*" "*Mais non*!" "*Oui, oui!*").

He appeared to be wargaming—preparing for a battle at the park. He then picked up one of the movable pieces and popped it in his mouth. "*Meeerciiii*," he drew out in surprise, "*parfait!*"

They were tiny French pastries. Petit fours, profiteroles, canelés, and madeleines across the table. Len must have dressed up as a general-emperor to have a snack in the street. In no other earthly context would that previous sentence make a lick of sense. But when you're dealing with ol' Blowtorch, *c'est la vie*.

As Pith and I sat watching His Imperial and Royal Majesty sample delicacies, I grew angry. McGregor just likes to mess with people with his dress-up fantasy-land routines, I thought.

"*Oh la la*," whispered Len, inspecting his next bite.

Anything to keep his neighbors guessing.

"*Tres bien*," said Len, devouring another morsel.

Tangling others up in wild, dreamed-up escapades for his own enjoyment.

"*Magnifique*!"

He needed to know I was on to him.

But before I could open my mouth, Len looked straight into my eyes and said, returning to his New York-Irish brogue version of English, "History, *ma* boy, is just a set of lies agreed upon."

I had to catch my breath. I was pretty sure that was an actual Napoleon quote. Wait. Was McGregor making some profound statement about fact and fiction? I could feel my mind bending. Pith saved me from the depths.

"Sounds good, Mr. McGregor. Keep it tight," he offered and then started to drive us away.

Staring straight down the road, Pith said, "Best to let statements like that pass by, my man. Contemplatin' Lenny's adages is like exploring a house of mirrors in a wormhole. It'll fry your noggin."

I had collected my thoughts and calmed myself by the time we reached the path. "Appropriate that he was dressed as Napoleon," I said. "Len's always concocting a harebrained Russian campaign."

Pith didn't say anything. Pith doesn't have my education, so I explained my reference. "The Russian invasion was imposing and theatrical. But Napoleon lost his army, had to abdicate the throne, and was exiled to the island of Elba. It was just a fanciful disaster." I was very pleased with my analysis.

Pith took a sip from his red-plastic country-lawyer and replied, "But Napoleon escaped exile, raised another army, and reclaimed his throne, my dude."

I rubbed my chin. Hmmp. Indeed he did.

Pith eventually added, "Never forget, bro, Len's wily and resilient. Wily and resilient."

My mind wandered. Wily and resilient. That could describe Odysseus trying to get home. That cartoon coyote tangling with the road runner. Guerrilla forces fueling an insurgency.

At some point, as our golf cart slogged through the Ohunka wastelands, Pith said impassively, "Able was I ere I saw Elba." Again, I was speechless. "Always loved me a good palindrome," said Pith.

* * *

It's hard to do justice to the bleakness of the Ohunka swamp.

Grays and browns, rotting trees and wildlife, non-rotting plastic litter, stench. Oppressively muggy. Thick, mosquitoed air. As though the nearly departed souls of the terminally ill river and its expiring flora and fauna were forced to hover above the sludge until the merciful flatline.

Wetlands are nature's riparian guard—filtering water, thwarting erosion, slowing floods. Their meaning, their pride, is attached to the rivers they protect. Wetlands don't want to be praised for their beauty; they want to be admired for their utility. When the Ohunka River gave up, its wetlands lost their purpose. They were now attendants to an impotent king, armed guards of an empty vault. Created to serve a larger cause that no longer existed, the swamp, without a river to defend, had no reason to defend itself. It didn't become useless because it had deteriorated; it deteriorated because it had become useless.

Despite this desolate scenery and Len's lunatic Napoleon act preceding it, Pith's excitement about a night out in a marshy rathole could not be dampened. He ribbed me about various things as he navigated his beat-up cart along the tortuous, descending path and then over a rickety bridge—"No need to pony up for the ferryman, my man! I'm savin' us some ducats!"—until skidding to a halt in a gravelly lot.

The Dew Drop is nestled in what must have once been a clearing in the bog. But now vines and moss envelop it as though the natural environment, so perturbed by how this dank, moldering watering hole has devalued the mud and muck, is expending its meager energy to reclaim the land and what's left of its reputation. The Dew Drop's exterior wood is decaying; parking has been limited by fallen branches, growing saplings, and a gurgling creek that meanders the property like a drunk looking for her car. Outdoor electricity was lost in a hailstorm ages ago, so gas-light lamps provide the only illumination.

The Dew Drop is owned by a second cousin of a county commissioner. Initially, it had been allowed to stay open at 50 percent capacity during the lockdown because the county had designated it as a "Critical Sustenance Center" even though it hasn't been allowed to lawfully serve food since its kitchen was shuttered by state inspectors a decade ago. It did, however, have lemon slices, cocktail olives, and a vending machine.

Earlier that week, however, the Dew Drop had been authorized by the state to operate at 98 percent capacity because it had qualified as a casino under emergency state regulations. The owner had placed slot machines in each bathroom and converted half of the booths into poker tables. Roulette was in what had been the walk-in freezer. All clocks were removed.

Even before making our way through the pungent cloud of vape mist and body spray hovering inside the door, I could hear that business was booming. These were not the silent, sullen Wayfarers walking our circular, rural way of sorrows. No, this group would dig in and meet the pandemic Armageddon with sanguinity. Or at least indulgence. This crowd—let's call them the Steadfast—found freedom in hopelessness; they would smilingly forsake God right back. The Wayfarers sought the serenity of the murmuring river; the Steadfast welcomed the turbulence.

At first glance, the crowd looked to be a cross-section of the county—farmers, business owners, those on disability, police officers. But I quickly noticed that the crowd had an unusually high number of teachers and members of the clergy. Made sense. During the lockdown, that evil county executive, in the name of "extra precaution for the common good," had gone beyond the state's requirements and boarded up all religious establishments and schools. He thought he could ride his "Safety First" agenda to reelection in November.

He had based his decision partly on advice from the county attorney and the sheriff (his weekly golfing companions) who were both at the casino that night, kissing strangers in celebration of their blackjack hot streaks. The two had counseled the county executive that educational and faith-based facilities led to sustained close contact, and that was an unnecessary health hazard.

Seats at the Dew Drop were hard to come by, but Pith and I saw an empty baccarat table in the back. We made our way past a group of middle-aged co-workers by the karaoke machine confidently, spittily, and off-tune-ly singing "I Will Survive" to one another. Their leader—overdressed, tone deaf, and entirely ignorant of chord changes—was using one of her hot-pink Manolos to conduct the group. "People, I'm going to need you to hit the chord changes, mkay?"

I appreciated the Dew Drop's *esprit de corps*. The intoxication, the rule-breaking, the gambling away of government checks, the general devil-may-caring. The Steadfast were suffering in solidarity. Like Londoners finding community in the Underground during the Blitz.

Pith and I squeezed past the spiritual leader of the county's megachurch. He was playing Texas Hold'em, drinking a vodka sour, and smoking a blunt. "Good to see you're staying busy, pastor," I said admiringly.

He pushed a stack of chips into the center of the table and piously replied, "Idle hands are the devil's workshop."

Chapter 13: Guile

A redheaded waitress, about 50 years old with a tattoo of tumbling dice on the inside of her left wrist, made her way to our table. She wore latex gloves, a mouth guard, and a steel mill-grade face shield. Before I could ask, she merely said, "Latest CDC regulations." We ordered. Pith must've been thirsty.

He asked how I'd been doing, and I updated him on my newsletter and essays, a few groups I was forming, and a rally I was helping organize. He said, "Yessir, yessir, I wanted to talk to you about all that. I'm thinking some of this business you're gettin' yourself into don't make a whole lotta sense. We gotta keep it together. You know what I mean?" Pith was a good man, but he didn't have my education. I assured him everything was under control.

When the waitress returned, she was wearing a beekeeper suit and smelled like witch hazel. She took off her mesh hood and removed the swimmers' nose plugs. "A team of federal experts just offered new guidance," she explained.

Pith pulled out some stray cash and paid our tab. He then folded up an extra $20 bill, handed it to the waitress, and said quietly, "For the bartender, like usual." Her smile was embarrassed but grateful.

"He's had some good days lately," she explained. "Ups and downs. Still talks about trying his hand at writing again but..."

she trailed off and inspected the floor. "Dreams of the touchdown you didn't score, you know?"

Pith replied, "Well, you tell him my mama said hello, alright then? She does ask after him. Still talks about all that talent and potential. The good Lord must've given him my share!"

The waitress blushed and chuckled. But Pith's smile morphed into a scowl. I didn't know he was capable of such a look. He pointed in the direction of the bartender and said, "But now you listen here. You tell that S.O.B. that I still haven't figured out what 'guileless' means, but once I do, I suspect he and I are going to have words."

The waitress tilted her head back and laughed and laughed. She brushed some dust from her eyes and replied, "After 30-some odd years, you still can't let it go, can you? One innocent phrase in one run-on sentence in one clumsy column, and it's still a burr under your saddle?"

Pith stood up radiating naughty kindness, and she accepted the bear hug with less embarrassment than the $20 bill. She put her hand on his cheek and felt no need to say another word. He said, "I know." She walked away to tend to a gang of Chads playing keno and drinking hard seltzer.

I asked Pith about the $20 bill. "Ahh, it's nothin', my man," he said, lowering his head and brushing the air with his left hand. "You know them ladies. They're always trying to separate me from my money!" I laughed and told him that he didn't have much money to be separated from.

"Ain't that the truth!" He shook his head faux-remorsefully. "But that only makes their schemes more poignant."

I smiled and told him not to worry: A long, content life is worth more than all the money under heaven.

Pith said, "Real talk, for real," and then downed his drink and stared at the bartender for about ten seconds. "But the tragedy," he said to the bottom of the glass, "is when acute excellence is limited at 18 and everything afterward savors of anticlimax."

* * *

Pith and I got to talking about the neighborhood. "I'm a lifer," he told me. He lives in the house he grew up in. Even delivered newspapers in the community as a kid in the '80s. "It's why I know all my peoples! I know everybody's business from way back!" He laughed at himself. But, to be honest, he did seem to be on bear-hug terms with just about everyone. "For real, my man, I'd try to extort 'em, but they're all boring as drying paint. Bro, if them folks had any juicy secrets, I'd be rich as jeweled cheesecake, believe that!"

He told me about Barb's shortened career and her saintly husband, who is apparently the most uncomplicated and decent man in America. He told me more about the Little Free Library fracas, which really was as uncomplicated and indecent as it sounds. He told me that Len McGregor—before earning the nickname "Blowtorch"—had started Community Day decades ago to bring neighbors together. Pith also briefed me up on Butch Tweed, the corpulent, corrupt, 19-term member and 10-term president of our HOA—the only man I've ever heard Pith disparage: "Cutthroat to the weak, lickspittle to the strong. Heaven help us—dastardly down to the roots."

When I jokingly asked Pith about the backstory of ever-anxious Nelly and why she seems to have it out for him (including snubbing him back at the park), he raised his eyebrows, frowned, and then tilted his head down with eyes closed as though he were about to say grace. Or confess his sins.

"Oh," I said, getting it.

"Yesssssirrrr," he drew out over several beats.

"Were you two serious?"

"First time I knew what love was, and that's just being real. Honest-to-God connection. Sincere affection, I'd say." I didn't know Pith could be a softie.

"Nelly'd been divorced for a few years and wasn't fixin' to head down that road again. Ain't no education in the second kick of a mule, ya know?"

"But you won her over?"

"Yup. Wonders never cease! I could calm her, make her smile. She liked that I liked liking folks. I guess that's a rare breed. She made me want to act right, too. She didn't even mind my coarse ways, too much," he laughed to himself. I think I said that they sounded like a good match.

"On weekends, we'd take one of her dealership's teardrop campers up to the lake. We'd just be. Just be. Serene." I'm pretty sure I told him that he sounded good for her.

"It was brief though, bro. Too brief. Only six months or thereabouts. A 'lickety split' you might call it. This is back in 2005, after all that madness of the previous year settled down." He looked around the room aimlessly. At a blackjack table nearby, someone shouted in disgust after busting a good hand.

"Nelly had plans, my man. Big plans. She was going to start with that first dealership and then grow it. She used to get starry-eyed about running a 'transportation empire,' she called it." He smiled sincerely and used air quotes. "She had big hopes and ambitions. Great expectations."

I watched a dapper young gentleman who was shooting craps ostentatiously play to the crowd and then urge his date to blow good luck on the dice.

"And I had..." Pith stopped and looked at the empty glasses in front of him.

I wasn't sure what to say. I tried, "Sometimes the timing of these things just doesn't work out."

Pith smiled at me kindly, finished off his current drink, and replied, "Yeah, but sometimes the clock and calendar ain't to blame."

* * *

Pith started up with my inquisition again. "Everything been OK since your wife left town?" We laughed about all the pizza I'd been eating and my staying up late and missing work from time to time. We talked about how his shop had lost business, but they were holding on, what else can you do. I told him I'd been shopping at the strip mall with his store a couple weeks back and meant to stop by.

He said he'd heard I'd been around and that maybe I shouldn't have bought it without talking to my wife. I was starting to understand why so many people had misgivings about Pith—all this meddling. I told him things had gotten crazy in the world, and I needed it for safety, not a big deal. It's my right.

"It's just," he said softer, lowering his eyes as though avoiding the sun's glare, "that maybe you shouldn't have brung it into the house without a conversation of some kind with your lady. That's a powerful weapon, can do some serious damage. And accidents happen. Oughtta be a family-level decision, know what I mean, my man?" I didn't respond.

He continued, "And, listen here, that big event, that rally against the county executive you're fixin' to attend? I got a bad feeling. That thing might be trouble, see what I'm sayin'?"

I realized I'd misjudged Pith's judgment. My wife had been right to doubt him.

Chapter 14: Service

"We were sitting here, pal."

Pith had gone to powder his nose, so I'd been sitting alone, mulling over some new ideas for columns. A group of 10 were suddenly hovering above me. They seemed perturbed.

My new "pal," the oldest, sourest, and pot-belly-est of the gang, sporting several days of stubble and a long graying ponytail, announced gruffly, "I'm holding a private meeting at this table, so you'll need to move along." He looked like the kind of guy who'd speak extra-loud on his phone at an airport so you could hear his side of the conversation.

I saw the bartender glowering at this group's leader. I suspect he just didn't want a mob to bully me away from my table. One member of the group, a history teacher at the local high school, recognized me from my prior membership on Grangerford's 300th anniversary committee. He said he was sorry about how that had turned out for me. I appreciated the sentiment. The county executive—that bastard—"exited" me from the committee because of petty, trumped-up charges. He had just launched his reelection campaign and was being totally political about everything. He really had it coming, that guy.

Anyway, I assured the teacher it was no big deal. The moral arc of the universe bends toward justice, I explained. Everyone gets his due. In the meantime, I was busy on other important projects. I reminded him that in 1666 Sir Isaac Newton, who was also a bit of a homebody, did his groundbreaking work while shut away during a plague. The teacher smiled. He told his ringleader I was OK.

Two others in the group, a school counselor and the elementary school's music teacher, recognized me from one of my recent essays about the county executive. My writing was still polarizing, like all pioneering work, and these two troublemakers loudly denied my OK-ness. They even got vaguely threatening. Like I said, I needed to think about my safety.

Anyway, their pony-tailed leader was about to issue a ruling on me when Pith returned. He looked the group over, smiled broadly, and exclaimed, "Not since Jefferson dined alone, I'll tell you what! Local nobility. Honor and pleasure to be with y'all. Grateful and blessed."

He bear-hugged everyone within arms' reach as well as the rest who weren't. Once the group understood that I was with Pith (whose OK-ness was known by one and all) the leader decreed that Pith and I could both stay and play. But we couldn't vote. I didn't understand what he meant, but seeing as we were in a casino, I let it ride.

As we made room around the table, the leader introduced himself to me with a handshake. His grip was light, his skin soft. "I'm the skipper of this crew," he swaggered. He exuded leadership with his yellowed Bernie Sanders campaign t-shirt and jean shorts. "Name's Michael Powers—that's my *nom de guerre*—but comrades call me 'Mikey P'." He explained that he'd taught English composition and life skills at the local high school for 30 years "before getting bumped upstairs to lead the workers' struggle."

Since all the tables had recently been covered in fresh green felt, each member of the group used a mask as a coaster. Our local Catholic priest arrived and stood above the table, radiating chastity, poverty, and obedience. Pith shouted, "God above! Now I got the earthly *and the heavenly* powers surrounding me. Grateful and blessed, grateful and blessed."

Father Dante smiled and made the sign of the cross above Pith's head. Pith looked down, clasped his hands, and said solemnly, "Bless me, Father, for I have sinned: I'm too danged good lookin' for this world. No penance necessary: Eternal beauty is my cross to bear." Everyone laughed.

The priest took his seat. I figured he must be moonlighting here as the chaplain of the Steadfast. But it turned out he was the table's dealer. "Place your bets. Player or Banker, my children, Amen."

As the cards flew across the felt, Mikey P declared, "I hereby call to order an emergency meeting of the board of directors of the Grangerford District Educators Association. We have three resolutions on the agenda."

It seemed that Pith and I had stumbled into an important voting session of the local teachers' union's leadership. Public-school educators were receiving their full salaries despite only teaching online a couple of hours a day, three days per week, so I appreciated that they were still engaging in important district business.

"Banker wins," said the priest, collecting chips from the table.

"Resolution 1," said Mikey P, raising his left hand and revealing the "Labor Strife is LOVE" tattoo on his left forearm. "We hereby condemn the district superintendent and board of education for trying to rush educators back into schools during this period of grave medical risk."

As the group mulled over the resolution, the high school health teacher sneezed on the bus drivers' representative. The maintenance staff delegate and the middle school's technical-education teacher simultaneously reached into the communal bowl of stale pretzels.

"All in favor, please high-five in the center of the table," said Mikey P, moving the previous question. It passed unanimously.

He continued, "Resolution 2: We demand that the superintendent begin contract renegotiations immediately to provide double funding for our members' preventative health care." In unison, members of the committee gulped down the kamikaze shots that Father Dante had ordered for the table. The physical education teacher from the junior high returned from the vending machine with several bags of pork rinds.

"All in favor, in the spirit of solidarity, spit on your right hand and shake with the brother or sister on your left," said Mikey P. The resolution passed, sloppily and unanimously.

To quiet the table's cheers, Mikey P raised his right hand revealing a "No Justice No Peace" tattoo on his forearm. He cleared his throat and announced: "Resolution 3: Given the enormous financial distress of our members, we demand the school board use the influx of federal funds to provide bonuses to all employees who sign the petition to keep schools closed."

Several members placed large stacks of chips on the board. The high school's financial-literacy teacher, who was wearing a "Workers of the World Unite" shirt, flagged down our server and ordered five bottles of champagne for the table. Mikey P said, "All in favor of the resolution, in loyalty to this thing of ours, please use the knife in front of you to cut your palm and then..."

I looked at my broken watch and announced apologetically that it was time for Pith and me to excuse ourselves. I thanked the group for their dedication to public service. I raised my fist and said, "A victory for one is a victory for all!" They basked in the glow.

Mikey P saw our server walking nearby and shouted, “Darling, can you get me all the receipts from our table?”

He turned to me and said, “These are business expenses. We can submit all this to the district for reimbursement.”

* * *

Sounds good, it’s gotten late.

RECORDING CONCLUDED: 4:31pm
Monday, January 4, 2021
Uncorrected transcript
Interview by Elizabeth Jones

Chapter 15: Recalibrate

From: Dr. Jennifer Davis, MERCY STATE, COMS
Date: January 4, 2021 at 5:49 PM
Subject: RE: Night of 11/1/20, Community Day [CONFIDENTIAL]
To: Elizabeth Jones, Esq. OFFICE OF THE PUBLIC DEFENDER

Ms. Jones:

Yes, certainly. That is not uncommon. In exigent cases like this, on-site law enforcement officials are rushed and stressed. Their initial documents can be incomplete or unreliable.

Your client was our patient at Mercy for less than a week. After the events of his neighborhood's Community Day on 11/1/20, he was detained and transported here for evaluation. Mercy was the nearest medical setting certified for inpatient services of this type. Given the five deaths at the park, our initial medical assessment, and accounts provided by the local deputies, the state police, and the Federal Bureau of Investigation, he was involuntarily committed.

After a week of treatment, our staff deemed him medically stable. Responsibility for his care was then legally transferred to the state Department of Health under the supervision of the state's Attorney General. Judge Thomas approved their joint recommendation that your client be held at Capital City State Hospital (CCSH) pending criminal proceedings. That is the only state facility with suitable psychiatric and carceral resources (Mercy was built in 1920). He has been housed at CCSH since 11/7/20.

Your client presented to us on 11/1/20 with symptoms consistent with psychosis, including mania, delusions, and perhaps hallucinations. The file from law enforcement confirmed that he had been unstable and threatening for some time. His primary delusion since admission (and perhaps before) is that "the entire world has gone insane" and he is the only one able to understand that. This is not uncommon among those suffering similar mental-health episodes.

I recommend that you listen to his account earnestly but skeptically. Your client has always been a fabulist. His stories routinely mix fact and fiction to entertain or make a point. Even when he is in good health, it can be difficult to know exactly what to believe. In this instance, it will be even more difficult. During the type of episode he suffered, memory and other cognitive processes are compromised, often seriously. His recollections of Community Day (and perhaps from weeks or months earlier) are likely impaired. Any part of any story he tells you could be imagined. And he could believe it to be true.

Bear in mind, though, that the primary reason he dismissed his two previous attorneys was their unwillingness to listen to much of his story. They planned to argue in court that he should be found not criminally responsible due to his distorted sense of reality. That is unacceptable to your client; he is convinced that he has something important to say.

Dr. Davis

Chapter 16: Anthology

START: 12:54pm
Tuesday, January 5, 2021
C.C.S.H.

I was thinking after we finished talking yesterday: What we're doing here, this conversation, this is just like *The Decameron* by Boccaccio. It was written in 1353. It's a collection of stories told by people quarantining together during the bubonic plague in Florence. One of my authors for the magazine wrote about it in a poem a few years back. Eerily familiar: I'm telling you pandemic tales, keeping you entertained in the face of death. History doesn't repeat but it rhymes, right?

You take a lot of notes. I appreciate that. The other thing about *The Decameron*—I looked it up this morning—some people called it "The Human Comedy." Ironic nickname for stories during a pandemic. The collision of tragedy and comedy. Anyway, you see now how I'm like Isaac Newton and Boccaccio: Providing insight during a time of pestilence.

Ha! I knew you'd write that one down! Insight during a time of pestilence. Good line, huh?

Alright, back to the plague tales. Pith's bad knees always flare up late in the day, making it tough for him to walk straight after dark. He was leaning on me as we made our way to the Dew Drop's exit when I heard, perpendicular to our path, boisterous laughter from a table near the video poker terminals. And it was aimed at us. I was about to tell them how cruel it was to tease Pith about his joint problems when I noticed Matty's mom Kim was at the center of the taunting!

I shouldn't have been too surprised. If you remember, she and I had been thick as thieves for a hot second after I praised her sausage platter and creepy clock collection. But it was downhill from there. First, she got cross about the way I treated her precious prince. Then she had several letters published in the neighborhood newsletter exaggerating my role in the "spectacle" at the party. Then she started criticizing my recent political writing and calling me offensive names. I blew this off, deciding she was just hyper-sensitive. But this Dew-Drop Kim was *very* different than thin-skinned, security-blanket-sweater Kim.

She was wearing a baby-blue tiered ruffle gown with lace and rhinestone opera gloves. She had sunglasses resting on her head where a crown might go. She was surrounded by an adoring group of sleepy female senior citizens and what appeared to be Ritalin-ed theater kids from the community college. Honestly, she looked like a deposed royal who had to rebuild a wardrobe while possessing a limited budget and reassemble an entourage while retaining limited public esteem.

She pointed at Pith and me and said to her table, "Focus my fabulous friends! Our fair community's finest philistines and their ghastly garb!"

Evidently Kim was no longer charged by the word or double-charged for adjectives. In fact, she seemed to be getting a discount for speaking in alliteration. She also pronounced "fabulous" and "ghastly"—*fahhbulous, gahhstly*—like she was on an English estate not in a disreputable saloon.

Her throng snickered in delight at her gibes. I liked her better in earth tones. But I had to admire Pith's restraint. To demonstrate how little he cared about the taunting, he simply pretended to be passed out.

One of Kim's artistically affected hangers-on, a soft-featured boy of about 19 wearing a scarf and eyeliner, pointed to us and announced, "I just love these authentic dad-bod yokels! They're so kitsch! We should call them 'Bud Light and New Balance!' They could be in a buddy-cop film or play classic-rock covers here on Tuesday nights!"

The table mostly roared in gleeful approval. But at the end of the table, a young woman with black lipstick, Vans, and a septum piercing rolled her eyes, "Nah, instruments are cheugy. This place needs a DJ. I'll text my cousin, she's dope."

Kim ignored the musical discussion, preferring to pursue Eyeliner's initial line of abuse. "Yes, yes, I like that clueless-middle-aged-male direction. I could see them doing commercials for cargo shorts or double cheeseburgers."

The entire table guffawed. I overheard one of Kim's older admirers say in a side conversation, "It's awfully late. Do they have hot tea here? They really do need a davenport in this tavern, that's what I told Marla, they need a davenport."

Kim raised her chin and hand in unison, and the elderly lady on her left with pearls and penciled-in eyebrows filled Kim's Manhattan glass from a carafe and added two maraschino cherries from a jar in her purse. I was dumbstruck. In this pack, Kim was some kind of abusive alpha diva. And if I'm not mistaken that Eyeliner character had made fun of my New Balance.

The teasing continued—for the record, my beard did not look

like a rat's nest—until the depressive bartender came to our rescue. He was about 6 feet and had a disconnected goatee and close-set eyes. His hairline had receded to the crown of his head; what remained was cut short along the top and sides, but it was left a little long in the back. He was top heavy. His thick shoulders and barrel chest testing the seams of his black Dew Drop dress shirt. His athletic shorts revealed scrawny, hairless legs.

He scolded our *fahhbulous* tormentors. "Alright, alright, enough already. Leave these two be, or I'll have to ask you catty thesps to choreograph a closing number out of here."

The table giggled and apologized. Kim and the bartender locked eyes for a half second too long. She then cleared her throat and conceded his point about bullying. I accepted her apology, and Pith agreed with a snore. She waved us away with the back of her hand. Her rhinestones sparkled under the neon Margaritaville sign.

I bowed at Kim and thanked her for granting us an audience. She smiled ever so slightly, pleased that I publicly recognized her standing. Her courtiers levitated with pride. They found their proximity to Kim's faux-power intoxicating.

Now that we were all friends again, I put my hand on the bartender's shoulder and announced, "*Garçon*! The finest summer-sausage platter for the lady and her retinue! And see to it that Eyeliner gets a sassy vest!"

Kim did a spit take. Then sneered. But I noticed that she shifted in her seat and dropped her eyes. With trembling fingers, she fished a cherry from her glass. She tensed herself and glowered at me, "Oh, you think you're *so* funny, don't you? We are not amused."

Court jester Pith hanging on my shoulder whispered in my ear, "Bro, bro, her use of the 'royal we' ain't grammatically proper. Believe that. I keep my majestic-plural rules tip-top. That's real talk."

When she saw Pith and me snickering, Her Highness gave up the Queen's English for the vernacular, "I think you're stupid. Not funny at all, just stupid." Repeating the word seemed to have given her courage. "None of this is funny, it's just sad. I feel sorry for you." She was seething now, but she couldn't square her shoulders to me. She scrunched her cocktail napkin into a tight ball.

Eyeliner did not like this tense turn of events. "Sis, vibe check," he groaned at Kim. He seemed to have a position in her royal court that blended the job descriptions of snarky attendant, stern palace guard, and grumpy eunuch. He clapped three times to reset the table's mood and announced, "More drinks! Where's our server? That ginger needs to bring some jiggle juice! Where is she? The one who looks like a discount-carrier flight attendant—you know, seven years past pretty and crammed into a Lycra skirt."

Rather than escalate matters, I bit the bullet and apologized to the table for my bad manners. I asked Kim for forgiveness. She seemed to decompress. I smiled as kindly as I could and said, "I've seen some of your friends in local musicals. You've really got some great singers around this table." Kim was touched; her crew pretended to be embarrassed by the compliment, but they devoured it whole.

Since we were all friends again, I offered Kim an idea. "Maybe you could put together a barbershop quartet. I hear 'America's Got Talent' has an opening."

Kim was incensed—all snarled lip and squinted eyes. But she was boxed in at her table so she couldn't storm out with a flourish. Instead, she collected herself and executed a pose of gracefully aggrieved. Under the circumstances, it wasn't a bad substitute. I have to hand it to her: Kim is scrappy when it comes to conveying umbrage.

But I think we all recognized that the scene would've felt incomplete without a dramatic leave-taking. Duty called, so I mustered. I hoisted Pith up, tipped my imaginary hat, and called for our carriage. Pith said softly, "Dude, it ain't no carriage, just a golf cart. And it'll stay that way too. Golf cart 'til the cows come home. No pumpkin transformations, no mouse coachmen. No matter the hour. Golf cart, ride or die."

As we left the table's company, I overheard one of them say, "This cast truly is like family, and I *adore* them all, but I shouldn't join a barbershop quartet. I really need to be on vocal rest."

Someone else said, "I'm just going to rest my eyes for a spell. A davenport would help."

* * *

The bartender escorted us to the door and said, motioning back to Kim, "Don't mind queen bee. She's a special woman deep down. Bright, decent, caring." He had a distinctive vocal tick. In the middle of sentences, he'd inhale sharply, air passing through the corners of his mouth and then between his cheeks and bottom teeth. The quick inflow irritated his larynx, because he'd finish with a growly throat-clearing—*aherrm.* It served as a natural if involuntary firebreak, allowing him to pause and cool his words.

"Always was a special girl... *aherrm* ...I mean, woman. I knew her back in high school. We were close for a New-York minute." He hesitated and got sad eyes. He scrunched his forehead and raised his left hand just above his eyebrows, his thumb and unadorned ring finger each rubbing a temple. "But she changed... *aherrm* ...dang, how could she not? —after all the trouble with her husband years ago. But she's still in there somewhere, under that costume... *aherrm* ...."

He wanted to edit that but didn't know how. "Anyway, she's a regular. I thought she'd stop coming in once she knew we had gambling here now—given everything with her ex..."

He trailed off and looked back to her table. Kim laughed effortlessly at the conversation around her and, as she scanned the room disinterestedly, her eyes periodically, accidentally settled on the bartender before moving along.

"But she keeps coming in... *aherrm* ...like clockwork," he finished. The redheaded server was tending to a table on the far side of the room, but she kept glancing back at the bartender.

His extended aside made me realize I knew too little about Kim's backstory. I decided to probe. "For someone so prickly, she sure does have some devotees, huh?"

"That's for sure. Ever since her appearances before the county commission back in 2004... *aherrm*...she's had a cult following among dramatists, pet enthusiasts, and second-wave feminists. I guess that's understandable when you theatrically stand up for animals and yourself in front of an all-male board," he replied impassively, as though he had said something completely reasonable. "Her squad comes in here once a week. They roast everyone."

I'd been curious about Kim's background ever since Pith's reference to her "home-brew animal camp" and her son Matt's "aluminum pinwheel" escapade—both of which apparently took place at the park. At the consignment shop, Barb had also mentioned Matty's pinwheels and something about lawsuits and rabies. Now, this bartender had taken Kim's mysteriousness to a whole new level with these vague allusions to gambling, high-school relationships, county-commission appearances, and her motley crew of disciples.

Pith briefly quit playing possum and cradled the back of the bartender's head and said, "You're a good man. Good man.

You shoulda been homecoming king, and that's real talk." Pith turned to me. "You shoulda seen this cat back in the day. A blonde leonine mullet to beat the band, I'll tell you what. Looked like Daryl Hall at Live Aid."

The bartender was touched. It was the first and only time I saw someone get the drop on Pith and initiate a bear hug. After a few seconds, Pith pulled back and pointed at the bartender's nose. "Don't think we're all chummy now. I'm going to figure out what 'guileless' means one of these days, and then you and me might have a duel!"

The bartender smiled and choked up. At the time, I didn't know what to make of the second reference to "guileless" or the homecoming king thing. I wouldn't figure it out for a while. But once I did—wow.

Before I could thank the bartender for his help, a middle-aged guy stumbled away from the bar and pointed at prima donna Kim. He leaned forward red-faced, teeth showing and yelled, "You'll get yours in time, lady! I promise you that! I still got a scar from that mongoose!"

Kim took that indecipherable threat in stride; her coterie was similarly unperturbed.

The bartender rolled his eyes and said, "Goodness gracious. You could set your watch by it: Kimmy and her troop start up the sass, then my other customers begin airing ancient animal grievances. Excuse me." And then he left to deal with whatever in God's name that beautiful lunacy was all about.

Chapter 17: Wayward

As soon as I got home, I fired up my laptop to study up on Kim. Thanks to the archives of the local paper and the neighborhood newsletter, some police reports, court filings, chat rooms, and fan sites, I learned that her past was, well, complicated.

One day, early summer 2004—not long after Barb's summit with the plumber-ninja-spy at the picnic table—Kim started an unauthorized "animal camp" at the park. They say she'd been known as an animal lover for years. Her home always seemed to have a few dogs and an assortment of rabbits, hermit crabs, and hamsters. But gathering an assortment of creatures for semi-organized activities in a public place was a different kettle of fish. So to speak.

So far as I could tell, it was open enrollment. At the start, it seemed to be part free play, part counseling. It began with a neighbor's unruly border collie and a few despondent feral cats she'd found under porches. Eventually, it grew to include an astonishing diversity of God's creatures: lizards, pigs, chickens, rabbits, foxes, deer. Obviously, no one could've predicted this, but things quickly went awry. Some of the animals were untrained and others were wild, so they didn't always heed the camp's boundaries marked by four plastic cones. Kim had no relevant training and certainly no license to run such an operation.

One day Barb, who has a master's degree in public health, confronted her acquaint-opponent Kim about her qualifications to gather unleashed, undisciplined, unvaccinated animals in a neighborhood park. Kim replied, "My qualification is love." Hmmp.

Kim and her husband had recently separated (*he abandoned her* is more accurate). He was beastly. So to speak. Somewhat understandably, therefore, the community was unwilling to raise much of a stink about her project, particularly after she started calling it her "ministry." But her "wards" soon reverted to their iniquitous ways. One morning, three people waiting for the early bus wound up on the business end of wild animals not interested in Kim's morning calisthenics class. Two men heading to work at the wastewater treatment plant got chewed up by a family of ferrets, and a retired nurse going to the senior center learned the hard way why a male sheep is called a ram.

Over the course of the following week, in the face of several cease-and-desist letters from the HOA, Kim persevered in her heavenly vocation. In fact, she seemed downright energized by the persecution, adding to her slate of offerings Bible study, shuffleboard, and art therapy, which she claimed worked miracles for all marsupials but wombats in particular. She told the next four bus-stop bite-victims that they were overreacting and, anyway, "suffering brings you closer to Yahweh."

Things came to a head when a young woman taking the bus to her job as an assistant manager at the local ice cream shop had her ankles mangled by an adolescent raccoon. Kim was anguished by the incident: She had invested a great deal of time in mentoring that raccoon. The creature, sadly, had proved impervious to cognitive behavioral therapy, so Kim felt absolved: She had tried her best; no one could have asked more of her.

But the ice-cream woman's next-door neighbor was an accountant for the local branch of the department of natural resources. He was saddened by what he heard about the attacks, but he was appalled to learn that one of the campers was a nutria, an invasive species notorious for destroying wetland habitat: Bitings and maulings were one thing, he thought to himself; ecological degradation by a non-native species was another thing entirely. He threatened to bring down on the HOA the full force of his satellite office of a mid-level state agency unless they shut down Kim's health hazard immediately.

Within 24 hours, there was a negotiated neighborhood settlement. Kim's camp was shuttered, and the HOA established a fund to cover the medical bills of all those who agreed not to sue. But several victims refused to play ball. So to speak. They filed a lawsuit against the county and the bus line whose schedule was immediately reduced and whose ridership cratered. There was talk of ending the bus line entirely.

And then things started to get a little weird.

* * *

A handful of local Good Samaritans wanted to ensure a soft landing for Kim. Not exactly a golden parachute, mind you; more like a bronze airbag. She was, after all, responsible for 17 attacks, and that's excluding the non-violent perversions of a randy wallaby. Since her husband had emptied all of their accounts before disappearing, the group worked to find her a job, ultimately arranging for her to take over as executive director of the county's animal shelter on July 1.

Viewed one way, this was a natural fit; viewed in another, it was unfathomable. Barb resentfully asked to see Kim's C.V. Kim responded, "My résumé is love." Barb replied, "Hmmp!"

and fetched her transcripts from her own master's degree program, which was in public health.

Nelly got hives whenever she was aware of an argument anywhere; that her friends were feuding was torture. She took Barb to dinner that night at her favorite Italian restaurant (and Dairy Queen for Blizzards) and bought a white-orchid plant for Kim as an office-warming gift.

At first, Kim seemed to be getting acclimated to her new position. Her staff did most of the real work, so she was able to focus on "evangelization," spreading the Word of Dog. So to speak. She even started paying down some of her soon-to-be ex-husband's debts. And little Matty, who had suffered from his family's turmoil, showed signs of turning a corner.

But in August 2004, and continuing through most of the fall, Kim started showing up at the weekly public meeting of the county commissioners to speak out against the scandalous claims being made against her management and leadership of the animal shelter. She was hurt. She was indignant. She was determined to stand up for herself. The only problem was that no one was aware of any scandalous claims being made against her. There had been no newspaper stories with accusations, no officially filed complaints. No one had the slightest clue what scandalous claims Kim was talking about.

She was still a sympathetic figure locally—she and Matty were alone and penniless. The community outcry about the "unpleasantness at the park" (as the neighborhood newsletter diplomatically termed it) had died down, and medical bills were being paid. The idea of an organized smear campaign against her seemed unlikely.

But you could set your watch by it: Every Tuesday night at 7:30pm, Kim would arrive at the commissioners' meeting at the county's administrative building. It's still there—on Vanitas Street between that boarded-up bank and the Dollar General. She'd sign up to speak during the public-comment portion of the agenda, and then, when called, launch into a vociferous defense of her sullied reputation: Her behavior, she argued, was unassailable; her leadership record lacked even the smallest blemish. She fought without rest against scurrilous charges that—as far as anyone could tell—didn't exist.

The poor, befuddled commissioners didn't know what to do. The five-member board—all white, male, 67ish, and balding with wide, paisley ties and dress shirts with sweat-stained collars—didn't have jurisdiction over the nonprofit animal shelter. They certainly didn't have any recourse against mythical perpetrators of mythical slanders. Since Kim didn't abide by the convention of keeping public-comment statements brief, the commission eventually instituted a three-minute limit for all speakers. Obviously, Kim sued over the policy, which was stayed until the litigation was resolved. Eventually, a state appeals court watched videos of Kim's presentations, said the videos had to be fakes, were assured they were real, unanimously ruled for the commissioners, and strongly encouraged all government bodies in the state to adopt some version of a "three-minute Kim Rule."

While the litigation slogged through the courts, however, members of the commission had to endure the mortifying experience of sitting dumbfounded, their contorted faces broadcast via cable access television, as, each week, Kim took as much time as she deemed necessary to passionately refute baseless charges that hadn't been made.

* * *

According to my sources, over the course of her weekly presentations that summer and fall, Kim grew increasingly unmoored—unmoored from her community and therefore unmoored from reality. She was now a single mom with all the stress and shame that the status carries in such an area. Maybe in earlier days, when the county was confident and open, Kim would've been taken up by a network of friends and neighbors and had a freezer stocked with meals prepared by strangers. But for whatever reason, once an area becomes insular and vulnerable, it feels stronger when it makes its circle smaller. By some, she was shunned. By some, she was forgotten. Even those with whom she'd had a hugging relationship now kept the equivalent of six feet of social distance. Kim occupied a vanishing part of the community's attention.

But strangely, while testifying to the commission, Kim appeared composed, even satisfied. Fending off imagined foes strengthened her. There's an old saying: "We'd care less what people thought of us if we realized how seldom they did." I think Kim had somehow internalized the opposite of that lesson: She was tortured by the idea that that no one was thinking about her. She cared enormously that she might never cross others' minds. But if she had antagonists, even if fictional, then she must be at the center of something. She must matter.

So the more she understood herself as a victim, the more her confidence swelled. If self-worth rises and falls with public attention, then any audience—even an army of prosecutors—is steroids for the ego. The story Kim told herself (important public figure) was the only counterbalance to the message she had been receiving loud and clear from everywhere else (abandoned middle-aged mom).

There was, however, a sliver of a splinter of a silver lining to this tragicomedy. Despite their strained relationship, Barb came through for Kim, increasingly so as the latter, lost in an ostensible conspiracy, tended less and less to matters at the office and home. Barb put aside all her gripes and jealousies. She stepped in and just tried to love and care for little Matty as best she could. She regularly watched him after school and on weekends, including him on her various outings with her own son and daughter. Since Matty loved animals, she bought memberships to the local wildlife center and the state's zoo. Barb was as attentive as Kim was negligent.

After his dad left, Matty began wetting himself. Mostly at night, but also in stressful situations. Kim pretended it wasn't happening or scolded him, telling him to pull it together or else he'd be in trouble. Barb would hug him and laugh it away. "Just an accident!" She kept wipes and extra little-boy pants and underwear in her cavernous bag just in case. Barb's sainted husband never complained about scrubbing the couch or the back seat of the family minivan.

Barb had the time and flexibility to play the surrogate mother because she was no longer working outside the home—a decision precipitated by events she had resented for years but now saw as divine intervention. In the late '90s, when she unexpectedly got pregnant, Barb and her husband agreed that she'd postpone her promising career at the clinic. She had grown up poor, and her shiftless parents were in and out of jail and rehab. Her career was just about everything to her. It was her paycheck . . . her identity . . . the only reputation she had. But she was about to become a mom, and, as she'd promised herself for 20 years, she would prioritize her family. Her baby . . . all babies . . . deserved that . . . and needed . . . That's what was important . . . that child needed his family . . . sorry . . . and so . . . excuse me . . .

. . . and so . . . and so in exchange for Barb's sacrifice, her husband gave up his budding but uncertain career in music. He found something steady and agreeable, if not inspiring, in management at a factory about an hour away. He made extra money on the side in the most wholesome ways: as a math tutor, as a house painter, as a vocal coach. During Kim's troubled spell, he noticed Matty's God-given perfect pitch. Over the next decade he taught that little boy—and then young man—music theory, gave him weekly singing lessons, and introduced him to a cappella, never once asking for even a nickel in return.

According to all involved, Barb's husband was a godsend . . . just what the little guy needed. Twice a week he'd leave work early to pick up Matty at school and take him to a park or to dinner. He calmed Matty during his outbursts . . . exactly what a dad should be. Always there for him and helping. . . [inaudible] . . . he took Matty to basketball games, he always hugged Matty, bought him milkshakes . . . [unintelligible] . . . made Matty feel safe. Things were hard on Matty, he was there to [hug him?] [tuck him in?], protect him no matter what . . .[unintelligible]

RECORDING PAUSED 2:06pm
Tuesday, January 5, 2021
(Transcription edited for clarity)

Chapter 18: Bewitched

RECORDING RESUMED 4:06pm
Tuesday, January 5, 2021

Thanks, I'm good. I want to keep going. I was just getting tired. No big deal. I'm off caffeine, so I get a little sleepy in the afternoons. Back to the story.

Though Kim's extended cries from the heart debilitated the commissioners, they became the stuff of legend in some circles. Her fantastic claims attracted not just attention but, somehow, legions of enthusiasts. She became not exactly a hero but a strange kind of victim-celebrity. She was famous, she was adored, not for achievements so much as for endurance—even though she wasn't really enduring anything.

But Kim was a heckuva storyteller. Hypnotizing. For that brief period, the county's cable-access channel became must-watch television for her diehards. They were transfixed by this valiant citizen who, by day, inattentively managed a nonprofit animal shelter and, by night, warded off imagined plots. To this day, there are remnants of a dozen online communities dedicated to various aspects of her performances—one providing biblically focused exegesis on her written remarks; several comparing her persecution to the trials of Socrates, Galileo, and O.J. Simpson; another interpreting her adventure as a modern version of Joseph Campbell's hero's journey.

Her fanatics heralded her for surviving this crucible, but in time they weren't the only ones bewitched. Others began watching occasionally out of curiosity or voyeurism; soon they watched zealously. The longer Kim went on, the more people actually believed her allegations. Her repetition of false claims proved as powerful as evidence of true ones. More and more people grew terrified of the invisible forces terrorizing Kim. Before long, they worried that they might be next. This quiet rural town was morally panicked to the core. Thank heavens Goody Kim never named a tormentor; her disciples might've erected a county stake and collected firewood.

But the damage was done. A part of Kim—the baby-blue-tiered-ruffle-gown-at-the-Dew-Drop part, not the earth-tones-and-security-blanket-at-home part—was forever addicted to attention by any means. And a part of our county—whatever poised, trusting, cooperative part had remained—was forever degraded.

During the era of her presentations, local stores reported more shoplifting and returned merchandise, restaurants reported more excessive drinking and fights, churches reported fewer congregants and donations, and the police reported more run red lights and tip-line calls for suspicious behavior. The radio waves carrying Kim's presentations to local televisions amounted to an airborne toxic event, spreading to homes a social contagion to which our county's residents were unusually susceptible.

* * *

Butch Tweed (the corpulent crook Pith had warned me about) had been elected HOA president the month before Kim's presentations started. He twice showed up at the commissioners' public-comment period to distance himself and the neighborhood from Kim's exploits. He wanted the viewing public to understand that he ran a peaceful, sensible, family-oriented community. He played the tough guy to the hilt. During both appearances he celebrated his own "intestinal fortitude" and "strong jaw line." The scuttlebutt at the time was that he knew lots of people (i.e., potential voters) were watching the cable-access channel, and he was building up his reputation for his imminent campaign for the state legislature.

Some of the broader public commentary about Kim's performances was tongue-in-cheek (and therefore heartless given her family circumstances). But her devoted supporters hung on her every unhinged word. Level-headedness was needed, but half of the people were too cruel, half too credulous. But I found an archived blog that restored my faith. It was penned by someone playing the role of a simple, plain-talking member of the community. It focused on Kim's travails and the nature of suffering—how pain is senseless but unavoidable, how misery builds character, how withstanding adversity is what it means to be human. The blog was earnest and humane, serious about the subject and sensitive to its main character.

The anonymous author had an accessible, lively writing style. Though the short posts showed study and reflection, the author never referenced lofty figures or fanciful theories. And the author never discussed himself or herself. The blog was solely about the ordeal of the subject. But it's impossible to read the posts and not sense the author's own struggles. The blog, titled "Resolve on Tap: One Barkeep's Take on the Purpose of Grief," announced last call and then turned off its lights with Kim's final appearance before the commissioners in November 2004.

* * *

According to multiple sources, suddenly, unexpectedly, after months of presentations, Kim arrived at the commissioners' meeting dressed in white from head to toe and announced that this would be her "final deposition to a candid world." She asked the commission's indulgence should she take a little more time than usual since she had long endured "like Odysseus's beloved Penelope, like the canonized Joan of Arc, like Rose from *Titanic*."

She spoke for five hours and 18 minutes. A local reporter, on hand for what should've been the commission's discussion of the county's annual budget, wrote that Kim's "speech-ballet-allegory-performance-art" took the meeting past midnight. He assured readers that, even if the clock had not run out, commission members were in no condition for fiscal business by the time Kim closed with a medley of "We Shall Overcome" and "My Heart Will Go On."

When Kim announced that it would be her last appearance, the chair of the commission quietly asked the staff to prepare a citation commending her gallantry and indefatigability. When it became clear that Kim would go on for a while, the chair sent staff out to have the citation notarized and framed. After two hours, the commissioners emptied their wallets and pooled their resources so staff could purchase a slab of granite from the local quarry and hire an engraver. Such was the county government's zeal for immortalizing in stone its guarantee that Kim would forever stay in their thoughts and its assurance that she need never, ever feel any obligation from that point forward to ever return to public-comment time ever, ever again.

* * *

It was probably about 11am by the time I finished all this online research about Kim. I could still smell the Dew Drop on me. I had lost track of time again, so I called in sick to work. Most campus employees were working remotely during this part of the pandemic, but the college administration knew I was key to the magazine, so they wanted me in the office every day. But missing a day wasn't a big deal. This research was important. I think it was a Wednesday. My wife was supposed to come home from her sister's that day. She had said over email that she was looking forward to talking or something along those lines. I was really hoping she'd come home...

My dad never came home.

He left on a Sunday night before bedtime. My mom's sickness was too much for him. I don't blame him. No one should have to go through that. Her screaming, her obsessions. Imagined sins she couldn't shut off in her head. Locking herself in the attic. Cutting. He didn't know what he'd find each day when he got home from work. She couldn't help that. Brains can get sick just like bodies get sick. That's what the nurses told us. He needed a life. I understood that. Even as a 10-year-old. I could understand. It was alright. I was fine. It wasn't a big deal. I could handle it. Isaac Newton lost his dad. Look how much he accomplished. The two musketeers just had more adventures. I could always come up with stories to keep my sister's mind off things. I was OK.

It took time for doctors to find the right blend of medicines for my mom. We had nice neighbors. They helped. I still have a blanket that one gave me this one bad night. With the police and ambulance. Once they got the right medications, my mom could hold it together mostly. I got to see her creative mind at work. When she was in a good spell, we'd sometimes do adventures of the three musketeers. My mom would say something like, "Oh no! There's a report that Martians have taken over the ice cream shop!" We'd rush to investigate and save the day.

We'd pretend we had vanquished the aliens. She'd buy us milkshakes. I loved that. It made me feel warm inside my shoulders. My hands would tingle.

Around that time, my sister started having issues at school. Trouble kept finding her. That was too hard on my mom given everything she was dealing with. The medicines never worked for very long, I don't know why. Things started unraveling again. But it was fine for me, I was able to keep it together for everyone else. I've always had that ability. When I cried at school once after the eviction, I told the counselor that I was OK and not to worry. I was fine. I sat in the nurse's office, and I wasn't a bother to anyone for five hours and 25 minutes.

Even now, today, after all these years, sometimes at night I imagine my dad is tucking me in and kissing me on my forehead and telling me his love for me is bigger than a mountain. He says he'll keep me safe and always be there for me and everything will be good and that God is there for me. And then I imagine my dad hugging me tight and telling me he'll always be proud of me. I haven't seen him since that Sunday night when he had the hard blue suitcase and I was in my basketball pajamas and eating cereal. I wonder if he thinks about me.

Yes, let's stop for the day.

RECORDING CONCLUDED: 4:47pm
Tuesday, January 5, 2021
Uncorrected transcript
Interview by Elizabeth Jones

Chapter 19: Reconsideration

From: Dr. Jennifer Davis, MERCY STATE, COMS
Date: January 5, 2021 at 5:59 PM
Subject: RE: Prior mental health [CONFIDENTIAL]
To: Elizabeth Jones, Esq. OFFICE OF THE PUBLIC DEFENDER

Hi Ms. Jones, yes, it was a lifetime struggle. He has multiple risk factors. These include mental illness among multiple family members, substance abuse, and extended childhood trauma. If he discusses childhood (his or others'), he may become agitated. He also tends to edit parts of his past, erasing or rewriting the most difficult periods. These are all standard coping mechanisms.

The behaviors associated with Community Day mark his third significant psychotic event. He had been treated for a severe anxiety disorder since his teens, but he suffered his first event in his early-20s during graduate school. He was hospitalized here at Mercy State for two weeks (December 2001 – January 2002). He was stabilized and discharged. His ongoing treatment plan included medication and intensive therapy. He recovered and, as you know, had a successful career in public service for a decade.

At some point in 2011, we believe, he ceased taking his medication, precipitating his second episode. A series of stressful events caused his condition to deteriorate; his behavior concerned his wife and others by late 2011. He avoided rehospitalization through significant lifestyle changes, including new medications, sobriety, and a less stressful career. This is when they moved to Grangerford and he took the job at the college. He recovered and was stable for nearly a decade.

In early 2020, his wife once again expressed concern about his condition. But after a video consultation, a physician determined your client's behavior could be considered in the normal range of those struggling with isolation and anxiety during the pandemic. Upon reconsideration, we suspect that had his in-person treatments not been suspended due to public-health protocols a different conclusion might have been reached. We now assess that this was likely the beginning of his third episode.

Take care,
Dr. Davis

Chapter 20: Distress

START: 12:44pm
Wednesday, January 6, 2021
C.C.S.H.

OK, I know you've had enough of Kim's story and that you want me to move along. But I have to give you the coda. It matters for Community Day.

Remember, down at the Dew Drop, I'd seen Kim's capacity for theatrics. You know, the fugazi gems and hammy clique. Then I stayed up that night reading about her past. But a little voice in my head told me to go find the recordings of her appearances before the county commission. Honestly, I was expecting them to just provide some entertainment. But they offered so much more.

I was finally starting to see how the dots could be connected. I was locked in. But at about noon, my "boss" called and ruined my concentration. He wanted to yell at me about missing work again. But I wasn't having it. You know, the college president desperately recruits me to campus to take over that journal, I succeed like no one could have imagined, and then she installs this awful vice president for administration or whatever as my "supervisor." This guy was a real piece of work. Humorless, spiteful. I told him I have the right to take sick days and that he'd been confrontational lately. I told him that I understood that the pandemic had been hard on some people, and I was willing to be compassionate. But I wouldn't be treated that way. He got defensive.

Anyway, I was able to find video of 12 of Kim's 15 appearances before the commissioners. For the first few weeks, only digitized copies of home VHS recordings of the county's fuzzy broadcast are available. But by her fourth appearance, members of the public had begun attending the meetings with their own recording equipment. For her last several appearances, you can find professionally produced videos that incorporate up to four different cameras and include originally scored soundtracks.

It's one thing to read about her performances; it's another thing entirely to experience these one-victim shows for yourself. Each is a testament to the resilience of the human spirit no matter what non-existent threats it faces. But together, the corpus of Spartacus-Kim's martyr cosplay is a mood wrapped in a gestalt tied with a bow of self-parody. It is autobiographical hagiography—the exploits of a living saint told in the first-person.

Until the magnum-opus final installment, each appearance took the same form. She would introduce herself and thank her family and her supporters. She would then allude to her unmentionable suffering and then transition into an extensive mentioning of her suffering. She'd then spend the remaining time explaining how she refused to ever submit to the forces aligned against her. Each week she'd add a fresh element to the presentation—marble columns, a fan to blow her hair, mood lighting, a Greek chorus for the 11th appearance. She'd typically end with a misquote from the Bible or an inspirational lyric from Mariah Carey.

But something else stood out in the videos: Nelly. Nelly had befriended Kim years earlier. As professional women in a traditional community, they'd bonded over personal and work challenges. Both ended up with no-account husbands. Like Barb, Nelly was quick to the scene when things went off the rails for Kim. In the online archives of the state courts, I found a copy of Kim's divorce and subsequent bankruptcy filing.

While Barb cared for Matty, Nelly helped with Kim's legal issues, lent her money, and donated a shoulder to cry on. Nelly, it turned out—as someone once told me—could be loyal, tender, and conscientious. When she could focus on someone else, Nelly's anxieties seemed to vanish. As I've gotten older, I've realized that there are two types of people who are born for the storm. Some proudly, defiantly yell into its gales. Others provide blankets and cocoa, set up cots, and help rebuild neighbors' roofs.

I heard that Pith also quietly lent a hand during these tough times. He mowed Kim's lawn, took out the trash, changed lightbulbs and wound clocks around her house, cajoled case officers from the collection agency. He helped so discreetly that Kim never found out about it. As is Pith's way, he never wanted any credit. "Just doin' unto others, my man," he once told Barb's husband. "Golden Rulin' ain't deservin' of no extra attention." Nelly paid it attention, though, and thought maybe he might make for a caring husband and dad someday. As I mentioned, they gave dating a try, and the timing just wasn't right.

Anyway, at some point in just about every one of the videos, a camera would scan the commissioner's chamber, typically to catch the audience's reaction to one of Kim's rhetorical innovations. In all the early videos, Nelly could be seen sitting stoically in the front row. She didn't seem to understand what was happening. But that didn't matter; she was there to provide moral support to a friend in distress.

But at each successive meeting, Nelly looked more uncomfortable. Then pained. As her friend's claims grew more outlandish, Nelly would wince and drop her head. For those watching from a distance, literally and figuratively, Kim's performances were like an exhibition at the museum of the absurd. For Nelly, they were no such thing: Her friend Kim was unraveling before her eyes. Nelly stopped attending after the 9th appearance.

But one attendee was there for every single one of Kim's appearances—storm or shine—from the very first to the very last. In the back, left corner of the room, Blowtorch Len McGregor sat silently in a sarong, aviator sunglasses, and leg warmers. From time to time, he would tip his bowler hat at one of the cameras, perhaps out of respect for the audience, perhaps to take credit for the mayhem. Who knows. But one thing was clear: He always seemed to be very, very pleased with the spectacle playing out in front of him.

As it turns out, Len *had* been spreading stories about Kim. He was punishing her for what her animal-camp debacle had done to the park and the bus. Indeed, this is how Blowtorch exacts revenge.

And that is what you must understand about Community Day.

Chapter 21: This Whole Time

"My God! You've been down here this whole time?" My wife was home. She was yelling. Her trip to her sister's hadn't helped, I guess.

"We've been back for like eight hours. I thought you were at work. My God, you didn't go to work again?" She'd found me in my basement office. By this point, it was Wednesday night. I'd lost track of time again. Doing research and watching Kim's videos. That happens when I get in the zone. She was crying. The pandemic had been hard on her. I explained that I'd called in sick since I'd been doing important work. That didn't calm her. The pandemic had been hard.

I like being alone. I like the quiet. Emptiness. You get to be in control without anyone else's voice or body. The space and the time are yours. Time is different, too. It's not a burden or prod; there's no difference between this second and the next or this hour and the next. Time is agreeable. The clock isn't tracking you. Time is smooth, supple; no jagged edges; each moment flows into the next, no border between the two; a thought can spread as far as it needs; the time is yours, not the other way around. I love the quiet...

[...EXTENDED PAUSE...]

My wife's hands were rigid, palms facing the ground. She didn't blink. She was really struggling. She was taking short breaths. "I don't. Please. What is happening. Please. I need you. My God." It made me feel good to hear how much I meant to her. I knew I could help her through her troubles. We'd all be delivered from this ungodly plague eventually. She'd be fine. I tried to hug her. But she...and she wouldn't stop crying. She just kept going and going. Each instant was its own barb, distinct and sharp. A new word or sound each moment. Grating. A thousand pin pricks. I needed her to slow down. But each second was discrete, an opportunity for a stare or movement or noise. I kept telling her she could do this, that she'd be OK, but she just kept going. She wouldn't stop. I was getting so...I needed her to stop. She had to stop. This never-ending succession, this infinite spiral, I was getting lightheaded and hot, and...

Wait. Why?

What's wrong? We haven't done much today.

Wait. Please. No.

RECORDING CONCLUDED: 1:17pm
Wednesday, January 6, 2021
Uncorrected transcript
Interview by Elizabeth Jones

Chapter 22: Reverberations

From: Dr. Jennifer Davis, MERCY STATE, COMS
Date: January 6, 2021 at 2:59 PM
Subject: RE: Violence? [CONFIDENTIAL]
To: Elizabeth Jones, Esq. OFFICE OF THE PUBLIC DEFENDER

No. None whatsoever. Like many children brought up in unstable conditions, he developed the dispositions and habits of a peacemaker. He avoided confrontations and sought to deescalate tense situations. He was passive in the face of direct conflict. We've interviewed all his previous physicians and counselors, and none foresaw anything like his role in the events of Community Day. His complete lack of remorse for his actions that day is inconsistent with his character.

With that said, serious mental illness does run in his family, and several of his close relatives were prone to aggression. His mother was voluntarily admitted as a patient at Mercy State intermittently between January 1982 and December 1987. She frequently had physical altercations when she was unwell. The family moved a great deal as a result. Your client's sister has a long arrest record and a history of self-harm.

Your client's maternal grandfather—his mother's father—was

involuntarily committed to Mercy State from May 1951 until his death in June 1980. Though he was diagnosed as schizophrenic at the time, his records suggest he was also an alcoholic and had PTSD, likely from the wars. He was non-responsive to early anti-psychotic drugs and remained aggressive.

Hang in there.

Dr. Davis

PS: You might have already heard but there's likely to be another rally tomorrow outside of the hospital calling for your client's release. His celebrity is growing. You can enter the facility through the small lot in the back. I've asked the hospital's administration to clear you. Bring your state ID, and give yourself extra time. They'll have tighter security.

Part 3:

The Gazebo

Chapter 23: Relativity

START: 2:09pm
Thursday, January 7, 2021
C.C.S.H.

Late start today? Are you OK?

Good. Good.

Alright, before we get to Community Day, we must talk about the night at the gazebo. I saw everything differently after that crazy conversation. I learned so much. God, so much. About the neighborhood. About these people I thought I knew. Their relationships. Honestly, sitting here now, knowing what I know, I can't imagine how an outsider could even begin to understand Community Day.

It's so easy to think you know a place just because you're there. Or you think you know people because you see them every day. But there's a whole lot more to a community than locations and bodies. You have to understand why those people are there and what they mean to one another and why certain places and things matter to them. You have to understand the stories they tell one another and the stories they tell themselves.

I think Spinoza wrote that peace is more than the absence of war. To have *real* peace—true and lasting—you need justice, harmony, security, opportunity. It's not enough to stop the shooting. In the same way, I think community is more than the absence of loneliness. It's not community if you have a room full of people who don't know each other or don't talk or are afraid of or hate one another. Human proximity isn't enough.

I must admit: I learned a lot about community from Nelly and Barb's friendship. From what this county did to Kim and what Kim did to this county. From the endless generosity of Barb's husband. From every single fiber of Pith's being. And, maybe most of all, from Blowtorch Len—of all people, Blowtorch Len! Who would've imagined that? And I learned most of it during Gazebo Night.

You sure everything's alright? You're not acting like yourself. Just excited about the next part of the story? You have that apprehensive look. Probably amazed that I'm able to do all of this from memory, huh? OK, back to it. This part is legendary.

One evening, maybe a month or two after the Dew Drop night, Barb and Nelly were chatting over at the park's gazebo. They'd never done that before; not that I could remember anyway. Maybe they were struggling and needed some socializing. Maybe they'd been crying a lot and napping all the time, things of that nature that were happening.

The entire neighborhood had just gotten an email saying Community Day had to be postponed again. There had been a wave of infections or a new variant or something. The county had probably leaned on our HOA to scuttle the event. I heard that this latest delay had rattled a lot of people—they really needed the pandemic to end, they wanted things to go back to how they were. But like I said before, Community Day didn't matter that much to me. I had my projects.

My wife wanted me to join Barb and Nelly over at the park. She said I should get out of the house and get some fresh air. She didn't use her funny "qualify for recluse status" line, but it was in the same vein. I wanted to show her that I appreciated some of her recent efforts. Over the previous few weeks, she'd been trying hard to be positive, forcing a smile when I was around, rubbing my back, saying, "Things are going to be fine." She had also started working part-time to keep herself busy. Doing bookkeeping for a couple of places that hadn't been shut down. A landscaping company and an auto-repair shop, I think. She'd been having a hard time, so I was glad she was trying to turn things around.

But I had no interest in going over to the park. I never liked the gazebo. Adults gossip, teens get high and shoot fireworks from the roof. A year back, I sent a letter to the HOA telling them they should knock it down and replace it with bocce ball courts. You know the drill: "We'll keep your suggestion on file." But tonight especially I had no desire to chat with Barb and Nelly. I was neck deep in some important work and didn't want to get distracted.

I told my wife that I just wasn't up for drinking vodka Red Bulls with our friendly neighborhood yentas, much less reading the entrails of consignment-shop donations. She laughed for the first time in a long while. That made me happy. She'd be OK. It was all good.

When she smiled, I could still see the girl in the burgundy turtleneck. She'd grown her hair out a little over the years—she was now sporting a short shag with a little chemical color assistance. She didn't wear a cross anymore, and her lips weren't as full as they'd once been. But those hazel eyes were the same.

She assured me that Barb and Nelly were drinking merlot and eating chips and guacamole and that I could always diplomatically shift the conversation in a more charitable direction if they veered off course. She conceded Nelly's nonstop anxiousness, referring to her as "Calamity Jane." Well, I nearly fainted out of shock and fury: I explained in no uncertain terms that it is dehumanizing to make up nicknames for people. She tried to stifle a giggle as I announced that I was going to tell Pith and Masonry about her callousness.

Ultimately, I agreed to go to the gazebo, but I made it abundantly clear it was only to distance myself from her toxic nicknaming. I stormed to the kitchen to get my own food and drink, muttering—just loud enough—that I refused to get over there and have Public-Health Karen and Nervous Nelly telling people for the next year that I was a mooch. I was still cursing under my breath when I got to the front door with my snacks.

My wife doubled over laughing. "You're taking buttermilk and frozen peas? Lord, what will Barb and Nelly say!"

Anything to make her smile.

I deadpanned, "Don't tease my goodies. I have a refined palate and a temperamental valve."

She walked over to me with a stifle-free giggle, wiping the side of her index fingers under her bottom eyelids. "I still love when you make me laugh," she whispered as she hugged me around my ribs.

I let this go on for about five seconds and then pulled away and shouted spartanly, "Back off, woman! I'm heading into battle! Kissy-face will only make me soft! I shall return with my shield or on it!"

She got on her tip toes and kissed my forehead. I told her not to get too comfortable because I'd be back in a flash if Nelly tried to get me involved in her money-laundering schemes.

She playfully yelled, "Oh, stop it, you! Nelly is so innocent and pure she wouldn't even know what money laundering is! She sells recreational vehicles, floor mats, and tree-shaped air fresheners for a living!"

I squinted. "The lady doth protest too much, methinks..." I said pregnantly, using my finger to lift my eyebrow.

She rolled her eyes and blew me a kiss. As I fake-stomped outside, I could hear her saying to herself, "Things are going to be OK. We just need to hold on a bit longer. Things will be fine."

I believed her—she was strong, she would get a grip on things and get through her troubles. And I'm eternally grateful that she made me go over there. It was so good for me. Like I said, over the next 12 hours—at the gazebo and then through my online research at home—I got priceless information about the park, the neighborhood, and, ultimately, the meaning of Community Day 2020.

* * *

Barb and Nelly had the same awkward, upright posture and offered the same semi-smile as I approached from our driveway. It looked like they had a specific seat in mind for me, too. The un-spontaneity of this spontaneous gathering was fishy. Maybe the lockdown had gotten them out of practice at socializing. Who knows. Nelly's dog was over there too with his blank, witless stare, so at least something was unscripted. They were visibly thrown by my buttermilk and peas, so their advantage was lost. Barb snuffed out her cigarette.

Crossing the street, I had seen one of Nelly's huge Class C RVs standoffishly parked halfway down the block, refusing to get too close to the park. Maybe her lonely inventory and the abandoned bus stop were in a spat about which was the county's most depressing transportation project.

I also noticed that same mysterious stranger—Jimmy Callahan—over at the resurrecting memorial garden again. The sky was autumn-gray, and he had on a navy-blue pullover and a herringbone Gatsby cap. He was packing up his gear for the night.

The arbor looked better than ever. He had also planted a variety of perennials—daylilies, hibiscus, lavender—around the edges of the garden and what appeared to be an apple tree sapling on the north side. The sun was very low on the horizon. It had found a crease in the cloud cover, and the day's last rays lit up his handiwork and stretched his shadow long across the entire garden. I waved; he gave me a friendly thumbs-up.

As I climbed the two small steps up to the gazebo, Nelly and Barb motioned to a laminated sheet and newly installed wooden box affixed to a post by the entry. The notice, with an oversized image of the county's seal centered at the top, was from the county health director—the same local authority who prohibited repairing the memorial garden, turning Jimmy Callahan into our own woodworking Antigone.

I remember that the sheet read:

> Dear Subjects!
>
> Protecting the public is my most solemn duty! Because of my love for you and my selflessness, I have promised to do everything to stop this fiendish pandemic! Therefore, all outdoor assemblies are prohibited! Gathering spaces give the false impression that we should spend time with neighbors during these unfortunate times! They also undermine this government's ability to help you help yourselves! You're welcome!
>
> However, this virus must be understood in the broader context of fairness, oppression, and dignity. As you might know, my daughter is getting married, and it's not cheap let me tell you and we've had to postpone it like 50 times and we lost our deposit on the reception space at the country club, that events manager over there, she's a piece of work, it's been

> this whole thing, I'm going to talk to her supervisor, believe me. And now my husband is all worked up about these bills and I told him to calm down and we'll pay when we're ready and he said that attitude is how I got my credit score and that they should just elope and save everyone the hassle. But this wedding is my special day and no one is going to ruin this for me, don't even get me started on collection agencies. Therefore, if you contribute to the county's Nuptial Equity Fund, you may convene in this outdoor facility.
>
> When your donation in this coffer rings, the cause of social justice sings!
>
> In righteousness,
> Scarlett Bennet, MPH
> Benevolent Director
> County Health, Well-Being, Justice

I apparently came up a little short with my initial expression of commitment to this noble cause because Barb yelled, "Watch your language!" and Nelly screamed, "Oh dear! Oh dear!" To keep the peace, I pulled out a $5 bill and subsidized our public leader's effort to advance the common good.

During the first 10 minutes of gazebo small talk, I learned that selling a hutch is a marital death knell and that the couple that just moved into the neighborhood has odd trash-disposal habits and you have to wonder what's going on there. I mostly played with Nelly's dog, who, I realized, knows like 15 commands. I guess I'd been too tough on him. I probably saw that dangling tongue and pleasant stare and assumed he was dimwitted; saw him palling around with Nelly and charged him with ridiculousness by association. But that's not fair; he's not responsible for his surroundings. He's just dealing with them. It dawned on me that never once had I seen him act unruly.

Never barked at another dog, never pulled to sniff a tree, never chased after an artless squirrel engaged in completely standard squirrel behavior. Maybe he was perceptive, disciplined. Maybe he was just playing the rube. Clever boy. I'd keep an eye on him.

Nelly must've just finished with her evening scurry. She had on a blaze orange t-shirt with the short sleeves pushed up above her shoulders. Her evaporated perspiration had left behind the faintest streaks of salty residue on her forearms. I listened quietly as she and Barb chit-chatted about unintriguing neighborhood intrigue.

Barb, as per usual, did not lack for certainty. "Hmmp! Unless they reroute the drainage canals along Poplar and Harvest, we'll never get sewer lines." "Ack! An oak's roots can damage a sidewalk three miles away." "Pssht, I can tell you how much time a couple has left just by looking at their dinette set."

Nelly spoke haltingly. Herky jerky. In choppy bursts. It was as though her mind had horsepower and fuel to spare but her nerves messed up the clutch. "Yes, for sure…well, you, uhhh… you know…it's…I see the other side…Einstein's General Relativity explained the precession of the perihelion of Mercury's orbit…I'm not…oh, but…gravity and time…complicated…you know?"

I sort of zoned out and thought through a few of my newer ideas. I ended up with the makings of several more columns for my newsletter. I was going to lacerate that wicked county executive. There's no way I'd stand by and allow him to get another term. Election Day was just around the corner, Tuesday, November 3. I had it circled on my calendar, believe you me. It was nice to have something productive to occupy my mind since Barb and Nelly were mostly talking about virus-related sob stories.

Barb was fretting about her son. He had just made the personal decision to step away from college at the insistence of his academic advisor, the admissions office, and the student disciplinary council. I remember him as a gawky, chipper adolescent who volunteered at the senior center and was passionate about board games and the bass guitar. But he'd recently gained 50 pounds and turned sullen. I saw him a few times down at the Ohunka walking loop. I'd been going to the river most days. Usually around lunch until late afternoon. I never got the chance to talk to him, though. He knew the protocol of the procession—like I told you, no one talked there. He'd see me but keep some distance so we wouldn't be tempted to talk. I liked silence with the Wayfarers. My mind slowed.

But all that came to an end when the county executive shut down the Ohunka loop, declaring it a health risk: too many people too close to one another. His administration put up fencing and yellow police tape. But that very same week, the county executive was photographed with a group of 20—including health, well-being, and justice director Scarlett Bennet and most of his high-dollar campaign donors—maskless and in a private room at the swankiest restaurant in the county. Everyone in the region was furious about that. The smugness and the hypocrisy. Everyone was saying that something had to be done about him.

Anyway, Barb was listening to Nelly explain how her ex-husband—that pious man who'd performed rituals with nuns in an hourly motel—was getting lost in video games and pain pills. She said her neighbor across the street doesn't get out of bed some mornings and sometimes spends hours crying. I guess a lot of people were crying for no real reason.

Honestly, I didn't want any part of Barb and Nelly's mopey talk. I didn't give up a night of research to listen to them wallow in misery. Self-pity doesn't do anyone any good. Move on and focus hard on other things. Make the best of your situation. I remember getting more and more frustrated and thinking that they needed to cut it out with the drama. Pull it together already. They must've gotten really sad about their stories because I eventually realized both of them had gone silent and had tears in their eyes. The pandemic had really done a number on people.

Chapter 24: Abandoned

I had to break the god-awful silent tension. I told them I had studied up on the events of 2004: I'd read about Kim's infamous animal camp (which, I realized was based literally paces from where we were sitting) and watched her famed county-commission videos. Neither Nelly nor Barb said anything. Both kind of shifted in their seats. I'm good at picking up on things like that. It was probably still raw for them. They witnessed it first-hand.

Barb, who was wearing an electric-green poncho, white yoga pants, and sparkly flip flops, stared through me and said quietly, "Hmmp. Animals are more reliable than most humans."

Nelly didn't reply. Her mind seemed to have gone elsewhere. She squinted and turned away. She probably hadn't even been listening to me. I bet she was conjuring up some catastrophe to fret about. She reached behind her head and freed her ponytail and slowly raked her fingers across her head. I'd never seen her with her hair down. It was wavy and fell to her shoulder blades. She blushed and shifted in her seat again. She put on the reflective running jacket that had been tied around her waist.

A storm cloud settled over Barb's face, and she blurted out, "Did you know that Kim hasn't spoken to me in nearly 17 years?"

No, I didn't.

"She got it in her mind that Nelly and I weren't supportive enough during her hard times. Pssht!" Barb thundered.

Nelly cleared her throat and said, "Barb and I...together...we jointly...see...we went to one of Kim's presentations... gut-wrenching ...I couldn't...it tore me...we had to do something." Nelly's nerves were going to strip the gears. "We told her...Barb and I...the two of us...tried...look, we said...I think I said that she needed some help...we were there for her...I said that...we tried...I wanted to hug her." Nelly stopped herself.

"Gah! She refused to talk to us about it! She said we were attacking her! She said she didn't need that. *Real* friends wouldn't do that to her, she said. Argh! She raged at us!"

"I spent...God...for the next year...how I tried to fix...time and time again...you know, I tried so hard...I just wanted to patch...I needed to help her."

Barb touched the corners of her mouth with her index finger and thumb and said, "Nell humbled herself and accepted all the blame. Hmmp! Even though there was no blame to accept, Nell accepted it." Barb's face went from rain clouds to ice storm. "I refused. Refused! We didn't do anything wrong! I wouldn't apologize. I was strong. Noble. We tried to..."

"She needed a friend!" Nelly's interruption of Barb surprised them both.

Nelly put her elbows on the table with both palms facing up like she was holding a platter with the correct answer. She dialed it back. "It's just...see...I didn't mind apologizing...what mattered...I know Kim needed someone...like me or Barb... I would...truly I said this...I would do anything...she needed help...friends...someone...that was most important."

Several beats later, Barb said matter-of-factly, "Kim didn't invite me to Matt's high school graduation." And then, choking back tears. "My husband got invited. I didn't."

❋ ❋ ❋

"Bleh! Davey was a jerk. Slimy charmer. Such a politician. Gah! I always hated him. Disgusting." After a bottle and a half of wine, Barb didn't feel the need to invent furniture intrigues before weighing in on Davey and Kim's collapsed marriage.

"Oh...no, no...yes, I know, but...he was...he was a good man... I know, *I know*...it was so sad," Nelly responded plaintively. "He loved Matt...he did...to the moon and back. And you know... you know this...you saw it, Barb...he treated Kim like royalty... devotion...you know he called her 'my queen'...'my queen'..."

Barb stared down the empty street. Nelly exhaled and half-shrugged. "He was careless. Careless. I know that...we saw...we saw it. He got himself in a hole...he dug it...I know that. But... Barb, please...you know...he just couldn't climb out." Nelly glanced at me and then looked at her hands. Her nails were painted lavender.

"Ack!!! Careless? *Careless*? Anyone can be careless—you should see my husband fold his socks! Davey was vile. *Vile.* And what has gotten into you? Why are you changing your tune on Davey? You know better. You know better than that." Barb sensed her advantage.

Nelly responded sharply, bugging out her eyes, "Circumstances change." She finished another glass of wine and clenched her jaw. "Have sympathy."

Barb was unmoved. "Pshht. Sympathy. Ha."

Wine and indignation were helping Nelly operate the clutch.

“Mercy... sweet mercy is nobility's true badge,” she replied.

“Geh! I don’t know what you’re talking about. He was an idiot blackjack addict, plain and simple,” seethed Barb, blood and revenge hammering in her head. “He ran through every red cent she had saved! Destroyed the business her grandfather built. Hmmp! Sixty years of her family’s work down the drain. Why? *Why*? His stupid card games, that’s why.”

I was beginning to side with Barb. Since the Ohunka loop got shut down, I’d been spending more time at the Dew Drop. I liked the people and the energy. But I saw lots of gambling problems. Folks lose and lose but keep betting. The tables had neither sympathy nor mercy.

“I know...listen, I know...he caused so much pain...God, all that debt...but truly...he was good, and he was suffering.” Nelly’s tone and cadence had changed. Slower, smoother delivery. Deeper voice. Now she was tripping up on human contradictions, not self-doubt. She took a long sip of wine.

“Ha! Suffering? *Suffering*? He just up and leaves his family high and dry? Takes the dogs but leaves the humans behind? His wife falls apart! A successful, confident, generous woman—she used to put on full make-up just to go to the grocery store! A stately, composed lady reduced to...making up stories to try to reclaim some power and order! Embarrassing herself publicly! And *he* was suffering? *He* was suffering? Guh!”

Nelly sat calmly. Said nothing. Ruminated.

Barb did her thinking aloud. “Ahh! And another thing while I’m at it! That precious boy? That little prince? God, Matty idolized that rotten excuse for a father. That child wouldn’t stop crying when Davey left. At the kitchen counter. Where he had eaten breakfast with his dad. At bedtime. Hours of apologies, promising to be a good boy if his daddy would come home. Wetting himself as soon as he’d fall asleep! Wetting himself whenever he got scared!” Nelly closed her eyes and put a balled-up hand in front of her mouth.

Barb pressed the gas. "Screaming fits at school. Christ almighty. At church! Desperate tears out of nowhere. Watching television. It was months...*months* of that. He's never been the same. That poor boy was permanently damaged by that dirtbag."

"Yes...but...yes, of course...it was...it is unfair...little Matty... I know...I get it...but his dad...Davey needed help." Nelly continued equivocating, but I couldn't help but stare at Barb. Her neck was getting red, and her fingers were clenched around her thumbs. I'd never seen her like this. A few times I glanced over at Nelly to see how she was processing Barb's display. Each time, she was staring back at me. We were probably thinking the same thing.

"All joy was wrung out of him. Boys don't recover from that." Barb wasn't done. "Thank God in heaven my husband was there. He was that child's guardian angel. I believe that. I believe that in my soul." Barb made the sign of a small cross on her chest plate. "That precious little boy was old enough to know he had been abandoned, that his *father* had put his sick obsession above his own child. Wretched man. Selfish man. *Evil* man. Damn him. Damn him to hell"

I had been writing a lot. That's why my hand started vibrating a little bit. I only noticed it because I was zoning out Barb's yelling. My hand thing was subtle. Not a big deal at all. I was totally unaffected by her theatrics. I've always been good at keeping my cool when other people are worked up. Anyway, I had been typing a lot recently. My newsletter was important. Influential. That's why I had that small hand cramp. I just grabbed a few chips and brought both hands down onto my lap.

Barb uncrossed then re-crossed her sturdy legs. I could hear her yoga pants chafe. She brought her left foot down hard on the wooden planks of the gazebo floor. Her face changed. She had an idea. She lifted her left arm just above the tabletop and used her right hand to first adjust her wristwatch and then clear crumbs from the table in front of her. Then she struck. "Hmmp. Cut it out, Nelly," she said cuttingly. "Just stop it. You darned well know that you were terrified by Kim's bankruptcy."

Nelly didn't visibly react, and that perturbed Barb to no end. Barb fiddled with one of her huge gold hoop earrings then drank some wine. "All this forgive-and-forget nonsense you're now peddling," she said to Nelly, "is just the guilt talking."

Nelly's left eyelid twitched. She rubbed it, hoping it would settle. But it hadn't been listening to meditation podcasts. "Maybe…I guess…perhaps, it is." Nelly allowed.

It was getting chillier. The clouds were clearing, and the waning gibbous moon rising to the east over the memorial garden lit the sky. Nelly looked ashamed, but only briefly. She exhaled and clasped her hands in front of her on the table. "Anxiety and anger…they are liars…they mislead good people…and selfishness and stubbornness, too…they deceive." I imagined Nelly practicing those therapeutic lines in front of a mirror. They almost came out fluidly. Muscle memory.

Nelly turned up the collar on her running jacket and looked straight at Barb, who, unsettled, involuntarily sucked in air through her nose as though her olfactory system had temporarily lost the scent of Nelly's fear. Slowly, firmly, Nelly said, "They can make you do foolish things. I did unkind, selfish things."

Chapter 25: Compassion

Eventually, Nelly continued, muttering, "That little boy... sweet child...he deserved better. Childhood innocence...colliding with...ruined by adult problems."

I admit I was losing my temper at this point. All their wallowing in gloom and doom. That's not how I operate. Self-pity is weak. I can't stand that. But I just held it in. Stayed composed. That's why I lost my breath. It takes exertion to keep control. I just blinked a bunch and clenched my jaw to get my breath back and vision right. It was fine. I explained to them that I was alright. But they kept asking. If anyone tells you about my hands or my breath or whatever that night it was only because I was getting frustrated by all the self-pity. Body stuff like that's normal for me. It's not a big deal. Just how my body works. Like little adrenaline surges. Lightheadedness sometimes, you know? Doctors checked my heart years ago. It's in good shape. No problems. I can easily manage by focusing on a task. Blocking everything else out. It's like meditation. That's what I've told my wife. My style of meditation. My research and writing help a lot. When my mind is occupied, everything goes quiet. Time slows and smooths out. No barbs.

"Innocent...collateral damage..." Nelly went on, burbling to herself. "Suffers because of someone else's selfishness...and meanness...and blindness..." She looked at the bus stop sign and trailed off.

Part of me suddenly expected to see Len standing over there. I don't know why. The brain works in strange ways. But he wasn't there. It did seem, however, like Nelly wasn't just talking about Matty anymore. I think that was the first time I wondered if Nelly was hiding something. Well, other than her money laundering.

"Aha! Finally! You're coming to your danged senses, Nelly. Welcome back to the real world, lady! Nice to have you. Hmmp!" The wine had loosened Barb's pink shimmery lips. She uncrossed and re-recrossed her legs again and then straightened her blinding, neon poncho by grabbing it along her hips and pulling down crisply. Neither spoke.

We needed some levity, so, referencing tidbits I'd picked up over time, I said, "There was an incident with Matt and pinwheels years ago? Saving foxes or something? Was that about the same time as his family troubles?"

It turned out this wasn't exactly comedy gold. Barb harrumphed and crossed her arms. Nelly put her head in her hands then slowly pulled her fingers across the sides of her scalp through her black-with-two-inches-of-graying-roots hair, gathering it together along the nape of her neck, twisting it, and then bringing it across her right shoulder. She pulled down her sleeves at the wrists, turtling her hands back into their nylon shells. Both Barb and Nelly then acted like I hadn't said a thing.

Barb returned to staring at Nelly. Barb believed she had won their argument about Davey's wickedness. She wanted Nelly to acknowledge it. But Nelly sat with her eyes closed, rhythmically bumping her wrists together.

Frustrated by Nelly's silent obstinance, Barb rolled her eyes and turned to me. She leaned across the table, bringing her chin low as her elbows slid apart. She semi-whispered to me, “Soooo, I’ve been meaning to tell you how sorry I am that the hospital wouldn’t let you be with your mom when she passed last month. These Covid restrictions. It must’ve been so, so hard for her to be alone while she was... These regulations. Well, the county executive is just trying to keep us safe” — heavy sigh— "...what are you gonna do? We just grin and bear it.”

Barb smiled, satisfied by her display of compassion, drank some wine, and added. “I was at the nail salon when I heard that news. It was packed. I told everyone there how sad I was for you.”

OK. Yes, now would be a good time.

RECORDING PAUSED 3:47pm
Thursday, January 7, 2021

Chapter 26: Gravity

RECORDING RESUMED 4:43pm
Thursday, January 7, 2021

OK, a little while later we heard a quiet rumbling and then saw a floating figure in the shadows above the street; it was moving rapidly in our direction. Naturally, Nelly shrieked and tore for the woods. Her dog, humiliated that he hadn't sensed the imminent non-danger, continued to lay peacefully. Fortunately, it was just Pith on a skateboard.

I hadn't seen him in a while, and he looked paler and gaunter than usual. He had a bag of pretzels under his arm and was carrying a Super Big Gulp instead of his typical red cup. I filled in for the evacuated Nelly and joined Barb in motioning him toward the county's health-and-fancy-wedding-subsidy-fund notice. He read the sign carefully, protruded his bottom lip, and nodded in agreement. Wow, I thought, Pith contains multitudes; I hadn't realized that his political consciousness had been raised. But then he started to unzip his jeans and prepare to relieve himself on the donation box.

Barb yelled, "Ack! My God, no! That's a health-code violation!" Maybe Pith had forgotten that Barb has a master's degree in public health.

He folded his seven-foot frame onto the bench on my right. He did a triple-take at the bag of thawing peas. He pulled off his fishermen's beanie and rubbed his scabbed hand across his bare dome. The peas still wouldn't compute, so he looked at me for answers. I rolled my eyes dramatically and nodded at Barb as if to say, "You know Barb and her thing for half-frozen starchy legumes." He smiled broadly, appreciating my non-sense, and then coughed. Barb was none the wiser; she had her head down, digging in her purse for her tape measure.

Realizing the non-crisis had abated, Nelly cautiously returned to the gazebo. Her dog turned his head away, too embarrassed to make eye contact and knowing a justified scolding was on its way. But rather than turning her attention immediately toward her negligent protector, Nelly stopped as she reached the steps and looked again at the county's notice, biting her bottom lip and deliberating. Eventually she said to the universe, "Moderation in pursuit of justice is no virtue." She reached into her pocket and put another $20 dollars in the box. "I have to do the work," she said quietly.

By this time, Barb had finished chalking each person's six-foot buffer zone, so Nelly was able to return to her seat across from me and between Pith and Barb. Nelly and Pith locked eyes. Briefly. She took a gulp of wine. He downed about 12 ounces of his drink. Both smiled sheepishly. She went first.

"I'm sorry...I am...I do apologize...see...sincerely...it was really dark....I was startled...ahem...that's no excuse...I know...so I, uh, I regret screaming 'We're all going to die, Voldemort is going to kill us' when you...you were just skateboarding... when you approached...ahem...when you came to the gazebo." She adjusted the zipper on her jacket but still couldn't look anyone in the eye. "It's been said...look, I know...yes...I have been known to overreact...a little...from time to time." Her dog exhaled loudly.

The moonlight made Pith's bald head glow. He replied, "I'm sorry about what I done to your flower bed again last night. I need to get them golf-cart brakes fixed."

Barb uncrossed and re-crossed her legs. Nelly allowed her hands to turtle out from their sleeve shells and then lifted her eyes toward Pith and cocked her head. He took another pull from his cup and then looked over Nelly's shoulder to the center of the park to where the sundial had been.

He sat still for several seconds, lowered his head, this time like a penitent, and finally said softly, "I'm sorry about everything, Nells."

* * *

Barb caught her breath as she saw Pith, drawn and sallow, under the gazebo's fairy lights. A sore on his upper lip stood out. He'd lost weight that he'd been in no position to misplace, and his teeth didn't look great.

[...EXTENDED PAUSE...]

You know...I haven't talked to my sister since I drove her home from rehab three years ago.

[...EXTENDED PAUSE...]

"So, how've you been lately?" Barb asked Pith while staring at the wine she swirled in her glass.

"Truth be told, not so hot. Tough days. Tough stretch," wan Pith replied. He was hunched over, his chewed-off fingernails picking at shards of wood in the tabletop. "We can't open back up. Inventory's sittin' there. I got debts no honest man could pay. I do a lot of sittin' nowadays, too. Lots of hours in the day, you know what I mean? Time's like a mule in molasses." He paused and then confessed. "Waking up is hard sometimes.

Body feels heavy."

Barb cleared her throat and attempted to smile. "We're all trying to hold on until it ends. This too shall pass," she offered with more hope than reason. "My family...yes, indeed...we're trying...we're doing our best...gritting it out." Barb had suddenly broken into an unintentional Nelly impersonation. Her eyes welled up.

Nelly cleared her throat and said to Pith, "I was starting to tell these two...I was about to say...things went downhill for me... I was no longer myself...back when my dealership was first in trouble years ago. I didn't recognize myself...didn't know... who that woman was..."

"Yessir, yessir. Know the feeling. In times of trouble, the mirror becomes a stranger. No doubt," agreed Pith.

"As soon...first thing in the morning...when my eyes opened... it was like the Earth had doubled in density...pulling me down...plastered to the mattress," confided Nelly.

"I'll tell you what: The gravity of the times. Real talk."

"Hmmp," added Barb softly.

Everyone went quiet. A few teens on bikes rode down the street laughing and instigating one another. Pith must've gotten to the bottom of his cup because he added to it from a flask he'd had in the front pocket of his sweatshirt.

Barb looked at Nelly, who bumped her wrists together a few times and then turned toward me, "So then...how are things... how, I mean...how have you been doing given the..."

"Good. Good. Staying busy. Staying positive," I replied. Barb brushed more crumbs from the table. Nelly's dog got up, walked in a circle, and sat against my right leg. He moaned quietly and then put his head on my lap.

The recurring silence threatened to dampen spirits, so I tried to keep the conversation going. I got Pith caught up. "Right before you got here, I asked about Matt and the aluminum pinwheels. We'd been talking about the animal incident at the park all those years ago and Kim's infamous shows at the county commission. She must've had some serious problems."

Pith must've really been struggling. He started to half-stutter. Pith might stumble but never over words. He said something like, "Yessir, bro…yessir. After all that went down with Kimmy…yup, yup…all them years back…the three of us—me, Barb, and Nells—we made us a pact. Took a blood oath…swore it then and there: We'd never let a friend…see here, now…go through…have that type of situation again…"

I don't know what he was getting at. Like I said, he wasn't being clear. He was stumbling over his words. I could've pressed him, but I knew he was struggling, so I just let it be. But honestly, I was getting even more frustrated by all the gloom and doom. That's why my body started shaking a little bit. If someone mentions this to you, it was just one of those sudden adrenaline surges when I get frustrated. It can make my body tense up and rattle a bit. It's not a big deal at all. Like when the priest yelled at my mom. My body got tense because I was mad.

It's like, you know, when you get a fever, and the chills make you shiver a little even though you're not cold? That can happen when I'm starting to come down with the flu or something. Especially when I was young. As a kid, if I had a fever while I was sleeping, I'd wake up shaking and with a weird taste in my mouth. Sometimes, I'd be in the middle of a nightmare but not know I was actually awake. This one time, I was half asleep and feverish and got out of bed and came down the stairs. The stairs didn't end in my dream, but they did end in real life. I ran into a wall. I chipped my front tooth. My dad wasn't mad. My mom was in the hospital then. He told me he loved me. Cooled down my head with a washcloth. He held me and told me that everything would be fine. And that God would take care of us. He said we have to give it to God since we can't handle it ourselves and God will take care of us...[unintelligible]...fell asleep in his arms...I needed [that? him?]...made me feel safe...

Maybe a year later, after my dad left with the hard blue suitcase, we were staying with our neighbor. I woke up one night and I was shaking. She said we all have anxiety dreams sometimes. I didn't have a fever that time. She checked with an old mercury thermometer. The glass clinked my bottom teeth. She said I didn't have a fever. She said I needed to stop worrying so much. But I had been sleeping, I hadn't been worrying. She didn't know what she was talking about.

Anyway, I didn't want to tell Nelly, Barb, and Pith that I was getting frustrated by all their moping. I didn't want them to be embarrassed. When they asked if I was OK, I just told them I'd gotten a little chilly. The night air was getting crisp. But I didn't have a fever. I know that. I checked later that night with our battery thermometer. I was completely fine. I was just a little irritated by all the sad-sap talk. I wanted to keep the conversation going so I asked, "So, what's the story of Matt and the foxes?"

Chapter 27: Ark

Pith probably recognized that he wasn't making much sense because he rubbed his right hand across his scalp, patted my back a couple times with his left, and said, "Alright, alright." And so began his explanation of the adolescent trials and tribulations of Matty.

"You already know about Kim's crazy-town circus, right?"

"Please…stop…don't call it…please…it was so sad," interjected Nelly, closing her eyes.

"C'mon, Nells! That lady had kangaroos loose in the paddock—figuratively and almost literally! With respect. But word." Nelly lowered her head, put her elbows on the table, and raised her hands to her forehead like they were a visor.

Pith went on: "After Kimmy's illicit animal-camp operation got shut down, but before them people arranged for her gig over at the animal shelter, folks still had to clean up the mess she left here at the park. Remember, we're talking about dozens of species running loose—feisty, skittish." Pith put his palms forward, opened his eyes wide, withdrew his head into his shoulders, and tilted his body to the right. Then he bobbed side to side like a boxer dodging jabs. It was easily the best pantomime of animals avoiding capture I'd ever seen.

"Anyhow," he continued, reprising his role as neighborhood historian, "animal control did regular sweeps of the neighborhood for weeks picking up whatever stragglers they could find."

Barb had to add: "Hmmp! That alpaca broke my fence. She also spat at my husband. I told him she was probably scared and missed the mountains of Peru." I appreciated Barb's imaginative compassion. "Gah. But my husband said spitting is an insult in any culture. He said that, of all people, I should know the public-health consequences of spitting animals. He got his shotgun."

Pith belly-laughed. "I was there! Barb ain't lyin'! Gentlest man on God's green earth, her husband. But he was loaded for bear! Only time I ever seen him ready to throw hands! Talking about defending his honor from llama saliva! It was a scene! Goodness gracious."

Barb drank some wine and conceded the point, "I *should* know better, I *do* have a master's degree in public health after all. But I'd hate to see an alpaca dead. I wanted to talk it out."

"Problem was," Pith continued, "a bunch of them varmints got spooked and hid out under this very gazebo, including a whole family of foxes." Pith stomped his ratty right flip-flop three times. "It was like Noah's danged ark down there! A bounty of God's animal kingdom seeking refuge together, living in peace. Beautiful, really. Glory be." He looked up at the stars and drank his 7-Eleven sacrament.

Barb had to exert her authority. "Bah! It was a public-health hazard! We couldn't have wild animals under the gazebo. Kids play here for God's sake!"

Pith pressed ahead. "That ol' hefty prevaricator Butch Tweed stepped in. He'd been on the HOA board since 1984, but he was in his first term as board president in '04." Pith paused and smiled. "It took that crook 20 years of scheming to convince the board he should take the helm. He wore 'em down. Woowee! Wars of attrition are won by the stubborn not the strong."

Two decades of work to be president of a sleepy neighborhood's association? I was dubious. "That's a lot of effort for a lousy reward," I replied. Pith belly-laughed. "Yeah, bro, but if you play silly-ass games, you win silly-ass prizes."

"Dude must be thirsty for attention," I half-laughed.

"Truth, champ. Truth. The word on the street was that he lusted, hot and heavy, after a seat in the state legislature. But that never came to pass. And that gutted him. They say he gets depressed every four years at election time. Pines over the one that got away." Sometimes the timing of these things just doesn't work out, I thought.

Pith grimaced and clicked his tongue, continuing. "But Butch Tweed ain't one to wave the white flag. He just lowered his sights and settled for the HOA presidency. Sad fact of life: Some people need power. It don't matter what kind—just need to be at the switch. I bet you seen that plenty back when you were a big deal in the gub'ment. People anglin' for any stray bit of juice."

He wasn't wrong. Just before I got tired of working for the government and wanted to leave, I was working at the state's transportation department, and my wife was overseeing public debt for the state treasurer. We used to joke about legislators who couldn't find the time to make sure their shoes matched their belts, but they'd hatch elaborate plans to become deputy assistant associate caucus vice chair of some worthless workgroup. My wife came up with a medical term for it: "Desperattention." Like hypertension but for people dying for the spotlight. She used to joke that the only cure was eating fresh greens and going back in time to get your parents' approval.

"Anyhow," Pith went on, "Butch Tweed saw this animal disaster as his one shining moment, his coming-out party. Boy, he started talkin' like an Old-West sheriff, saying he's going to 'clean up this cow town and make it safe for justice and harmony again.' That mug was actin' like he's about to Wyatt-Earp some ruthless outlaws when we're just dealing with some agitated wildlife." Pith balled up his hands then extended his index fingers and thumbs like six-shooters.

He continued, "So Tweed makes a big show of hiring professionals to smoke out them critters hiding under this gazebo, cage 'em up, and take 'em out to the country. This was the last part of the legal agreement that would close the book on Kim's bootleg zoo—"

Nelly pressed her middle fingers on her temples, "I asked you… I did…Please stop…please stop calling it that…it was sad, not funny…"

"—and then things could get back to normal, bro. That was the plan. All them animals would be 86'ed, the HOA could settle all them lawsuits, and the bus line could get its riders back. Good, solid plan, I'll tell you what, sensible and firm."

Nelly must have been typing a lot recently too. Pith noticed. He exhaled and rubbed the top of his head with his left hand. He reached out his right like he was about to steady or hold Nelly's, but he stopped himself. They both retreated their hands to their respective laps.

Increasingly drunk Barb said to no one in particular, "Hmmp. It would take a long time to dig a hole big enough for a dead alpaca. And I don't know the funeral rites for that either."

Pith stared at the memorial garden. Nelly lowered her head and rubbed the tops of her shoulders.

When I couldn't handle the suspense any longer, I nudged Pith and said, "*And*? What happened with the animals under the gazebo?"

Pith took a swig. "Matty happened."

* * *

"You have to...I mean, please try...try to understand," Nelly preempted. "We'd been spending...all of us...a lot of time with Matt...doing our parts...since his family disintegra...since all of that happened. And Matty just loved animals...adored them."

"Hmmp. The hole would have to be six feet deep and six feet wide. An alpaca can be the size of a small horse. God only knows where you'd find a suitable casket. And who would say the prayers? Alpacas come from South America, so I assume they're Catholic by upbringing. Maybe we could've found a priest. A zoo might have a chaplain."

Nelly pressed on. "Talking about animals...looking at pictures in books...drawing them...animals were the only thing...nothing else worked...that kept his mind off everything. Barb, you took care of him...you know...you took him to the wildlife center a hundred times, right? We all talked about animals...it made him smile. He loved foxes the most...oh, the foxes..."

Barb closed her eyes, exhaled sharply, and explained, "Wfff. The best we could ever figure out is that Matty must've overheard and misunderstood a conversation. Everyone was talking about getting rid of the animals, including the foxes. He knew the hawks around here prey on baby foxes."

Barb craned her neck to look out of the gazebo and to the sky. She used an upward pointed index finger to trace circles, tracking an imaginary predator's path. "Matty must've thought the fox family was in danger. The wildlife center said reflective, moving objects can scare away birds..."

"They were abandoned! Matty...and his mom...both of them! ...tossed aside...forgotten!" Heartbreak, not anxiety, not contradictions, were now choking up increasingly drunk Nelly. "Animals gave them love...companionship. Hurt people do irrational things." Nelly's dog whimpered and pawed at her thigh.

Pith grabbed the baton. "That little dude makes a whole mess of them pinwheels on the down-low. He steals a box of straws from his school cafeteria and uses up all his mom's tin foil. He went to town, too. I'm talking a good hun'red, hun'red-fitty of 'em. And them pinwheels were tight, my man. Gotta give him credit. Meticulous production and at scale. Arts-and-crafts talk."

Barb sucked in air and pointed eastward into the darkness, "Hmmp. That angel sneaks out of his house. Comes to this field. In the middle of the night. Sticking all those homemade pinwheels in the ground to protect foxes from imaginary birds. The sweetest little boy..." —she cleared her throat— "...he makes up a story in his head to try to gain some control."

Pith brings it home: "It was *late*. Matty falls asleep on the soccer field. When he wakes up, animal control was on the scene, rootin' 'round under this gazebo tryin' to get at any animals still on the lam. Well, Matty straight *loses* it. Bonkers." Pith blinked rapidly, tensed up his neck, and vibrated. "He thinks he's on a holy mission for them animals. He kicks one worker, runs over to the cages in the back of the truck and frees some of the critters they'd already caught. Rest of them varmints under the gazebo hightail it outta there. That fox family, a whole mess of cats, beavers, a parakeet, a *got-dang wolverine*. Like a mutiny at a circus, I'll tell you what!"

"And that...that was it...that was pretty much the last straw," Nelly shrugged her shoulders.

"Them workers running all over hell's half acre tryin' to corral scared, pissed-off animals..." continued Pith half-laughing.

Nelly continued, "Every mom in the neighborhood...worried the park is dangerous. All of them...I felt the same...I never got to be a mom, though...they all spoke up."

"Hmmp. I was one of them."

"New lawsuits...from bite victims...from residents saying their annual dues should have prevented this...from parents... everyone furious...everyone saying that the county and HOA didn't take the risk seriously..." Nelly added.

Pith goes on, "Kim wakes up that morning and can't find her boy. Poor kid had been volatile as drunk mercury lately, so she thinks he's run away from home. She shows up at the park, sees Matty fixin' to hit these workers with a stick. Little boy screaming about 'tyrants.' Mercy, mercy! Kim pitches a fit with a tail on it!" Pith was laughing so hard at this point his eyes were watering. He was half standing, pretending to wield a stick like a sword. En garde.

"I'll tell you what, the owner of the company hired by Butch Tweed comes screechin' up to the park in a beat-up Datsun truck. Brown and orange. Good godamighty! She can't believe her men are under attack by a boy with a fallen branch! Now she's meaner than a wet panther!"

"Hmmp. If you didn't want to bury a dead alpaca, you could feed it to a panther," brainstormed drunk Barb. Then, after a moment of contemplation, "Less digging required. Much messier though."

Pith continued. "Then of course, that rat-bastard himself, Butch Tweed rolls up on the scene tryin' to make like a swashbuckler with a walkie talkie." Pith sat down and extended his arms toward the center of the table, palms facing inward like he was trying to hold the story together. "Som'bich is yelling about 'cease and desist' and then gets a golf club from his trunk and starts hollering about his powers in the bylaws to put down insurrections..."

"A shambles...no winners...complete disaster," said Nelly.

"Yessir," said Pith, exhaling. "Situation went from bad to worse. The workers from that critter-catching company sue the neighborhood, claiming their lives were endangered by Matty and his stick. The county says it's going to revoke the HOA's covenant because it's been negligent..."

"Gah. Biggest mess I'd ever seen," added Barb.

"Wild-ass animals ransackin' the neighborhood like the Mongol Horde, the state's departments of health and natural resources launch a joint investigation, and this bus stop..."

"The bus stop is killed," Nelly and Barb said in unison.

"Yessir, done. Finished," Pith said, first sounding like he was stipulating the facts of the case but then sounding like he was mourning the verdict. "Everyone agreed—the state, riders, the HOA—that the neighborhood couldn't have a bus stop at the park no more. Too expensive, too much liability. The county said it was making other transportation plans anyhow, so when the HOA voted unanimously, led by Butch Tweed, to pull the plug, the county commission permanently removed this stop from the Blue Line. Real talk: No bus returned to that spot..." he pointed toward the sign, "...ever again."

We sat silently.

"There should be a daggum tombstone next to that bus-stop sign. 'Born 1985. Died 2004 of unnatural causes,'" added Pith at last. Barb wiped her eyes. Nelly was ashen.

Pith reached down to pet Nelly's dog, but he wasn't there. "Bro, you know cynicism ain't part of my make-up, but I know Butch Tweed enjoyed shuttin' down that bus. Vindictive, obtuse man. The kind that could be guilty as sin and still demand to lead the prayer, know what I mean?" Yes, I knew the type. For some folks, self-awareness is an area for personal growth. Pith sighed loudly and added, "Tweed had been gunning for ol' Lenny McGregor since 1985."

I still didn't get it. Why would Pith, Nelly, and Barb get so sad about the end of a bus stop? And what in God's name is the weird connection between Len, the bus stop, and Butch Tweed? But before I could ask, an unexpected voice was added to the mix.

"I hope she gets left at the altar and is forced to join a convent!"

None of us had realized that Masonry Brown had ambled up to the gazebo and was weighing in on the soon-to-be-bride mentioned in the pandemic-and-nuptial-justice fundraiser notice.

Yes, it's late. We can start with Masonry tomorrow.

RECORDING CONCLUDED: 6:25pm
Thursday, January 7, 2021
Uncorrected transcript
Interview by Elizabeth Jones

Chapter 28: Restock

From: Dr. Jennifer Davis, MERCY STATE, COMS
Date: January 7, 2021 at 7:12 PM
Subject: RE: What happened in 2012? [CONFIDENTIAL]
To: Elizabeth Jones, Esq. OFFICE OF THE PUBLIC DEFENDER

Ms. Jones, it was very nice to meet you in person (well, almost in person) on the video call this morning. We all appreciate how difficult this is. No one should have this as a first trial. You've handled it like a seasoned professional.

The update from the medical team was encouraging for all of us. At least there will be one survivor from Community Day. And based on the surgeons' comments, I think they may be able to bring him out of the induced coma soon. Even one adult witness will help enormously. Once he can communicate, many holes will be filled in.

As for your question, I need to sort through some old files to piece it together. But the short answer is that your client and his wife had gone through a very difficult period, and they relocated to Grangerford to get away from their past and try to start over. You might not know that prior to joining Mercy, I was an attending psychiatrist at CCSH. I treated your client on an outpatient basis for a year starting in early 2012 (after his second major episode). This included counseling with his wife. They fought hard to keep it together.

I'll get back to you soon with more specifics.

Jen

Chapter 29: Relocate

From: Dr. Jennifer Davis, MERCY STATE, COMS
Date: January 7, 2021 at 11:48 PM
Subject: RE: RE: What happened in 2012? [CONFIDENTIAL]
To: Elizabeth Jones, Esq. OFFICE OF THE PUBLIC DEFENDER

I found all of my old files. This may be more than you wanted.

First, by way of background, I'm from the state so I had known your client by reputation. We're about the same age. He was a local legend. Basketball star, first Rhodes Scholar from the state college in like 50 years. Became state secretary of transportation at 29. Wunderkind.

His agency had a budget in the billions. At 33, people were already recruiting him to run for county executive. Everyone said he would be governor someday. He was the poor kid made good. If the story weren't true, you'd think it had been written in Hollywood.

In late December 2011, his wife, sister, and his mentor (the state legislator he had worked for) staged a mini-intervention and convinced him he needed help. He had been acting erratically again. He had stopped taking his medications but then started self-medicating when things got hard at home: Their young son had not yet bounced back from the chemo, and the medications that had helped his wife's depression were no longer effective. There was also an issue at work.

The huge public transportation project he had been leading (you might have read about it: new light rail, bus lines, subway for the city) had had major delays and cost overruns. The state's newspaper assigned its investigative reporter to look into your client's past. She pulled some dirty tricks and found out about his troubled childhood and hospitalization in his 20s. She got leaked medical records, interviewed neighbors who had known your client as a child, and got quotes from people at the transportation department saying your client had been acting bizarrely in recent months.

The paper decided the public's right to know all of this trumped his personal and medical privacy. By the time the reporter interviewed your client, she believed she had all the evidence needed to write that his history of mental-health issues was at the root of the project's problems and would eventually cause even bigger problems for the state.

You have to understand that your client's career was everything to him. He came from worse than nothing, so it was not just his income; it was his identity, his status. He said he couldn't imagine living if the only good part of his reputation was tarnished. So he secretly struck a deal with the newspaper's publisher: He would resign his position as transportation secretary and never serve in public office again, and in return the paper would not publish the story. The paper could feel good about protecting the public by scuttling your client's career; your client could protect his name by saying he resigned to spend more time with his family.

His wife had already been unhappy. She had her own mental-health issues, and she was having trouble dealing with his. It was becoming too much for her. Things got worse when he didn't tell her about his negotiations with the paper or discuss the idea of resignation. She nearly left him. She had a divorce lawyer. But she stayed.

They agreed to build a new, quiet, uncomplicated life in a new, quiet, uncomplicated place. They moved out to Grangerford in 2013.

Hope this helps.

Jen

Chapter 30: Bouts

START: 12:53pm
Friday, January 8, 2021
C.C.S.H.

Hey. They just told me about the commissary funds. Thank you. You didn't have to do that. Very nice of you. They must've told you I need my Pop Tarts!

No, seriously. It helps. I appreciate it.

Back to it?

* * *

I used to see Masonry regularly during my walks around the neighborhood. I'd stop by to say hello while he was expertly managing the logistics of unnecessary brick-moving. He always seemed to have a new, pressing gripe. I'd provide him an audience. He appreciated this. But to keep up appearances, he'd tell people I was a "pestering nuisance produced via generations of inbreeding." We'd gotten to be good friends.

He seemed to be not entirely himself that night at the gazebo. Preoccupied maybe. When he tossed a bag of salt-and-vinegar potato chips on the table, he merely said, "Hands off, knuckleheads." That translates to "nice to see you" in English or a bear hug in Pith-ish.

But upon seeing the seating dimensions, which were not exactly custom-made to his ample form, his mood reverted to sour. He indignantly adjusted his board shorts and gray-and-brown flannel, sucked in, and then wedged himself into a space between Barb and me, cursing to high heaven the gazebo's incompetent architects and carpenters. During his heaving and cramming process, the rest of us were rewarded with a view of his Superman underwear and lower-back tattoo. My good friend Masonry is complex.

Once situated, he stared irritably at the warm buttermilk and thawed bag of peas. I delivered my now practiced pantomime implicating Barb. No one was the wiser: Nelly was staring sleepy-eyed into the middle distance, Barb was occupied anew with her tape measure, and I'd already sold this false bill of goods to Pith. Pith leaned across me and said quietly to Masonry, "Come see me at the shop, bud. I'll get you a deal on a better toupee. We got the finest collection. I'd take my oath on it." Masonry accepted Pith's business card and then turned to me.

"Well, I'm supposed to ask you how you're doing." Maybe he'd been working with a counselor on social etiquette.

"I'm good," I said. "Keeping busy. Doing a lot of reading and writing,"

Masonry isn't one to mince words, even if he doesn't know what he's talking about. "You need to quit all your conspiracy talk. And that demonstration of yours against the county executive got completely out of hand. That's his house. His kids live there," he said, showing his ignorance. I'd gotten used to stuff like this at the Dew Drop. Uninformed people spouting off.

Barb wanted to stop Masonry from embarrassing himself any further, so she interrupted his off-base speech and said, "So, then, what a pleasant surprise to have you here with us. We didn't expect you to be able to make it."

He glared at me for a moment, muttered something about my newsletter, and then replied to Barb, "I had absolutely no intention of coming here, to be frank. But I had to get out of my house. That creepy old bastard is dressed up in a purple leotard and an eye patch, and he's been serenading me with 'In Your Eyes' for the last six hours."

* * *

This had Blowtorch Len written all over it. Barb shuddered. Nelly closed her eyes. Pith smiled broadly and shook his head in disbelieving belief. All three simultaneously took gulps from their respective beverages. I leaned in and implored Masonry, "Tell. Me. More."

"I was out in the yard, working on my brick project..."

"What exactly...pray tell...what is your brick project..." inquired inebriated Nelly.

"Ope! Hush now, girl!" snapped even-looser-lipped Barb.

"...and that decrepit coot on his ridiculous foot patrol walks by my house," fumed Masonry.

"Yessir, here we go," replied Pith, rubbing his hands together.

"I'm just saying...my only point...is that it *could* be a crypt. We don't know...we can't say that it's *not a crypt*. It's not unreasonable for me to ask," whispered Nelly to Barb in the way drunk people are unable to whisper.

Masonry continued, "I say to him, 'How's it hanging, Len?' and then I just go about my business."

"Whoa! That's neighborly! Too familiar, but neighborly. Especially for you," replied uninhibited Barb.

"For sure. I didn't know you could be that almost-polite," I added, agreeing with Barb for maybe the first time ever.

"You just wait one minute," snapped Masonry, surprised by our unsurprising responses.

"Awww, no, no, no, my guy! I bet McGregor didn't appreciate that idiom one bit," said Pith.

I turned to Pith, "What in God's name are you talking about? *Appreciating idioms*?"

"My point...listen...anyone with that many bricks and nothing to show for it has to be up to no good. That's what I'm saying," Nelly explained to the table.

"Easy money, bro! '*How's it hangin'*?' The origins of that saying are *personal* in nature, if you catch my drift," explained Pith, pointing affectedly below his waist. "Len don't want folks alluding to his nether regions. Len McGregor does many things, but he don't ever work blue. Persnickety something fierce about bodily discretion and decorum, real talk."

"I resent the implication that I'm not neighborly. I give everyone the respect deserved. It's not my fault I'm forever surrounded by mouth-breathers," said the suddenly scandalized Masonry.

"You're out of your mind!" I diagnosed Pith. "McGregor's so old he couldn't tell his privates from a wicker stool. And since when do you track the moral sensibilities of Blowtorch Len?"

"Oh my God, don't call him that! Don't ever call him that!" cried Nelly.

"Hrrmmmpppfff. Wicker stools and teak vanities signify marital troubles," slurred Barb sadly, her eyes sagging.

Masonry continued, "McGregor stops dead in his tracks and spouts some garbage like, 'The status of my bits is my concern alone! Do not presume to inquire about my undercarriage!'"

"I lost bits of my car's undercarriage when I rear-ended that harvester. I had been singing along to Miley Cyrus. I should know better than to drive distracted. My master's degree taught me that. It's in public health." Drunk Barb was trying to track the conversation but was quickly losing the trail.

"Yup, yup! I told you so," gloated Pith. "Len don't play with lascivious language. I once saw him offer to jiu-jitsu fight a mechanic who referred to his own package as 'the Ambassador.' Len said 'anthropomorphizing privy parts is an affair of honor demanding a duel.'"

"My God! That makes no sense! Zero sense! That has got to be fabricated!" I screamed.

"I told that rotten gaffer that I presume to declare he should be institutionalized and tended with a cattle prod," said the now worked-up Masonry about the elderly man who had given him chivalry lessons in the middle of the road.

"Woo-eee! Get some! Get *sooooome*!" gushed Pith. "Dang son! Tusslin' with Len McGregor! That takes rocks, I'll tell you what!"

"My wife would agree with you about tending Blowtorch Len with a cattle prod," I conceded.

"Don't call him that! In the name of all that's holy, do not call him that!" shouted the now fluid-speaking Nelly.

Masonry, red-faced and sweating: "McGregor straightens his back, extends his arms from his sides, and says right to me—right in my face, 'You are nothing but a brick-moving nincompoop, and I am the rightful heir to the Portuguese crown!'"

"Good night!" exclaimed Pith with what appeared to be absolute seriousness. "He invoked his royal claims?!?"

"Good God almighty! Len has no foreign royal claims!" I

shouted. "He's a totally homegrown, domestic madman! What is wrong with you people?!"

"Speaking of royal claims, Queen Victoria was the patron of the Royal Society for Public Health," offered Barb, now on her own conversational excursion.

"I'm not going to take guff from that ancient gimp, so l let him know what I really think about his 1980s getup, his asinine walkabouts, everything," bragged Masonry. He opened his bag of chips and daintily removed one, inspected it, and finding it to his liking, consumed it in one crumbly bite. "My language was salty. But he had it coming, so I gave it to him with both barrels. That scaredy-cat just slunk away," Masonry concluded with more satisfaction than I thought him capable.

"Awwwww, nah, nah, nah, dog! You got it twisted, my man. You thought the game was over, but Len was just warming up," said Pith knowingly. Nelly's dog sighed loudly.

"Of course, I thought the game was over!" replied Masonry, now offended that someone could imagine his vicious insults were not the final word. "That old loon left the scene with his tail between his legs. I dominated that creepy kook..."

"Ack! No, no, no, no, no, don't ever let it be known that you called Len McGregor 'creepy'," interrupted Barb who was back on the trail.

"...and he understood that he'd been trounced by this guy." Masonry lifted his two beefy paws and extended both thumbs toward his cheekbones. "It was a manhandling! A knockout! I put his old rear end to sleep!" Masonry lifted his right arm to flex his bicep muscle, or to show us the yellowed armpit stain on the Minecraft t-shirt he wore under his flannel.

Pith laughed quietly and replied, "Nah, dude. You don't know Len McGregor. That was no knockout. That's the start of a rope-a-dope. He had you just where he wanted you."

Nelly, leaned her head back against a post of the gazebo, eyes still closed and agreed, “You don’t know Len McGregor.”

Chapter 31: Gratitude

"...AND...?!" I demanded of Masonry.

"And...and...and...McGregor shows up again in like half an hour. He's standing outside my house in that leotard, eye-patch, and ear-muffs ensemble with a 1980s boom box, singing his heart out. But I refuse to give him the satisfaction of coming out..." continued Masonry, thinking he was describing a defensive bob-and-weave technique while actually giving off some serious playing-hard-to-get energy.

"Nah, nah, sorry son, that stayin'-in-yer-house tactic ain't going to work with ol' Lenny Mac," said Pith, now drinking straight from the flask. "He'll overcook your grits 'til the house burns down. Best believe that."

"Then...then...he chucks one of his tasseled Ugg boots at my front door! That's the last straw, I say to myself. Fisticuffs it is, old man! I go out there ready to get it on..." Masonry held up his fleshy dukes like a 1920s prize fighter, confident he's a bruiser not a palooka with a glass jaw.

"I came in like a wrecking ball...I never hit so hard...in loooove..." sang drunk Barb to the cosmos.

"I get out there and roll up my sleeves. That crazy geezer is still singing. He won't stop. His heart was in it, too. And then, and then..." —Masonry is getting frantic now— "...and then he pulls out a feathered boa from somewhere and starts spinning it around his head!"

Pith looks straight at me, dead in the eye, with no emotion, half shrugs, and says, "Every bit of this story checks out if you ask me, bro. This is Len McGregor, by the book."

"So I get up right in his grill..." Masonry growls.

"You were gonna give him what for! Give him that smoke!" added increasingly animated Pith.

"Damn right! It was go-time. I was fired up. But then...but then..."

Pith starts laughing and slapping his knee, "You thought you were about to wreck shop!"

I'm leaning so far over the table I can hear Barb's quiet snoring.

"...but then...but then...he gets down on one knee and proposes to me!"

"Bingo! Yessir, yessir!" shouts Pith, standing up and clapping. "That's my boy! McGregor!"

"He's still out there singing right now. He's on a mission," concluded Masonry punch-drunk.

* * *

"Lemme ask you a couple questions," Pith paced around the gazebo, rubbing his chin. "Does Len typically walk past your house?"

"No, never. Never. I'm not on his normal patrol route," responded Masonry, growing curious.

"You recently talk smack about the bus stop?"

Nelly's dog whimpered.

"How would you know that? I mean, how could you know..." Masonry leaned back; his jaw went stiff. He grabbed a mittful of oily chips, lowered his face, and inhaled. The rattling of the chips through his teeth and down his gullet sounded like a vacuum sucking up Legos. His confidence and cholesterol restored, Masonry sat up straighter and puffed out his chest. The moonlight shone off his greasy face: "Yeah, I did. Damn straight! Two days ago, I told that lousy Butch Tweed that if the HOA was good for anything it would get rid of that eyesore bus-stop sign. It's a community sacrilege."

"Oh, no, no, no...no, no, no...no, no, no..." mumbled Nelly.

"Pop, pop!" Pith grinned and pointed his six-shooters in the air. He turned to me and nodded like a suspect's alibi had been verified. "That scans, my man."

"What in God's name are you talking about?" I demanded of Pith. Masonry grabbed my bag of peas and started pouring them directly into his mouth. Several got lodged in the rolls between his neck and collarbone. He was eating his feelings, a stew of fury, confusion, and fear.

Pith sat down and explained: "Listen close, buddy. McGregor's been increasing his activity lately. You seen it. You *seen* it with your own eyes. That broken-down-Camaro routine he laid on you right before the virus showed up? That Napoleon act we witnessed? This indecent marriage proposal and serenade tonight? That business he pulled at Matty's concert back in March—you heard about that right?" I had *not* heard about that yet.

Pith waited calmly for me to locate the unifying theme in that pastiche of craziness. When I couldn't find it, Pith dropped his eyes to the table and then raised them up in the direction of the bus-stop sign. "Something's afoot," he said quietly. "Sure as shootin', something's afoot."

I'd never seen Pith so serious. He continued, orating more than talking: "Imma tell you what. Len went dormant. Preparing. Fueling up. Now he's returning to the world. Like a cicada. Lenny's about to swarm."

I was flabbergasted. "This is madness. Why do you act like there's a rhyme or reason to Len's lunacy? There's not! He's a random-craziness generator!" Nelly's dog stood, stared at me, and then plopped back down.

"Listen here, Ace," Pith reached across the table, grabbed Barb's unattended wine glass, and drained it. "Let me tell you a little something about this bus stop sign," Pith straightened his back and pointed both index fingers into the dark like an Australian-rules football umpire signaling a score. "After Matt's pinwheel crusade and his mom's wildlife fiasco..."

"...please stop...please for the love of mercy...that's not funny..." Nelly pleaded.

"...I told that cur Butch Tweed and the HOA board that they should let the bus stop sign alone. 'You ended the bus line,' I told 'em, 'and maybe that was justified. I ain't here to re-litigate that. But that bus stop was part of this community. You can't just pretend it didn't exist. There needs to be mourning.' That's what I told 'em. 'It's now a cemetery of sorts, and it's a temple to reverent Len McGregor. So don't mess with the sign,' I said to'em. 'Just let it all lie fallow for a stretch. Let it be.'"

It was getting colder. The sky was entirely clear now. Above the memorial garden, I could make out the Big Dipper. "You went to bat for wacky Len and a bus-stop sign that serves no purpose?" I asked Pith.

"*My maaaaan,*" Pith winced and stretched out his disappointment over several beats. "Ain't you been paying attention? That sign serves a purpose. There's a time and place for everything under heaven, bud. Everything under heaven." Over Pith's left shoulder I saw the balance scale of Libra in the clear night sky. "And it wasn't time for that sign to leave this earth. It still had work to do. And that's the realest talk."

For the life of me I couldn't comprehend why this bus stop was so important. Why it had to be preserved. It was like I was alone on the outside of an inside joke. I just asked, "They let it be?"

"Well, Butch Tweed still wanted to yank the sign straight outta the ground and resod that entire area. He wanted to memory-hole all tracings of the bus. Wipe out a whole stretch of time." Pith pretended to erase a giant chalkboard with both hands, clapped his two imaginary erasers together, and then watched the imaginary cloud of dust rise and then dissipate.

Pith went on, "Tweed's a lackwit when it comes to emotional intelligence, I'll tell you what. His interpersonal calculations are one-digit addition problems that he gets wrong, if you follow what I'm saying. The rest of the HOA board of directors—good on them—they refused to go along with him. They told Tweed that he'd become fixated on Len and needed to let go. Tweed stomped around and accused everyone of being yellow-bellies, but—yessir—the HOA let it be."

"...He was down on one knee, telling me sweet nothings like we're teenage lovers..." Although Masonry's head was stuck in the potato chip bag, I could still track his narration of Len's courting.

Pith went on: "Now, don't forget, this is back in 2004 or 2005. But I remember what happened next like it was yesterday." Since Pith was on a roll, I didn't bother saying that he sometimes doesn't remember yesterday. "Real talk, I was having that pergola constructed behind my house. Thought it would class up my joint. I didn't want to have a bachelor pad no more." Nelly blinked rapidly and looked away.

Pith continued, "I was aiming to evolve into the respectable gentleman you see before you today." He pretended to stroke an imaginary handlebar mustache like he was a 19th-century aristocratic industrialist. "But—gather at the river!—that was an expensive project. Nearly bankrupted me. I almost had to start dancin' on the pole for some cash flow!" I tried to imagine Pith as an exotic entertainer, succeeded, grimaced, and then tried to unimagine it.

Pith briefly turned wistful. "Bro, I coulda made pole-dancin' lucrative. I got mad rizz. *Mad* rizz. You know that. Also got rhythm and curves that won't quit. I'd've made it rain fives and tens, not just ones. I know it in my heart of hearts." Spoken like a true respectable gentleman. Pith has the dimensions and grace of a tent pole, but I wanted to see where this story was headed, so I said, "Amen to that, brother."

He snapped back to reality, or whatever approximation of reality we had that night. "That pergola turned out nice, you seen it," Pith digressed from his digression. "You know, out near where my girl rides her bike 'round and 'round that circuit?" I said absolutely nothing about the sensitive topic of his daughter's right-turning abilities. As a wise man once told me, ain't no education in the second kick of a mule.

"Anyhow, the construction was almost done, and I'm wondering how I'm gonna find the money to pay it off. I had put some money down up front, but I still owed the builder like 12 grand." Yowsers. That's a lot of fives and tens, I thought to myself. Pith must've sensed my mental computations because he whispered to me, "If push came to shove, I was willing to dance the *champagne room*, too. But don't tell the ladies..."—he motioned his chin at Sleeping Beauty Barb and Eeyore Nelly—"...I don't want them thinkin' I'm a man of loose morals." I laughed and swore his secret was safe with me.

Pith was satisfied. But after a few seconds, he made sure they weren't listening and then said with some measure of pride, "But I could've amassed a loyal clientele. People would've lined up around the block for my sultry moves." To prove it, he twerked as well as a gangly middle-aged man sitting on a gazebo bench could twerk. My eyes watered I laughed so hard.

"Back to business," Pith said, concluding that line of craziness and returning to another. "So, remember now: I defended the bus stop to the HOA, and I owe this builder a small fortune. Two completely unrelated issues, right?"

"Yes, unrelated," I agreed with a statement that would've been obvious in any other situation.

"Well, one night, at three-dark-thirty in the morning, my doorbell rings!" Pith flicked his flask with his index finger, trying to mimic a doorbell, even though it sounded more like the clang of a wiffle ball hitting a gutter. "I'm fit to be tied! It's the middle of the blessed night! So I get outta bed in my ratty drawers and go to the door with a baseball bat and a starving cougar's mean streak..."

As anyone would, I thought.

"...and standing right on my porch is a dude in a top hat, wraparound sunglasses, tank top, and bolo tie. He says he's from the county inspection office, there to deliver my building permit."

I did not see that coming.

"Now, obviously, this ain't no county bureaucrat. And I knew we already had them permits. Jimmy Callahan's daddy was doing the pergola job for me, and he was always on top of his business. Fully buttoned up, ya know?"

For a moment, I thought the most interesting aspect of this story was that Jimmy Callahan—remember, that bowl-of-fruit-instead-of-cheesecake carpenter fixing the memorial garden?—was the son of the fully-buttoned-up carpenter who built Pith's pergola. But I quickly remembered that a bureaucrat impersonator in a top hat and bolo tie had been on Pith's porch in the middle of the night. That reclaimed the interesting-est top spot.

"I knew only one character on God's green earth would pull this kind of dress-up routine: Good ol' Blowtorch. And, honestly, I just wanted to get back to my shuteye. So I said, real simple to'm, 'Much obliged, sir.' And then this 'official' nods, hands me an envelope, and limps away in the moonlight." Pith smiled and stared wistfully into the night sky, as though nostalgia, not hives, is the proper response to such a memory.

"And the envelope???" I demanded.

Pith snapped out of it and replied, "So I open it up..."—he pretended to rip the top off an envelope—"...and pull out the contents." Then he stared at the imaginary document in his hands and looked up at me with play-acted bewilderment.

"*AND?*" I shouted.

"It was a cashier's check for $12,481. The entire amount I owed to Callahan for the pergola."

Now I was for-real bewildered.

"That's how Len McGregor says, 'Thank you for respecting the bus stop,'" translated Pith.

Chapter 32: Rescheduled

Pith's interpretation was crazy. "You're connecting dots that aren't connected! That's not a special McGregor 'thank you,'" I shouted. "That's a senile eccentric randomly doling out cash!"

"*Bro.* Come on now. You gotta understand at this point. As far as McGregor is concerned, there are two types of people in this world. There are those who respect this community, this neighborhood, this park, that bus stop." Pith's eyes got big. "And there are those who don't."

"You think he gave you 12 grand for being nice to your neighbors and protecting a sign for a bus that no longer exists?"

"Yessir."

I gave Pith my best "Oh, please" look.

"Buddy, you think it's a coincidence that my guy"—Pith tilted his head toward Masonry—"tells the HOA to get rid of the sign and then a couple days later McGregor scrambles his brain?"

Masonry mumbled, "I didn't even tell you about the ring he offered me. Big diamond. Clear and colorless. Refined tension setting."

I maintained my "Oh, please" look.

"Why do you think he's been after Matty, Kim, Nelly, and Butch Tweed for so long? In Lenny's eyes, they disrespected this place."

My "Oh, please" look was turning into a "Hmmm..." look.

"Remember when Lenny pulled that broken-down Camaro routine on you? Dressed up like Elvis in a unitard?" Naturally; that's not something one forgets. "What did he say to you, bro?"

"He asked me if I cared about this neighborhood. He said this is a community, and it can't afford any more selfish types."

Pith gave me a "See what I mean?" look.

It suddenly occurred to me that the Camaro encounter happened not long after I'd sent those two letters to the HOA requesting the removal of the bus stop sign and the gazebo. Pith must've seen this realization on my face because he leaned in and emphasized his "See what I mean?" look. I didn't know what to say.

"Listen, my guy. McGregor has drawn a line between the two sides. Between the good and the evil. The last battle is a-comin'." Pith looked shaken. I remembered Napoleon Len and the map of the park.

But this apocalypse talk was too much. I needed to dial things back. "Let's all just take a deep breath. We have no reason to believe that Len is capable of something serious. He puts on costumes and spooks people. That's all. And we certainly have no reason to believe that anything is imminent." Pith puffed out his cheeks and exhaled. Nelly closed her eyes and then lowered her head to rest on her arms crossed on the table.

"What?" I asked.

Pith replied, "Did you know that even though the HOA has refused to reschedule Community Day, Len took it upon himself to make it happen? He somehow got a barbecue food truck scheduled to come to the neighborhood for an afternoon event." I did *not* know that.

"It's coming, my man. It's coming. In two weeks. Locked and loaded. Sunday, November 1."

That didn't prove anything, I thought.

"Yessir. Signed and sealed. He inked a contract with the food-truck owner. Even got a county permit without the HOA knowing a lick about it. County's been denying all public-gathering requests like this, but Len testified during an online hearing. He even got fined $100 for talking for 20 minutes and breaking the county's Kim Rule. But a majority of the licensing board agreed with him that gatherings are important." I guess they'd be on the community side of Len's battle line.

Pith whistled, then said admiringly, "Woo-wee. Old-timer is kickstarting Community Day all by his lonesome."

"OK, so he reserved a food truck! Big deal! He just did something sneaky and outlandish. Oh my! Alert the media! Len has a new caper!" No one was laughing.

"Seriously, folks," I tried with a calmer tone. "This doesn't require fancy interpretations. McGregor is nuts, and he likes pulled pork and an audience. End of story."

"He's gathering people up, bro, and it *ain't* for a sense of community," replied Pith solemnly. Barb had a night terror. Nelly, fatigued by the wine and emotions, just stared at the bus stop sign and said, "Real talk."

Before I could even try to answer, Nelly's dog stood up and walked over to the gazebo's entry, sat, and offered a paw. We hadn't noticed that my wife, holding a pot of coffee and a stack of Styrofoam cups, was reading the county health director's marriage-justice-and-graft notice.

"A nuptial equity fund?" she said incredulously. Her lips were not inhibiting words from coming out. "A *nuptial equity fund?* You want money to help someone else's marriage? You have got to be..."

Pith finished off the contents of his flask, reached below the table, adjusted himself, and stared into the void, "Yessir, I got an equity fund for the county right here. Equal opportunity and plenty to go 'round, I'll tell you what."

Chapter 33: Confessional

My wife had such a strong reaction to the notice on the gazebo because she isn't crazy about weddings. Her parents' marriage wasn't a success. That's why she had such cold feet about marrying me. And then our wedding wasn't great. To put it mildly.

I told her we shouldn't invite her dad, but she wanted him there. She said that she had been an unruly kid and deserved the tough discipline and that his life had been hard. I didn't have the heart to tell her that that was her Stockholm syndrome talking. So I gave in. She hadn't seen him for years. He showed up at our rehearsal dinner hours late and high on something. The first thing he said was, "Look at that. Piggy thinned out."

He kept telling people he was there to celebrate getting his final girl off his hands. "They took away my best years and bled me dry," he repeated laughingly 20 times. The more he drank, the more he said things like, "None of you are better than me," and "If she's going to turn out anything like her mother, you better think twice about taking those vows." My groomsmen made sure he didn't come to the ceremony. It was a father-free event, and that's fine; we were starting a new family that wouldn't have all the drama. Her surviving sister walked her down the aisle.

When my wife stepped into the gazebo, Nelly drooped the sides of her mouth and eyelids, stood confidently if unstably, tottered over, and hugged her tight. Though passed out, Barb's public-health-violation senses tingled and, to protest the close contact, she snored and uncrossed and recrossed her legs. My wife accepted Nelly's hug with eyes clenched and arms outstretched—not wanting to scald Nelly's back with the coffee. Nelly pulled back, put her hands on the sides of my wife's head, and mouthed, "I know…I know," and hugged her again. Nelly's one of those emotional drunks.

My wife was also out of practice at social interaction, so when she sat down between Pith and me, she had the same forced, upright posture and pleasant smile that Nelly and Barb had when I arrived. She patted my right hand three times before holding on to it tight, pulsing it from time to time.

"I could hear the party from our porch. I thought I'd bring something warm to drink," my wife announced with good cheer. She was being nice so I didn't say out loud that dosing panic-prone Nelly with caffeine is like delivering a smallpox blanket inside Pandora's box via Trojan Horse. But Nelly's dog and I made eye contact; we were on the same page. Pith grabbed the coffee pot and poured everyone else a cup. He had a second flask in his sweatshirt, this one with coffee I'm sure, and he took a slug from that rather than taking from the communal pot.

"Soooo…" my wife began, tilting her head and nestling a lock of hair behind her left ear. "How's it hanging over here?"

"See! See!" shouted Masonry. "It's a completely acceptable idiom!"

"Wait, what?" asked my wife.

"He blames me! I deserve it!" announced Nelly out of nowhere and to no one, saving us all from another discussion of privy parts and undercarriages.

"Nah, girlsfriends," Barb garbled to Nelly as she woke up, sort of. "You had that new bid'ness. And you were just trying to protect the things. You had an idea, and you went with it! 'Just go ahead and go fer yer ideas,' is what I always say. Good doing."

When Barb lifted her head from the table, we saw that one of her strip lashes had become disconnected from her eyelid. It looked like a streak of mascara had grown centipede legs and inched toward her temple. Pith leaned behind my wife and whispered to me, "My shop already got wigs, toupees, and extensions locked down, bro. If I can corner that eyelash market, Imma dominate the region's false-hair game. Believe that. I'm building an empire on vanity and low-grade deception. Leveraging the human condition, my man."

Not your run-of-the-mill ambition, but I respected the hustle.

"By the way, bud," Pith whispered to me, "don't forget what I told you about cabbage. Same type of opportunity. Veritable gold mine." I laughed.

"I'm confused," my wife said, eyes darting side to side. "Did everyone have a good conversation over here? Did you talk about the things that you wanted to talk about?"

"Hmblrf! I had a thing I wanted once," Barb proceeded to build on her just-laid foundation of incoherence. "I was going to be the Florence Nightingale of rural public health. But I didn't want to wear a doily-lacy nurse cap-bonnet. I had a loose perm."

"You don't just propose marriage in the middle of the street to a married man," added Masonry, who had progressed to the bargaining phase of grief.

"No...no, no...I was selfish," Nelly, her eyes filling, dams about to break, replied to an idealized version of Barb—a Barb who was totally keyed in to the current topic of conversation. "I was selfish...cruel...I just hated those diesel fumes...I know...that's a silly thing...but the crowds at the bus stop...they made me nervous...I mean more nervous...I was so selfish...and mean."

What in the world was Nelly talking about? Where was all this guilt coming from?

"Starting a dealership...terrifying...all that investment...I was young...big dreams...I didn't know if people would buy RVs or campers...every day I worried...maybe I'd made a huge mistake," said Nelly, making the case for market research and a solid business plan.

"Yasss, queen. When you started it, I did think it was a dummy idea," stammered Barb, possibly trying to be supportive? "'Hblmp. An RV dealership?' I said. 'That's a dumb-dumb idea.' That's what I was saying. 'Dumbdididumdumdum.'"

"Whoa, Nelly! *In vino veritas* something fierce up in here!" yelled Pith.

"I'm sorry...are you all joking around...I'm having a hard time..." said my wife, who was trying, unsuccessfully, to find a marked trail into the discussion. In her defense, in the span of 30 seconds, the conversation had bounced from false hair and cabbage to Florence Nightingale and loose perms to a marriage proposal in the middle of the street to diesel fumes and crowds to dealerships and dumbdididumdumdum. Not exactly a well-lit path. To her credit, my wife was undeterred and tried to blaze a new trail: "Did everyone share thoughts and feelings about the virus and quarantine and holding on...?"

"'In Your Eyes' is a beautiful song—I have no problem admitting that—and he's got a mellifluous voice. Like a chorus of angels from on high. But we had just been arguing in the street." Masonry was now playing the part of the voice of reason in his one-man conversation.

"I started floating my idea to some people in the neighborhood...and everyone thought it would work...I had planned to tell Barb about it...but a British man lied to me about a gas leak and Barb got buttonholed by a plumber-ninja-spy." In any other context Nelly's last sentence would've earned her a straitjacket. But here it actually made sense. But I still didn't understand what had her tied in knots. I couldn't take it any longer.

"What did you do, Nelly? It couldn't have been so bad. You're loyal, tender, and conscientious."

And then Nelly revealed her plan and her years of remorse. Wine, confession, and an audience distracted by multiple simultaneous conversations enabled her to speak with no hitches in her get along. No potholes.

"I wanted to create a car-pool and park-and-ride service at my dealership to replace the neighborhood bus stop. Once that succeeded, I could replace other bus stops in the county. Soon I'd have a county-wide operation." Beneath Nelly's regret, there was still a hint of pride in the idea. But that soon gave way to guilt-ridden justification. Her pitch got higher, her words quicker. "It would be easy! It made sense! I'd go to the county and get all the permits. My lot had plenty of space. Then I'd use my dealership's excess inventory to help people commute in comfort. It would be cheaper and easier than public buses. It was a great plan! A great plan!" With each sentence the tears came faster.

"We can lean on one another, right?" my wife tried again. "But we all have to work hard to hold it together, don't we?"

"When Kim's animal incident happened..." Nelly continued.

"—home-brew animal camp—" Pith clarified for those just joining us for this evening's insanity.

"...I realized that the bus was in trouble, so the iron was hot, I had to strike. It was time to execute my plan," Nelly pressed on.

"Some peoples wanted to execute Typhoid Mary," edified Barb. "She infected two billion people give or take. I would've pardoned her. The guilt she felt was punishment enough. Public health is complicated. Good thing I have my master's degree."

Nelly continued, "The bus was dying anyway...why not have a rideshare? The public bus could go away peacefully...there'd be a private option ready...riders would be happy...my dealership would get some revenue. Win-win-win!" I wasn't sure whom Nelly was trying to convince.

She went on, "I put together a confidential report for the county commissioners. I had charts and graphs. I showed how expensive the county's bus service was. Personnel costs, gas, maintenance. I did my research. I showed how few people were using the Blue Line, especially our bus stop. I found survey data showing most county residents didn't like public transportation. I was convincing!"

"Nells had them reports printed in color. Spiral binding, clear front cover. Final product was on point, no doubt," added Pith supportively.

"But after all those meetings, all those documents and forms, all those printing costs...the bastards at the county denied all my permits and rejected my plan. They said it was unrealistic and unsustainable. My idea and my hopes were killed." Sometimes the timing of these things just doesn't work out, I thought.

"Then they twisted the knife," Nelly added.

Pith rubbed his chin and took another drink.

"The commissioners, those awful, sneaky...their next budget spent millions on a highway project. Leveled acres of forests, tore up fields...to make room for more roads and more cars."

"Subterfuge something wicked..." Pith added.

"They used the information in my report to not only kill our bus stop but slash half of the county's bus service, kill the entire Blue Line, and justify their highway construction plan," confessed Nelly.

"Mesmerizin' duplicity, I'll tell you what. We later learned that S.O.B Butch Tweed had been trying to get the county to undertake a massive road project for years," explained Pith. "He used the animal-camp situation to convince his buddies on the county commission it was time to cut bus service and start chopping trees, moving dirt, and laying asphalt." Gross, I thought.

"Tweed's construction business got a huge contract out of the deal. He made a fortune," fumed Pith. "He's just a high-end pickpocket." Hmmp, I thought. Pith exhaled hard like he was trying re-inflate a busted balloon. "From Tweed's point of view, Nelly's hopes were collateral damage, and Len's mental anguish was just an added benefit."

"Wait. Wait. What do you mean?" I asked. "How was Len affected by any of this? I still don't know why he cares about this bus stop!"

"I have self-respect. I deserve to be wooed in a proper fashion," Masonry asserted his worth.

Nelly, anguished, didn't slow down to acknowledge, much less answer, my question. "I know the death of this bus stop...and the Blue Line...it wasn't all on me. I know the bus didn't have many riders. I know Matt and Kim share the blame. And the county commission and Butch Tweed had their dirty scheme. Plenty of blame to go around." That was a lot of qualifiers before an admission. Nelly was straddling the depression and acceptance stages of grief. "But in my heart," she continued, "I understood that I deserved to be punished. I tried to kill the bus. I was devious and selfish. I didn't think about the consequences of my behavior. I was wrong."

"Yessir, for 17 years Nelly's been Raskolnikov-ing. Stalked by shame, always looking over her shoulder, always expecting retribution from the universe." Crime and punishment, indeed.

Pith continued with a fraction of a smile, "Oh, doggie, them Russian writers knew the shadow of guilt. You gotta give 'em that. They had that deep appreciation for contrition and conscience, I'll tell you what." Pith then furrowed his brow. "They also knew how to wear long beards and big furry hats. They made it look easy. It ain't. I've tried."

"But I didn't know! God almighty, forgive me. I just didn't know what I was doing to Mr. McGregor. I swear I didn't. I had no idea!" Nelly wasn't anxious; she was tormented. But why?

My wife and I looked at each other, disoriented. And then, of course, we turned to sage Pith. And it all came into focus.

Chapter 34: All These Evils

Pith obliged. "When Nelly was pullin' all that ride-share skullduggery, she didn't know that Len McGregor's wife and little girl had been killed in a car crash on Central Union Highway back in 1984. Len had been working late. Wasn't with 'em."

I could picture the two small white crosses solemnizing the side of the road by the Ohunka loop. Walking and suffering.

"Drunk driver and dense fog," Pith added quietly and then wiped under his nose with the back of his left hand. "Len's girl was a curly blonde. Freckles, too. I went to grade school with her. Had me my first crush." Deluges down Nelly's and Barb's cheeks.

Pith pointed to the bus stop sign, "Len was entirely responsible for this here bus stop. He wanted fewer cars on the road: Fewer cars, fewer crashes. Fewer lives ruined. He lobbied the county relentlessly. Said the neighborhood had to have a bus. Said no one should suffer like he had." My wife's hand trembled.

Pith continued, "The county eventually agreed outta sympathy. They came up with the money. Cleared that little spot. Cemented that sign in the earth. Reworked the Blue Line's route so it could stop here. Most generous thing a gub'ment ever done." Of the people, by the people, for the people. "On the first day of operation, Len paid everyone's fare. He loved that the community had something that brought them together. Sometimes, he'd come to the park just to watch people talk at the bus stop and climb aboard together. He said it made the pain almost bearable. Almost bearable, he said." Pith smiled and nodded toward the street. "For all intents and purposes, that was the Len McGregor Bus Terminal."

I imagined neighbors riding that bus together. It didn't much matter where they were going. It was mobile community. Like the Wayfarers.

"Yessir. Him and his wife were inseparable. And that little girl was the center of his universe. His life revolved around her. And, real talk, his life fell outta orbit after that accident. Dislodged by the combined force of guilt and shame. Careening in space, I'll tell you what."

I remember thinking to myself as Pith talked, "Maybe Len was the first Wayfarer." Circular neighborhood walks of pain and penance. Trying to pace the ache away. The palliative peripatetic.

"Len mostly held it together for a couple years. But he began to unspool, you know? Started actin' cockeyed and makin' up stories," Pith remembered. Nelly clasped her hands and rested her forehead on her knuckles. My wife gulped in air, then muttered, "Jesus in heaven."

"Eventually, he retreated and walled himself up," Pith said with raised eyebrows and a cocked head. "Just couldn't take the world one second longer. Needed to keep it all out." Then, like the voiceover from a documentary, "His compound is just a rampart, defending him from everyone and everything. Self-preservation. And all them crazy outfits he wears? All them characters he plays? That poor man just needed another reality. Make-believe as respite from constant sorrow. Stories as self-therapy."

I just couldn't square the abject grief with the absurd conduct. "But he's a grown man playing dress up, for God's sake." I tried

Sublimation, bro. Heckuva drug," explained Pith.

I rephrased it as a question. "What are we supposed to make of something so ridiculous and so heartbreaking at the same time?"

Pith poured himself coffee from the communal pot and said, "Human condition, bud. A tragedy to those who feel and a comedy to those who think."

* * *

"I didn't know…I just didn't know. I moved here in 1999. Years after the accident. No one told me. No one talks about these things." Nelly seemed to melt into the table like she'd gone boneless or was being sucked into a black hole under the gazebo. Her dog pawed at her hip trying to release her. But the singularity abides. "I couldn't have known…please believe me."

Pith put his scabby, compassionate hand on the back of Nelly's head, platonically. "Ol' Len's been in suspended animation for decades now. Poor man is frozen in the mid-1980s. A flashback stuck on repeat. Relivin' grief nonstop." Groundhog Len.

"Yessir," Pith continued somberly, "trauma distorts time. McGregor is a real-life Miss Havisham. Unable to move on. Basic temporal processing defect. It's no joke."

"Gravity distorts time, too," mumbled Barb, who was now plastered to the floor, staring up at the radial design of the gazebo's rafters. "Einstein talk."

My wife slid past Pith and hugged Nelly tight. She put her hands on the sides of Nelly's head, their eyes connected. My wife said, "I know, I know."

Pith locked his hands, turned to me, and whispered close to my ear, "Life yanks at us. Just the way it goes. Round-the-clock tugging and tearing. We all get loose at the seams. Nells, Len, Kim..." He pulled his hands apart, spread his fingers, and then latched his hands together. "No shame, no dishonor in getting stitched back up." At this point, I knew it was time to go. Everyone was drunk and hyper-emotional.

"None of you understand the gravity of this situation! My wife's going to think I'm cheating! But my relationship with McGregor has been entirely chaste so far," said Masonry, keeping his options open.

Nelly wiped her face with her sleeves and announced, "Ugly crying!" and laughed. My wife had her wrapped in a side hug, with her cheek rested atop Nelly's head. Nelly said, "I'm probably imagining it, but after they shut down our bus stop, strange things would happen at my dealership." Pith rubbed her dog's head and said, "You know better than that, Nells. Ain't no imagination about it. That's how Len does his work."

"Suddenly there were rumors about the low quality of my inventory. Stories that we were dumping toxic waste into the river. Then we couldn't sell a thing. No customers. The bank was after me—calling every day. I was all but bankrupt. It was over. It was over." She clasped her hands together and closed her eyes as though she'd just knelt in a confessional.

Barb, still splayed out on the floor sang to the stars, "Dumbdididumdumdum."

Nelly continued, "My dealership would've gone under if I hadn't gotten together with the American Legion on their bingo and gambling operation and started laundering money for the Legionnaires..."

"OH MY GOD! I KNEW IT! NO ONE LISTENED TO ME BUT I

KNEW IT! NO ONE BELIEVED ME! HA HA! I WAS RIGHT!"

"Legionnaires' disease presented a serious public health crisis, first afflicting veterans attending a 1976 bicentennial convention and likely caused by a hotel air-conditioning unit." Barb, unable to track the discussion, decided to answer a grad-school test question.

"I have to make amends...I must...I have to set this right." Nelly returned to crying into my wife's shoulder. Pith just looked at the table, shook his head, and said quietly, "Woo-eee. If Len pulls off this unsanctioned Community Day? Man oh man, we're all in for it, I'll tell you what."

I told Pith I didn't understand. He turned the flask over in his hands a few times and said, "This park is sacred to Len. And people keep desecrating it. Before the accident, he started Community Day so neighbors could bond. But this year, when everyone is scared and alone, the year that people most need community, the HOA cancels Community Day over and over again."

True, I thought.

"After his wife and daughter...after that...he engineered that bus stop to help the neighborhood. Then a bunch of wild nonsense shuts it down."

Yes, I thought.

Pith let out a long, descending whistle, tapped the flask on the table, and then pointed it into the darkness over my left shoulder. "Few people know this, but Lenny also made a quiet donation to pay for the new playground equipment. He said childhood is short and precious, and kids deserve a nice playground. But people fought about the equipment anyhow."

Yes.

Pith shook his head in disappointment and then pointed the

flask eastward. "Decades ago, he silently paid for the memorial garden. Wanted to help neighbors come together to remember their loved ones. But then folks vandalized it."

True.

"Bro, listen to me. Len suffers in a way that no one should ever hafta suffer. Loses his wife and his little gal. But he tries to do some good. He gives himself to this community, tries to make this park special. But this community disrespects the bus, the garden, and the playground. Even today, after all these years, more disrespect for the park—it's insult after injury! People fightin' over the Little Free Library. People tryin' to shut down this gazebo..." –Pith pointed the flask at the county's notice at the entrance—"...people still tryin' to have that bus stop sign torn out of the ground..."—Pith nodded at Masonry.

I couldn't disagree with any of this.

"'Love of power, operating through greed and through personal ambition, was the cause of all these evils,'" quoted Pith. Insightful, I thought. Sometimes Pith is on to something. "That's Thucydides. I've been tellin' you, my man: Them Ancient Greeks knew what was what." Nelly wept. I wasn't sure what to say.

Pith turned grim, "Listen up, bro, Len's makeshift Community Day? Daggone, it's bound to be *a show. A show.* Lord heavenly Father, I wouldn't want to be someone who'd disrespected this park or that bus stop. 'Reckoning Day' is more like it, Judge Len McGregor presiding. Meting out justice with a sword."

"Come on. What would Len actually do? What's there to be worked up about?" I asked Pith.

"Bro. *Bro...*" Pith stared at me.

"I'm serious. What's the worry?" I replied.

"Barb is scheduled to have a conversation about the park, and she gets hit with that spy-ninja-plumber routine. Kim organizes wild-animal day-care at the park, and McGregor spreads rumors about her, drivin' her to go *loco* in front of the county commissioners. Nelly schemes against the bus stop, and he tries to destroy her bid'ness. Matty interferes with the wildlife cleanup, and 17 years later McGregor pulls that stunt at his concert a couple months back."

Vigilante Len.

"*My guy*, Lenny dressed up as Napoleon and was starin' at a map of the park! You seen it! You ain't convinced he's got unwholesome plans?"

"I can't get in that man's head," I replied. "But come on, now. Do you really think Len McGregor has the capacity to pull off some massive punish-the-entire-neighborhood plot at the park?"

"Bud. You still don't know about the Compound Incident back in 1987?"

"I've only heard hints and whispers. Like everything related to Blowtorch Len, people act like it's spooky lore," I replied with an eyeroll.

"So you don't know what he done with them three journalists and his neighbors?"

"No."

"You don't know about Old Man Callahan's or Butch Tweed's involvement?"

"Nope."

"Bro, you ain't ever heard about how Kim and I got roped into that mess?"

"No."

"And I'm suspectin' you ain't wise to how Len McGregor earned that sobriquet 'Blowtorch'?"

"No idea," I said.

"Then, my dude, you ain't even got the outlines of what that man is capable of."

* * *

My wife grabbed my hand and explained how tired she was. She kissed the top of Nelly's head and then crouched down to hug Nelly's dog, saying quietly, "Be brave. She needs you. That's your job right now. Be strong." Then my wife stood, took a deep breath, and forced a smile. I took the buttermilk but decided to leave the peas for Masonry. I tried to wave to Barb but she was muttering something about a Soviet plumber saying the funeral Mass for a dead alpaca. I nodded to Masonry. He looked at me with the biggest, saddest eyes, and said, "The leotard was flattering. But if I'm going to upend my life, I'm going to need more than one song."

I half-smiled, and as my wife and I walked home, I heard Pith say, "Lenny's justice is coming, and there ain't no avoiding it. Lord, bless us and keep us safe."

Chapter 35: Curtains

"No. Please no. Don't go to your laptop. Please just come to bed." My wife was crying about Nelly's heartbreaking revelations at the park.

I tried to explain to her how valuable the conversation at the gazebo had been. I learned so much about Len's grief and Nelly's guilt. About Matty and Kim. Butch Tweed. I was buzzing. I could see all the connections. I told her that I had so much more to learn. I had to do some research. About what Len supposedly did at Matt's concert. About that event at Len's compound back in 1987. This was exhilarating. But she kept saying that she didn't care, that she didn't care about any of that.

To make her feel better, I explained how much I'd learned about the county government's corruption back in 2004. I thought she'd be glad I was also focused on work-related things. I told her that the commissioners probably got kickbacks from Butch Tweed on that roads deal. I could probably find some evidence of that. I knew I could find some incriminating records. I told her that the commissioners are probably still taking kickbacks today. And I just knew the county executive, that villain, was involved in something dirty like that.

I told my wife I needed to research this and write a column while the ideas were still fresh in my mind.

"God help me," she put her left hand over her stomach and steadied her forehead with the back of her right hand. She was really struggling. The pandemic had been so hard on her. The sad stories over at the gazebo made things worse.

"I was hoping...while you were over there..." She wasn't being clear. But I didn't want to interrupt her. Maybe if she talked things out she could settle herself. But she kept staring at me like she was waiting for me to help her. She went on with half thoughts and phrases. "Don't you understand...I've loved you...Don't you care...What am I supposed to think... God please." It was hard to listen to this. No matter how much I thanked her for nudging me to go over to the gazebo or told her about my new ideas, she was inconsolable. I wanted her to keep her voice down. I had to keep explaining that everything would be fine.

But this year had really worked her over. I guess she'd gotten her fill of hugs from Nelly because she didn't seem to want one from me. She woke up our kids when she was repeating how she couldn't take this any longer. But she wiped her face, stiffened her spine, and cheered up when she went to tend to matters. Like I've always said: Keeping your hands and mind occupied is the best remedy.

This gave me time to go down to my office and research and write. In no time, I was able to knock out a great essay about corruption in the county government. I was in the zone. I also decided to research what happened with Len at Matty's a cappella concert. Pith seemed to think that was important for understanding the upcoming Community Day. God, what I learned!

Before the sun came up, my wife came down to my office. She calmly asked me to close my laptop. She looked pale. Her eyes were swollen, but she wasn't crying anymore, so I guess she'd gotten a hold on things. I joked that if she was going to show up in front of me suddenly in the middle of the night, she should at least say she's from the county inspection office and have a top hat and bolo tie. But she didn't laugh at all, so maybe she wasn't there for that part of the conversation at the gazebo when Pith told that story. It was hilarious.

* * *

I didn't know the name of Matty's college a cappella squad. Since he went to Clemson, I guessed "Safety Schools"—but nope. With a little searching, I learned they called themselves the "Melody Makers." Dear Lord. But they differentiated themselves from other campus a cappella groups, billing themselves as "the *cool* troupe—with only the hottest theatre kids and dopest bops." Dear, dear Lord.

According to a campus newsletter, a Facebook Group, and the Melody Makers' video channel (and consistent with Kim's boasting) they'd made it to the collegiate semifinals. Their sectional was held in Georgia in late March 2020. Although much of the nation was already shut down by then, the American South evidently had special immunity to Covid so the competition was all systems go. They were going up against Auburn's Remedial Education, Duke's Topsiders, Emory's Intersectionals, and Liberty's Raptures.

Matty's team came in dead last place in the big show. I watched a few videos of their performance, and, though it pains me to admit it, they were solid. And given the difficulty of Matty's childhood, it was heart-warming to see him thriving on stage. Of course, they had some hammy choreography, their sopranos got tinny, and they couldn't help but add a few tritone substitutes. But their song choices were clever, and they pulled off an amusing mash-up of "Informer" by Snow, Vanilla Ice's

"Ice Ice Baby," and "King Without a Crown" by Matisyahu.

Did they actually like those songs or were they being ironic? Maybe they liked them ironically? Or they were being ironic about liking them ironically? Who knows. To keep your attention, an artist's intentions, like a woman's heart or a magician's hands, must keep you guessing.

Matty did himself proud. He looked sharp in his linen trousers and sequined vest. And Kim was right: When he delivered that natural sunshine, Matty seemed to have been made for the camera. And, I have to say, his singing would add immeasurably to any county-fair barbershop quartet. Anyway, I couldn't figure out why his squad finished at the bottom. The other teams were exasperating in their own ways. Maybe I had missed something in the Melody Makers' performance? So I watched every single video available online. I could find nothing to explain the judges' harsh assessment. Until I found a video recorded by the Emory Intersectionals.

They'd recorded the other teams so they would have incontrovertible video proof of their competitors' exploitation of unearned power differentials. But what they documented was disturbing in an entirely different way. When the Melody Makers were finished with their set, they received the obligatory audience standing ovation. This was captured by the Intersectionals' recording, which was taken from side-stage unlike the other recordings which were taken by audience members sitting in the crowd. As the Melody Makers were taking their final bows, the Intersectionals' camera panned to the audience. It showed Barb's benevolent husband in the third row, left side, cheering wildly, brimming with pride in Matty. I laughed and teared up.

But dead-center in the very front row of the audience was Blowtorch Len. He was wearing a floral muumuu, cowboy boots, and pince-nez. He had a fox-fur stole wrapped around his shoulders, and he raised a sign that read "Justice is Coming."

Matty, triggered, wet his pants right there in the middle of the stage.

* * *

Len was obviously punishing Matty for his role in bringing down the neighborhood bus back in 2004. As Pith had foretold at Kim's smoked-meat party, there would be payback for Matty's aluminum-pinwheel escapade, and while the universe had delayed settlin' accounts out of mercy, in time them books gotta be squared.

I did some more research and learned that concert was a turning point for Matty. His teammates not only blamed his stage-wetting for their last-place finish, they also said he had brought eternal shame to the Melody Makers' good name. They voted unanimously to expel him from the group. His a cappella squad had been everything to him. He'd been a loner since elementary school. His weight and accidents had made him bully fodder. Barb's husband, his only real friend, his only cheerleader, encouraged him to go away to college and audition for the group. And Matty had made it. It was his only community on campus. He'd even almost made some friends on the team. And there was this one girl. In his dorm-room mirror, he'd practiced giving her a compliment about her voice. He was quietly hoping that next year he'd be allowed to arrange a song for the group. Only late at night would he be so bold as to wish for a solo.

Matty thought he'd found his tribe. But they'd exiled him summarily. If he saw any of them on campus, they acted like he was invisible. Except the girl. Three times he saw her whisper and laugh at him. The team went to "America's Got Talent" without him.

Unfortunately, Kim didn't notice, much less understand, Matty's subsequent deterioration. At home, earth-tone Kim preferred to focus on keeping things ordered; she believed that acknowledging his sulking, yelling, and slamming doors would only encourage more of it. Out and about, she enjoyed being the center of attention, and her social obligations took a great deal of time and energy. We have no reason to believe she was aware of Matty's increasingly furious, threatening social media posts.

RECORDING CONCLUDED: 5:03pm
Friday, January 8, 2021
Uncorrected transcript
Interview by Elizabeth Jones

Chapter 36: Refract

From: Dr. Jennifer Davis, MERCY STATE, COMS
Date: January 8, 2021 at 9:12 PM
Subject: RE: Career and stories
To: Elizabeth Jones, Esq. OFFICE OF THE PUBLIC DEFENDER

Hi Liz—of course. I want to be as helpful as possible.

If we're lucky, we end up in jobs that match our interests and abilities. I loved science and wanted to understand why people do the things they do. This career found me. Same is probably true of your client. He ended up in jobs that allowed him to live in the world of imagination, where he's most comfortable and at his best. His storytelling becomes an asset not a liability. In his literary work, creativity was obviously important. But he once said public-service was no different. People want to be captivated and inspired, he said. They want "stories not spreadsheets."

When I was first treating him, we talked about honesty. I told him some of us want straight truth. He quoted a poet, something like, "Tell all the truth but tell it slant." He said he comes at facts from an angle. That's the only way to see all sides of the truth. He once said, "truth can be too bright," and stories provide information indirectly so we don't go blind. I raised my eyebrow. He laughed. He told me embellishment is the sugar that helps the medicine go down.

Combine this with the cognitive effects of his episode, and, like I mentioned at the outset, you should assume that much of what he's telling you is imagined or contrived. Events may have never happened. Particular people may not exist.

Now, with all that said, I realized at some point during his treatment that his stemwinders often have some kind of purpose. During our sessions, I'd find myself rolling my eyes at him, but later I'd see he'd made a point in a roundabout way. After working with him for a couple months, I started using a curlicue notation in my notes when he said something that seemed off. It was a reminder to give some extra thought to what he might be trying to convey. He used to say, "Take me seriously, not literally." That's a helpful, if frustrating, way of engaging with him. Hope that helps.

Jen

PS: I heard from my friend in the medical examiner's office. The toxicology report for Matthew is finally complete. You'll get a copy tomorrow. No surprises. High levels of prescription anti-depressants and Xanax. Also, evidence of alcohol, oxycodone, cocaine, methamphetamine.

Part 4:

The Compound

Chapter 37: Fortification

START: 2:12 pm
Saturday, January 9, 2021
C.C.S.H.

Now you're ready for the Compound Incident of 1987. Buckled up?

Right after Gazebo Night, word spread that Len had engineered a food-truck visit. Attitudes across the neighborhood brightened. For months, Community Day was a mirage; now McGregor's special brand of chicanery was making it real. Around the same time, I had more free time for my research. The economy had devastated my magazine. People weren't working thanks to Covid so fundraising dried up, and our subscribers had become difficult. Nothing I could do about the economy. I tried to explain that to my wife. Anyway, I had more free time.

I was keeping busy and doing interesting work. Honestly, I was at peak performance. I think it was the week before Community Day 2020 that I finally immersed myself in Len McGregor's backstory, including the Compound Incident. Frankly, he'd always seemed vaguely unearthly, so part of me wondered if trying to understand him was sacrilege. Or like breaking a mirror or opening a tomb or giving a clock as a gift —bad juju that would leave you cursed or mad. But onward I pushed.

The first thing I learned is that there is surprisingly little official information about Len online. It's almost like he doesn't really exist. The short joint obituary for his wife and daughter didn't even mention him by name. There was, however, a revealing story in a major outlet about Len at the peak of his career, a few decades back. He'd been promoted to executive producer of a national evening newscast, which earned him a short, gauzy media profile.

In it, Len explained that he'd been orphaned in 3rd grade. His mom died in childbirth when he was 7. His father was killed in an accident at a meat packing plant not long thereafter. This could've—should've—wrecked him. But, looking back, he said he saw how fortunate he'd been in subsequent years. He was quickly taken in by the nuns who lived in a convent attached to his parish. They smothered him in love and discipline. His close-knit community gave him everything else he needed. Never alone, never neglected, never hungry, never the odd kid out.

"I lost both my parents inside of 10 months," he explained, "but my kin grew. The 100 families in that four-block neighborhood adopted me. No one treated me like a burden, even after I got polio. I was theirs. Just a shared responsibility. That was that."

What struck me most, though, is how Len described the difference between family and community. He was proud of his last name, he said; it described where his DNA came from —"centuries of commingling of the Irish, Scottish, and English across the pond and in New York City." But his neighborhood was who he was. "My name didn't tell my story. My community did. I would've been happy to trade 'McGregor' for any cross street in that Irish ghetto on the Hudson. You could call me 'Leonard 10th Ave and West 51th and I'd smile."

The same publication, just a few years later, blurbed his resignation from that job. He wanted to spend more time with his family.

His wife, Francisca, had grown up outside of Grangerford, and she wanted to put down roots here. Len landed a job nearby. He must've known someone who knew someone. I looked online and found some old PDFs of the masthead of our state's big paper. For a few years at least, Len was the bureau chief for our tri-county area.

I was able to track down a few neighborhood old-timers who knew Len when he first arrived in the area. They all said that he was a natural-born convener. Unfortunately, the county just didn't have the same instinct for community-building as Len's childhood neighborhood. When he got here, Len founded and chaired the capital campaign that funded the construction of the county library. Others appreciated his effort, but he had to do most of the heavy lifting. He tried his very best —with limited success—to gather people up for a book club, weeknight cocktail hours, and Saturday night dinners. He even briefly served on the HOA board. But after the car crash, Len used his convening gift for a different purpose. A very different purpose.

The clearest, strangest example of that took place at the McGregor Compound on November 1, 1987, 33 years to the day before Community Day 2020. It's the only other episode of Len's life for which there is publicly available information. And for that extraordinary written record we have a hot-headed 17-year-old to thank. Were it not for him and his school newspaper, we'd only have whispered accounts of the time Blowtorch Len McGregor staged the most baffling gathering to, as best we can tell, punish some neighbors for neglecting him and three journalists for insulting buses.

* * *

First things first. Blowtorch Len has an extra-large lot in the southeast quadrant of the neighborhood. He lives in a modest, two-story midnight green American Craftsman with two chimneys. At least that's how older neighbors remember it. A more up-to-date assessment is impossible because his property is protected by a 10-foot, solid rebarred concrete wall that he had built in 1985. Right after the wall went up, children climbed nearby trees to try to peer over the fortification to see what he might be hiding. But Len's network of booby traps, trip wires, and sirens nipped that in the bud.

The barricade violates numerous provisions of the HOA bylaws related to fencing, building materials, neighborliness, good sense, and the migratory paths of sundry species. But Len — surprise!—began construction without the necessary permits and was about halfway finished by the time the HOA got its act together and issued a cease-and-desist order. It took another three weeks for the local clerk of the courts to determine that Len's counterclaim that "possession of an illegal wall is 9/10 of the law" was gobbledygook. And by then, *c'est fini*!

Considering the tragedy that McGregor had endured, most HOA residents at the time were willing to look the other way when it came to the wall. The problem, however, was that no one seemed to look his way, in a manner of speaking. No one reached out to console him or just connect. Good fences make good neighbors, I suppose. Or maybe the community just didn't know how to rally around a widower. Or maybe the area's post-Ohunka insularity and suspiciousness kept people from warming up to an outsider.

Whatever the reasons for their distance, his second loss of a family turned out very differently than his first: As a child, he'd been taken up by nuns and neighbors; as an adult, he'd been forgotten. As Kim later learned, it was devastating to no longer cross others' minds. But whereas Kim responded by fighting for the community's attention, Len would respond by punishing his neighbors.

* * *

As it happened, only one person took special interest in Len during his period of mourning. But it was not the kind of interest Len needed.

McGregor had understandably resigned from the HOA board after the accident, late 1984. He was replaced by a wealthy resident who owned several construction companies and desperately wanted a seat in the state legislature. This new board member, thick of hair and midriff and confident miles beyond his competence, thought the HOA would be the perfect political steppingstone. He wanted to make a name for himself, and he'd been looking for a confrontation to establish his alpha-dog bona fides. Len's wall was perfect for his purposes. Or so he thought. This new member convinced his board colleagues to petition the local magistrate for an emergency order allowing the HOA to demolish Len's fortification. "Something there is that doesn't love a wall," you know?

The district judge sent the two sides into arbitration. Len, naturally, refused to attend the session. Instead—oh, the mischief in him—he sent his "dueling second," a man who claimed in a court document to be "a lawyer of international renown and impeccable sartorial capacities." This "lawyer," however, looked an awful lot like Len dressed in denim coveralls and a hat a debutante might wear to the Kentucky Derby. Not his most inventive costume, but he was still green: This, it is believed, was Len's first time going semi-incognito to flummox a foe. One does not suddenly become capable of war-gaming pastries while dressed as Napoleon or invoking peace treaties while playing a ninja-plumber-spy; it takes years of practice to hone that craft.

His "lawyer" brought 37 boxes of "evidence and highly classified exhibits" that he claimed proved beyond a shadow of a doubt that Len's wall was lawful. The swaggering, bellicose new board member, Butch Tweed, was representing the HOA at the arbitration hearing. He walked in absolutely certain he could end this rigmarole in a snap. He was entirely unprepared for Len's show of fictional force. Though Tweed's comeuppance was richly deserved, those who've had similar encounters with Len could have some sympathy for Tweed. Trying to match wits with ol' Blowtorch is like trying to arm-wrestle soup.

Thinking he could prevail with his stentorian voice and unfounded self-assurance, Tweed was ill-prepared when McGregor's "attorney" demanded the arbitrator fine and imprison Tweed for arriving at the hearing with an "offensively weak chin." This wrong-footed Butch from the jump; he was then all but incapacitated when Len's attorney proceeded to argue that the wall's composition of "recycled papier-mâché and the ground-up bones of ancient Trojan warriors" guaranteed it protections under environmental laws and the local historical trust. In our county at least that was a novel argument in small-claims arbitration.

The arbitrator was a retired executive at the local bank who'd built a solid reputation over decades by calmly foreclosing on family farms and making meticulously documented and astoundingly unsound loans to friends at the country club. He had a tee time in 45 minutes and no interest in dragging out these proceedings. He interpreted Tweed's stunned silence as acquiescence. The arbitrator declared Len's wall to be permissible: The HOA couldn't touch it.

Sensing his advantage and the arbitrator's antsy-ness, Len's attorney made a small secondary motion. The arbitrator, who had already changed into golfing knickers and argyle socks, granted the request: Since the HOA bylaws were silent on the subject, McGregor was allowed to maintain a moat, 20 feet deep, around his wall as well.

Wait. What's wrong? What are you doing? We just got started. No, I don't want to stop. Please don't pack up. I need to tell you more. Please, don't go. Please. I don't want to be alone for the rest of the day. Please, don't leave me.

RECORDING CONCLUDED: 2:55pm
Saturday, January 9, 2021
Uncorrected transcript
Interview by Elizabeth Jones

Chapter 38: Rewrite

From: Dr. Jennifer Davis, MERCY STATE, COMS
Date: January 9, 2021 at 5:12 PM
Subject: RE: Too much
To: Elizabeth Jones, Esq. OFFICE OF THE PUBLIC DEFENDER

I understand. Believe me, I understand. It can be a lot. Innocent people were killed, and it seems like he's making light of everything. But try to understand how his brain is wired.

After graduating college, he had his pick of consulting jobs and law schools. He could've easily been a self-made millionaire by 30. But he used his grad-school scholarship to study literature abroad. He loved it, said his first year at Oxford was the happiest he'd ever been. His master's thesis was going to be a study of how aspiring fictional heroes grapple with mental-health issues. Sadly, he was his own oracle.

In his second year, he suffered a prolonged manic episode that went undiagnosed for much too long. Oxford sent him home during Christmas break (this was late 2001). His mother had him hospitalized at Mercy. He never made it back to England, never finished his graduate program.

While he was recovering at home, he turned his draft thesis into a book. It got published, won awards. I actually reread it when he was brought here after Community Day. It's called *Imperfect Hero*. Beautiful, tragic. It tells of the mental and emotional struggles of a dozen or so characters in high and low fiction—Antigone, Moses, Don Quixote, Hamlet. Gatsby. Ignatius Reilly. Raskolnikov in *Crime and Punishment*. Nelly in *Wuthering Heights*. Barb Gordon from Batman. It's clear that your client felt stalked by mental illness. He was trying to make sense of his fate before it happened.

Stories are how he thinks and copes. He has a troubled mind, and on some level, he knows it.

Jen

Chapter 39: Cross

START: 1:21pm
Sunday, January 10, 2021
C.C.S.H.

Pith came to visit yesterday.

After you left, they gave me medicine. I spent some time with a doctor I like. He's older, calm. Like a Jedi. He thinks I have sadness, anger about being neglected as a kid. He said my body and mind act on fear. He calls it "learned instinct." It's why I attribute bad motives to people. To make sense of people, feel in control. He said my brain developed this when I was a kid. Since I was alone so much. But I told him I was always fine when I was alone. That never bothered me. He knew my mom. He was a new doctor at Mercy State when she was there in the 1980s. I asked if he was one of the doctors my sister screamed "En garde!" at. He smiled but said he didn't remember that.

[...EXTENDED PAUSE...]

I talked to him about my storytelling. He said that's from loneliness. Also the abuse. Stories are a place for my mind to go. He said I write fiction in my mind with facts from my life. That's a safe way for my brain to deal with real things. He called it "secure processing." He agreed I got the storytelling gift from my mom. He said I got a lot from her.

He said I should see if a friend might visit me. Pith came straight away. He looked good. Better. He said he had tightened things up. "The bottom hits like a rock," he said. He's taking it day by day. He told me that my wife's sister has been staying with my wife. Things are up in the air. She said a lot depends on things here. Evidence and hearings, you know. I told Pith we can work all that out. I'll get it taken care of. I'm good at fixing things. Always have been.

[...EXTENDED PAUSE...]

Pith said my little girl is doing fine. My boy isn't crying so much anymore. Pith promised to help make sure he keeps growing up straight. Pith said my son told his teacher that he is fine and he can handle things. My boy said no one should worry about him. I'm glad he's being strong. We can get all this sorted out. People are worked up right now. Things will settle. We'll get it sorted out.

I've always been good at fixing things. I have an instinct. When my parents would argue at night, I'd sneak out of bed and stand at the top of the steps. I wanted to help. I'd say prayers. I'd apologize to God in case I had done something bad. Something to cause this. I'd drink little cups of water and pace. Silently, 14½ strides, down the hallway and back. That was one lap. I'd stop counting the laps when I hit 300. I hated their fights. Sometimes, I'd whisper-yell, "No more!" into the crook of my elbow. I felt better when I walked. It was calming. I liked when the heater would turn on or off. That sound made it seem like things were changing. My sister always locked herself in her room. When things got loud, she'd growl, trying to muffle the noise. The first time she got out of rehab, she told me that when they argued, she'd hide under her blankets and repeat stories I'd told her. When things got bad, she'd rake her fingernails across her legs until they bled.

One Saturday night, my dad stormed upstairs during one of

those fights to get his wallet and keys. So he could leave for a bit. He did that sometimes. I always had time to run back to bed so he wouldn't see me. This time I was sitting outside my sister's door whispering to her because I was worried about her. I couldn't get back to my room in time. He saw me sitting there with my little cups of water in a row. I stood up and said something to him. Like, "Are you OK?" Don't remember exactly. But he said, "Get out of my life." Got his things and left. It didn't bother me. He was upset. I understood. I was fine. I went downstairs and talked to my mom. She had her cigarettes and coffee. I could always make her feel better. I tried to talk to my sister, but she was walled up in her room. Her fortress of solitude.

My dad would always apologize after something like that. But this time he didn't. The next day, he had the hard blue suitcase. I didn't get to say goodbye. That's the last time I saw him.

[...EXTENDED PAUSE...]

Haven't seen my kids since November. That's OK. I don't want them to see me like this. Good news is she'll be too young to remember any of this. My boy's strong enough. He'll handle it. I'll get it worked out. They can be the two musketeers.

[...EXTENDED PAUSE...]

Pith gave me the gold cross my wife used to wear. He said she wanted me to have it.

[...EXTENDED PAUSE...]

I'd like to get back to my story tomorrow.

RECORDING CONCLUDED: 1:50pm
Sunday, January 10, 2021
Uncorrected transcript
Interview by Elizabeth Jones

Chapter 40: Retreat

From: Dr. Jennifer Davis, MERCY STATE, COMS
Date: January 10, 2021 at 3:12 PM
Subject: RE: heartbreaking
To: Elizabeth Jones, Esq. OFFICE OF THE PUBLIC DEFENDER

Your listening has worked. He must trust you now. He's not one to open up like that. (Success—I'll tell Judge Thomas. He'll be pleased.)

Because of your client's childhood, he thinks other people and God are aligned against him. He's convinced that when things are going well, the universe sets its sights on him. When he was young, every short period of stability ended abruptly. When he was finally content at Oxford, things fell apart.

He thinks the same thing happened when he worked for the state government. Probably in mid-2002, when he was in his mid-20s, he got the job with the legislator. As you know, she's governor now. At the time, she was about to take over as state senate president and was hiring a team, trying to find young, talented staffers. It's not clear how your client got connected to her. I'm sure he knew someone who knew someone. And I'm sure she thought it was a coup to hire him.

Remember, this is before social media so virtually no one knew he'd been hospitalized or left graduate school early. He was still seen as a rising star. Things were finally working out for him. He met his wife, kept getting promoted, and was confirmed as state secretary of transportation in late 2008. But then that reporter dredged up his past, and he had to resign in 2012 to stop the story from running.

He was never the same after that. He was furious at the world. He had a vendetta against journalists. He called them corrupt and said the newspaper had tried to ruin him for sport. He said that while others did real work, reporters destroyed people and the country.

He also became bitter about the government and politicians. He started buying into conspiracy theories. He thought he didn't get any credit for all of his public-service work, he thought bureaucrats and politicians had plotted against him, he thought his mentor had torpedoed his career. He couldn't take it anymore. He retreated and walled himself up.

But his wife and friends wouldn't let him give up. They worked overtime to find him a new job. The campus where he landed was in a quiet part of his home state. He'd known the college president when they were students together at Oxford. She was finishing her Ph.D. when he was in his first year. They'd evidently been close, but they hadn't been in touch much since he'd dropped out. She knew he was gifted. But she'd seen first-hand his first major mental-health episode, and now she was being asked to hire him after his second. According to your client's wife, the college president reluctantly agreed to have him run the English department's minor journal.

Ultimately, he took the job, but he wasn't happy about it. During the last counseling session I had with him and his wife, he said it was humiliating that his wife and friends secretly got him the job. He said they conspired to put him out to pasture in a college library in the boondocks. His wife tried to tell him it was a great opportunity and a reward for years of public service. I'll never forget this—he said it felt "more like a bronze airbag than a golden parachute." I told him he didn't need to be a young man in a hurry anymore, his new life would be wonderful if he slowed down to enjoy it. He said heroes need to keep moving or the demons catch them.

That was the last time I saw him until he was brought here after the events of Community Day.

-Jen

PS: Quick thought. Now that he trusts you, don't be afraid to ask him clarifying questions if one of his stories takes a "curlicue" direction. Just try to show curiosity not judgment.

Chapter 41: Reconsider

From: Dr. Jennifer Davis, MERCY STATE, COMS
Date: January 10, 2021 at 6:12 PM
Subject: Animal camp?
To: Elizabeth Jones, Esq. OFFICE OF THE PUBLIC DEFENDER

Hi Liz, I was just talking to my team about your client and the events of Community Day. One of my colleagues (he grew up in that part of the state) said the park where everything happened is the same place where a woman organized an illegal "animal camp" back in 2004.

Do you know that story??? It's almost unbelievable. I had forgotten all about it. It was all over the news back then. I think she also became semi-famous for her dramatic presentations to the county government. She went viral before going viral was a thing!

Anyway, that was a long time ago. Obviously, no bearing on your client's case. Just interesting. What an odd neighborhood!

Chapter 42: Distortion

START: 11:31am
Monday, January 11, 2021
C.C.S.H.

Good morning. Looks like you've got more pep in your step today, huh? Great to see.

And you have a fresh notebook! Well, today's the day for it. That's for sure. You're in for a show. Get comfortable. The characters. The setting. What an aggrieved Len McGregor is capable of. The foreshadowing. Lord, the foreshadowing. Honestly, if this story weren't true, you'd think it had been written in Hollywood. Or for a sketch show. Truly. It's nuts.

Alright. After the completion of the wall and moat, McGregor was quiet for the remainder of 1985 and 1986. Not necessarily by choice. Let's just say he didn't get any book-club, cocktail-hour, or dinner-party invitations. The view around the neighborhood from the "good fences make good neighbors" crowd must have been, "He's grieving. Leave him alone." Solitude, they decided for him, is sometimes the best society.

It was about this time that Len started his lonely foot patrols. I imagine that he still wanted to be part of the neighborhood but now understood that he had been consigned to its periphery. No matter how hard he'd tried, he was an outsider. He was left as an observer, traveling its perimeter in endless loops. And in time, this broke him. So this natural-born convener rebelled against community. He turned community on its head.

It was as though he concluded that the opposite of community is *not* loneliness but the distortion of togetherness. It didn't seem to matter to Len if he gathered people under false pretenses, ruined their events, or goaded internecine warfare. Whatever warped the sense of community was fine by Len. And of course it also had to amuse Len. I guess he wanted to laugh and punish at the same time.

I came across all sorts of crazy stories. Once Len called all the members of a Bible-study group and, pretending to be the pastor, moved that night's meeting to a new address. They dutifully arrived at an abandoned warehouse, and a circus clown greeted them with balloon animals. Once, a brawl broke out at the annual Kiwanis Club dinner because *someone* had spread stories that each attendee was having an affair with another attendee's spouse.

My favorite, though, was the Opening Day Fiasco of 1986. Len told the county's little league organizers that he had arranged for a "world-famous vocalist" to sing the National Anthem before the ceremonial first pitch of spring. After about 10 minutes, it finally dawned on the hundreds of adult spectators that the woman standing in a ball gown on the pitcher's mound with a microphone was only there to recite filthy limericks. Her performance became so legendary among the players that the middle school principal began suspending any student for starting a sentence with, "There once was a man from Nantucket..."

In a sense, the infamous Compound Incident I've alluded to started in mid-1987 when McGregor purchased a full-page ad in the local newspaper. He identified himself as "Sir Leonard the Just, karate white belt and rightful heir to the Portuguese crown." County residents were aware of neither Len's noble pedigree nor his martial arts training. But there you have it.

The ad explained that Sir Len was in the market for a contractor to design and build a "glorious shed" in his backyard. The solicitation seemed suspicious. But Len promised to pay in cash—a contractor's dream—and the ad claimed, "This is no penny-ante operation. I got a high-five-figure project on my noggin." Given how things turned out, no one is sure if Len actually ever wanted a shed. But a request-for-proposals of that size was uncommon in this depressed rural county 30 years ago, so the opportunity caused a stir in the local construction community.

But bidders found the process difficult. For instance, Len required all proposals to be written in Latin. His preferences also shifted wildly. At first, he wanted a modest 150-square foot structure but wanted it made of "marble, vibranium, and dark matter." Later, he said he wanted a shed that would "humiliate the Taj Mahal in size and scandalize a bordello in degeneracy." Even the most experienced carpenters found that challenging to construe.

After all the bids were in, Len's "selection committee"—don't ask!—chose a local family-owned business with a reputation for on-time, on-budget projects and handwritten thank-you notes. Once the firm promised Len that all members of the work crew would neither swear nor consume dairy while on the job, negotiations moved swiftly. The contract stipulated that Len would get an 800-square foot shed modeled on the Alamo, and the firm would get $76,455.76.

The firm's patriarch, an older, good-natured Christian man, had some misgivings about this undertaking. As one would. But, all things considered, he found Sir Len to be a decent, if eccentric, character. McGregor's final request was that they start the job on Sunday morning at 7:00am sharp "in accordance with the strictures of the Book of Leviticus." Mr. Callahan agreed, even though he was pretty sure the Bible was silent on shed-building.

Though he'd never admit it, Callahan was proud to have been selected. This was his reward, he believed, for decades of good, solid work in his county. He also suspected he'd had a leg up on the competition because of his ties to Sir Len's neighborhood: Callahan was the local craftsman who had recently built and donated several trellises for the new memorial garden at the park. McGregor, however, had picked Callahan for a different reason.

After doing that unpaid work at the park, Callahan sent a handwritten thank-you note to the HOA expressing his appreciation for being able to contribute to a project that had such personal meaning to him. But Callahan was a man of principle, he explained, and felt obligated to express his view that it was inappropriate to have a public bus stop so close to the memorial. The bus, he wrote, was loud and spewed noxious fumes. It was an insult to those paying their respects at the garden. And, anyway, he went on, people prefer their cars to public transportation; no neighborhood—especially a small, spacious neighborhood like this one—should have a public bus stop.

* * *

On the Friday morning before the Sunday construction of the martyr-venerating shed was to begin, a fax arrived at the corporate headquarters of *Cat Fancy* magazine. It was a press release announcing that a family had trained a refined, lethargic Persian and a live-wire, until-recently stray Siamese to meow along to Dolly Parton's hits. This feline odd couple was said to happily wear authentic cowboy hats and boots "after mild sedation and a good talking to." The unnamed impresario sending the notice closed with the most generous invitation:

Cat Fancy, because of its long track record of supporting the visual, fashion, and creative feline arts, was invited to send a reporter from its music and costumes department for the first public performance of this groundbreaking act.

Instead of assigning this to a junior writer, the magazine's editor-in-chief, the simplest, roundest, unmarried-est man in publishing, jumped in his car and began his road trip. He was so stirred that he even touched up his pencil-thin John-Waters mustache to disguise a few nettlesome grays. He believed that animals were proof of God's love and that cats were His clearest expression. This job was his calling. The editor had always wanted to be a great journalist, the kind that gave readers exactly what they wanted. He loved shaping and bending a story to get it just right. He would tell his reporters what to write, he would advise sources on what to say, he would construct and embellish to perfect the narrative. In this editor's able hands, a story would be catnip for his readers.

He had a soft spot for moody purebreds, vagrants made good, and country-and-western musical cat theatre. This event, he thought, had the potential to be a story of rejuvenation, redemption, *and* hand-crafted cat apparel, which, obviously, had the makings of a cover story. He was determined to be there in person, even if the show was slated for 6:30am on a Sunday. During the long drive, the editor had the chance to daydream about his magazine's finally being recognized as one of the nation's elite publications. He'd long resented its being pigeonholed as something for kids and ill-adjusted adults. "We do profiles just like *The New Yorker*," he thought. "We do commentary just like *The Atlantic*. We do fashion and glamour just like *Vogue. But we do it all with cats.*"

He was especially proud of his team's recent on-the-ground reporting. There was the terrific piece on "cats in hats in the workplace." Another focused on a Siberian who bullied a gorilla at the Memphis Zoo. And of course, he was waiting for his

National Magazine Award for his article on why cats should never be taken on buses. He'd recounted the academic research on feline brains and motion sickness as well as heartbreaking accounts of cats' heightened sense of claustrophobia. He also editorialized at great length on the general filth and noisiness of buses and the cat-unfriendly behavior of the riffraff who generally ride public transportation. By decimating buses and their advocates, he had done—he was absolutely confident—a service to humans and cats alike.

The editor felt like his Toyota Tercel hatchback was floating above the highway. It was gratifying to know a reader had been moved by his publication's outstanding recent work and thought to extend an invitation for what promised to be an unforgettable performance.

* * *

That same Friday, a separate fax arrived at *The Plain Dealer*, Cleveland's newspaper of record. It was from an anonymous source who claimed to have found "the *real* Al Capone vault —not the bogus safe that duped that mustachioed charlatan, Geraldo." (You're too young to remember this 1986 event; I'd explain it, but you wouldn't believe me.) This real vault, alleged the fax, contained secret government documents proving that Cleveland was the linchpin for America's westward expansion and had been slated by corporate and government bigwigs to replace Washington, D.C., as the nation's capital. What astonishing claims!

This news seemed to have been genetically modified to perfectly match the interests of the paper's top investigative reporter. Her editors were always looking for breaking news about mysterious subjects, especially those that might get national notice and convince the American people that Cleveland was more than burning rivers and regret. But this reporter's particular passion was Frederick Jackson Turner's "frontier theory." She was convinced that this niche academic concept introduced in 1893 explained everything that mattered in the United States—democracy, freedom of speech, Prohibition, wallpaper, corndogs, jazz, space exploration, organized crime, board games, concrete, cursive, long division. The list was endless. And she was eager to destroy anyone who disagreed.

As she regularly lectured coworkers, readers, and passersby, to deny the influence of the pioneer spirit, forests, and open horizons was tantamount to erasing American history. To refuse to see the world through the lens of unsettled land, gumption, and egalitarianism was to blind yourself to the real story of America. Though she saw herself as a hardscrabble journalist pursuing justice and truth, her colleagues mostly wished she would just stop making life miserable for everyone. Her habit, for instance, of filing HR complaints against anyone who disagreed with her rubbed some people the wrong way. But she understood that disrupting the peace and harmony of the newsroom was but a small price the community would have to pay for her mission. After all, she'd only gotten four people fired so far.

The reporter was especially passionate about the evils of public transportation, particularly buses. She was convinced that easily accessible, government-funded means of travel had made Americans soft and sedentary. It encouraged "lassitude, depression, and low testosterone levels." This and much else she wrote in her multi-part series, "The 1897 Project," that marked the opening of America's first subway in Boston as the beginning of the nation's unravelling. Yes, some of her facts were fabricated and some of her analysis tendentious. But, in her defense, it was all unfailingly faithful to her narrative. She won awards from wilderness groups, Daughters of American Pioneers, and the National Federation of Nomads.

Her editors were terrified of her. So when she submitted

paperwork for her employer to cover the costs of her first-class flight and triple the normal per diem for meals and accommodations, they immediately approved. Sure, the editors thought it strange that someone in a rural community had come across Al Capone's safe and planned to open it at 6:30 on a Sunday morning. But they also knew, because the reporter had told them many times, that it would be cause for legal action should they deny her request to advance her beliefs: It was this reporter's manifest destiny to prove our institutions and national imagination were entirely shaped by hardy itinerates, prairies, and river crossings.

* * *

At about 7:45 on that Saturday night, Ronnie was helping assemble the Dungeons and Dragons Club's float for the next weekend's homecoming parade. His mom shouted out to the driveway that he had a phone call. Ronnie's close-set eyes got big. He immediately stopped work on the giant 20-sided die and sprinted inside. He was more than a little disappointed to hear an older man's voice. "Whatever, I don't care about her anyway, many fish in the sea," he thought.

It wasn't *her*, but the voice on the other end did have a lot going for it: It was semi-hushed, ardent, and British. The caller claimed that stolen artifacts from King Tut's tomb had been found in the basement of a nearby home. Ronnie was the first and only call this sleuth was going to make—he wanted the news to be broken by a local journalist. This was almost too good to be true, Ronnie thought. Not only was he president of the Dungeons and Dragons Club; he was also the treasurer of his school's chapter of the Future Archaeologists of America *and* the editor of the school newspaper.

Ronnie was 17, 5'10', and baby-faced (but he was trying to grow a mustache). His teeth were perfectly straight, and his upper body was concave (but he was doing push-ups and shoulder presses nightly). He was chipper and generous though susceptible to bouts of melancholy (which he kept at bay through a full schedule and accomplishment). The previous year, his minister called him "clean cut," so in an act of light-touch defiance he grew out his sandy-blonde crew cut into a thick, flowing mullet. But most of all, Ronnie was a romantic. He dreamed of digging in the Giza Plateau. Of winning a Pulitzer. Of getting his crush in chemistry class to notice him. Breaking this story could help him progress along all three fronts!

"Of course, sir," Ronnie replied to his source. "*...aherrm...*I'll be there at 6:30am sharp tomorrow, Sunday, November 1, 1987. I'm writing this in my Trapper Keeper calendar. In fact, I think the Blue Line has a bus route that stops not far from that address."

* * *

At 5:53am, perfectly on-time, the Blue Line deposited Ronnie at a bus stop on the west side of a quiet park whose north end was covered by a dense mist that hadn't yet burnt off with the rising sun. He noted to himself that it was one heck of a luxury to have public bus service to such an out-of-the-way neighborhood, especially before dawn on a Sunday. Now that he'd taken advantage of it and found the bus clean, quiet, and punctual, he felt badly for writing that editorial a couple months back.

In a typical exercise of teenage certainty and rashness, Ronnie had suddenly developed passionate, though not well thought-out, views on the county's bus service. Unlike most teens, however, Ronnie had full control of Riverside High School's *Eagle's Nest*, giving him access to literally dozens of readers. He called the county's bus system "a colossal boondoggle probably lining the pockets of local tycoons." He'd been especially critical of the Blue Line, whose "inexplicable route and schedule seem to have been designed to so confound taxpayers that they'd be too frustrated to appreciate its waste." It would not be the last time he regretted his editorial decision-making.

As he began his walk to the address provided by his source (approximate 0.546 miles southeast by his reckoning—he was also the secretary of his school's Cartography Club), his thoughts wandered to his crush, Kim. No one in school could so effortlessly pull off the glamour of acid-washed jeans, baggy sweaters, and tasseled white boots. Back when they were sophomores, she once wore neon yellow leg warmers and a black mesh crop top over a hot-pink tank, and he committed himself to telling her that she looked "more elegant than Madonna and more effervescent than Molly Ringwald."

He practiced this compliment in the mirror for a week. To his pubescent ears and eyes, the content and delivery grew more spellbinding by the day. But he never got the chance to use it in real life. A senior named Davey, who drove a Pontiac Fiero, bet on basketball games, and looked like Billy Idol, snarled Kimmy's heart away, leaving poor Ronnie dancing with himself.

But now Ronnie was older, wiser, and smoother, and he was about to pull off the greatest journalistic coup in the history of the *Eagle's Nest*. He was willing to forgive Kimmy for responding to his latest note by having her friend tell his friend that she was probably about to have other plans for the homecoming dance. Ronnie reminded himself that when you're powerful and famous you need to forgive slights like that. And once she found out that he had planned to take her to Fuddruckers before the dance, she'd be doubly remorseful.

As Ronnie walked down the street, planning his Pulitzer acceptance address and deciding how best to publicly absolve Kimmy for insulting him, the reporter from *The Plain Dealer* happened to be driving by in a rented luxury sedan. She slowed, rolled down the window, and asked if he needed a ride. She saw Ronnie as a possible background source on this godforsaken neighborhood; maybe he'd even have intel about the shadowy figure who'd somehow come upon the cache of a long-dead Chicago gangster. Ronnie was hesitant at first to get into a stranger's car (he was, after all, the regional representative on the state's Junior Roadside Safety Commission). But when he realized that she was headed to the same address, he accepted the offer. Classic meet-cute.

It took little time for Ronnie to see she was a real one. Her crass newsroom talk, Virginia Slims cigarettes, and gravelly voice gave him a glimpse into the rough-and-tumble world of big-city journalism. Her tall bangs, heavy eye shadow, and boxy shoulder pads showed him what a true woman looked like. He almost blurted out, "Are all investigative reporters from Cleveland this foxy?" But he played it cool. If he'd had a mirror and a week, he would've practiced telling her that she was "as sultry as Kathleen Turner and classy as Whitney Houston." Kimmy who?

He was so smitten (and so nervous that he might inadvertently reveal how new he was to the breaking-news game) that he didn't ask her who this "Capone" was she kept talking about. He was hoping it was just another name for King Tut. Ronnie would've been even more confused if he'd had a chance to share expectations with the editor of *Cat Fancy*. But that goodly man had arrived at the Compound an hour earlier. He sat himself in the front row of folding chairs directly in front of the makeshift stage. He found it difficult to manage his glee. So focused on keeping his composure, Catman took little note of the 10-foot concrete wall or the older man walking about in silk hose, a long velvet robe, and crown.

Oh, OK. Sure, that's enough for today.

You alright? You stopped taking notes a while back.

It's almost hard to believe, isn't it? What a great story.

We'll get to the Compound Incident climax tomorrow.

RECORDING CONCLUDED: 1:09pm
Monday, January 11, 2021
Uncorrected transcript
Interview by Elizabeth Jones

Chapter 43: Reassess

From: Dr. Jennifer Davis, MERCY STATE, COMS
Date: January 11, 2021 at 5:42 PM
Subject: Familiar?
To: Elizabeth Jones, Esq. OFFICE OF THE PUBLIC DEFENDER

Hi Liz—unexpected event this morning. An older gentlemen came to Mercy first thing and made a BIG donation to our fund-raising campaign for community health clinics. He showed up with a check for the exact amount we needed to hit our Phase One target. Absolutely amazing, huh!?!

He said he had some mental-health issues back in the 1980s and a local clinic could have helped him. He wants people to be healthier than he was. And he's decided to start helping his community again. He made it sound like he used to donate to various causes. Anyway, he said he knows your client. They live in the same neighborhood apparently. His name is Leonard McGregor—does that sound familiar? Very nice man. But you should have seen the way he was dressed! I should've taken a picture. Lord, you wouldn't believe me!

--J

Chapter 44: Bait

START: 12:37pm
Tuesday, January 12, 2021
C.C.S.H.

Alright. Back to it!

Sunday morning, about 6:15am, November 1, 1987. Upon their arrival, Ronnie and Frontier-Theory were escorted past the folding chairs arranged between the street and the moat and into a special seating area of high-backed stools to the side of the stage. Their usher was a goodhearted but bemused 10-year-old paperboy.

Just an hour earlier, everything had been copacetic for the boy. He'd been delivering the bulky Sunday edition on his normal route and making good time while daydreaming about growing up to be a stunt-car driver. Then he turned a corner and saw what appeared to be an old man dressed up as a medieval nobleman standing in the middle of the road.

"Goodness gracious, I'll tell you what," the paperboy thought. "That there is a novel development in this neck of the woods, and that's just real talk."

This pleasant paperboy—proto-Pith—figured there was a chance he was about to get a big tip ("Aristocrats ain't typically in residence at the poorhouse, I'll tell you what," he thought to himself). So he decided to inquire further. He'd had little interaction with Mr. McGregor over the previous few years. Ever since his classmate Molly and her mom had been killed in the accident, the McGregor house—now the McGregor sanctuary—had been dark. He put the paper in the box each day, and payments were mailed to the administrative office.

The paperboy didn't even know the dressed-up man was Mr. McGregor until he heard that familiar voice serve up that familiar dad- (or former dad-) joke, "Come *heah*, son, I won't bite...at least not *hahd*."

Paperboy Pith got a crisp $10 bill, but it was not a tip, McGregor explained; it was for services to be rendered. Sir Len the Just told him to, first, direct two soon-to-be-arriving journalists to the VIP section next to the stage; second, at 6:30am, help the presenter wheel the trunk to the stage; and, third, when signaled, give each reporter a gift bag from behind the stage. This seemed very odd to the adolescent. In truth, it would've seemed very odd to any sentient adult. But $10 was a generous payment for such simple tasks, and his naturally benevolent disposition told him that if he could make Mr. McGregor happy, he should. So he said thank you for the money, bowed, and explained that he felt grateful and blessed to be part of whatever this was.

Before sitting, Frontier-Theory peppered this young usher with questions about the neighborhood, the moat, the old man dressed in Renaissance-festival garb, and the boy's views on westward expansion. But she could get no satisfaction. He kept replying, "I'll tell you what, that's above my pay grade, I reckon." She was frustrated but begrudgingly nodded to his caginess. Apart from that, all three reporters were thrilled.

Catman, nearly delirious about the feline extravaganza to come, joined the other two in the VIP section. He had just finished the task—placing name cards on dozens of folding chairs—assigned to him by the regally attired gentleman. Catman had also provided advice to Sir Len on proper stage lighting and the ideal entrance music. Yes, Catman was slightly concerned that, since he'd now helped prep the event, his objectivity as a reporter could be questioned. But he calmed himself; all journalists know professional ethics can be put aside when advancing your personal vision of justice.

Frontier-Theory was overcome with pride. She was confident that the documents in the vault would substantiate her previous reporting's unsubstantiated claims and mortally shame her detractors. Once there was finally proof that America's western expanse explained everything and that Cleveland was destined to be the new Athens, she could relax, get the chip off her shoulder, and simply annihilate her enemies.

Ronnie was just hoping no one would notice his schoolboy giddiness. But it was hard to keep it together. There was no question now: He had hit the big time. Just hours earlier he was preparing for a high school homecoming parade, but now he was in the VIP reporters' section of a major press conference. He was about to break international news. And he was sitting between a feline-magazine mogul and Cleveland's most seductive, most refined investigative journalist. He hoped and prayed that poor Kimmy would be able to get over him.

* * *

She speaks! At long last. Good question.

I've spent a lot of time thinking about that. Why would Len go out of his way to round up and discombobulate three journalists when he could've just kept hazing his neighbors? Sure, all three had publicly belittled buses. Maybe that was crime enough in Len's eyes. Or maybe Len was saying something about the state of his beloved journalism. I suppose he could've been aiming to make an example of reporters who had turned that respected, hard-nosed, shoe-leather profession into a cheap vessel for political activism, personal ambition, and fan service. After all, all three had been duped by Len's ridiculous stories that played to their vanity.

Or maybe there is no explanation apart from "Len snapped."

But I have a different theory. Bear with me. When the Ohunka was still flowing full and swift, this area had healthy interchange with the outside world. Goods, visitors, news, ideas. Our county was part of a larger community. And we were stronger as a result. All those points of contact, all those connections—those trusses and trestles—made us durable. Like that old wood-and-iron railroad bridge over the Ohunka. Engineered to be sturdy not flashy, to link our county to all beyond. I think Len was determined to wreck that. That was his ultimate revenge. Break those bonds and watch it all crash down and wash away.

I think he decided that the county's isolation wasn't the antithesis of community; destroying the county's relationship and reputation with the outside world was. What better way to accomplish that than humiliating three people who work for organizations that buy ink by the barrel. Here's what I mean: A man might have an affair to push his wife to file for divorce. A conniving coach can instigate a player into demanding a trade. John kept bringing Yoko into the studio to force the Beatles to break up.

See, sometimes the reaction is the goal. Len wanted the outside world to break up with our county. The Compound Incident was his Yoko. That's my theory at least. I could be wrong. I don't make up these stories, I only retell them.

Back to it.

* * *

But the reporters weren't his only targets. McGregor roped his neighbors into this goat rodeo, as well. And, of course, he used community against them. On Saturday, he sent personalized invitations to dozens of residents. To the religiously inclined, he said that he was hosting an ecumenical sunrise service at his home. Others got invitations tailored to their particular interests. A few older men who liked birdwatching were told there'd be an ornithologist with a rufous-headed hornbill. A few musicians were told Len had organized a gathering for trading bootlegs and swapping vintage records. Those with a passion for history were told there'd be a special lecture on—depending on each neighbor's tastes—naval vessels, German literature, the Civil War, or something else.

But all invitations shared two elements: The line "This will be a terrific opportunity to come together!" and a 6:30am-sharp start time.

And so it was that the three reporters were soon joined at Len's Compound by neighbor after neighbor after neighbor. Some came with books to be autographed by the lecturer, others with boxes of concert posters and tapes, others with a Bible or camera or notebook. Each neighbor found a folding chair with a card with his or her name.

Len, who was generally only seen during his lonely walks, sauntered around the seating area with the biggest smile imaginable. From time to time, he'd make an upbeat but vague announcement to the entire group, "So glad you all made it *heah*," "What a joy to *gatha togetha* in community," "You *ah* in for an *amazin'* show." Then he'd get close to a neighbor and whisper a personally tailored message: "Russian *nestin'* dolls—fantastic" or "So *excitin'* that Rabbi Weiss, *Cahdinal* Mancini, and the *Ahchbishop* of Canterbury are *co-leadin'* this service" or "*Wahms* my *haht* that you get to see a chess *grandmastah* play 10 simultaneous matches blindfolded."

The neighbors were overjoyed by the special treatment. How wonderful, each of them thought, that Len McGregor convened all these people for this thing I care about. It simply never occurred to anyone to ask anyone else if they were there for the same thing. In fact, no one was even skeptical until about 15 minutes into the event. That's when a few started silently worrying the entirety of the show might be this stupid mime pretending to be stuck in a box.

* * *

At 6:30 sharp, huge stereo speakers arranged between the moat and wall played a lively fanfare announcing the start of the show. The paperboy, as directed, helped the mime wheel toward the stage a cart holding a giant trunk. With the help of Sir Len, they hoisted the trunk onto the stage. Len and the paperboy then sat with the reporters in the VIP section. The mime began his act; it had all the hits—an imaginary wall, an imaginary rope. Classic stuff. Soon he found himself, tragically, in the imaginary box.

The crowd wasn't quite sure what to make of this. But every few minutes Len would loudly offer advice, like, "Maybe the box is locked!" or "You got an invisible *hamma*?"

Though their frustration grew, the observers were initially respectful. Some reasoned that this might be an opening act; maybe the art history professor or the vested country-and-western cats will come out next. Others were glued to their seats by the sight of the trunk: The Russian nesting dolls or the original Elvis demos or the Egyptian artifacts might be in there!

The reporters, completely unschooled in Len's brand of psychological warfare, might've watched the mime for an hour. But some of the neighbors who'd been previously duped or tormented by Len started raising a ruckus at about 6:50. They slowly realized each of them had been enticed to the

Compound by a different promise. As more neighbors understood what might be afoot, the clamoring swelled. At 6:55, Len took off his royal outfit and got on stage.

He explained that this mime act was, in fact, just an opener. The crowd relaxed. What each of you have been waiting for, Len explained, is in the trunk. He apologized for making them wait. He should've appreciated, he conceded, how eager they'd be. "No more delays," Len said cheerfully. The crowd got excited. Len pulled a key from his pocket, bent down, unlocked the trunk, and slowly lifted the lid.

And out popped a second mime.

* * *

The crowd was incensed. Neighbors accused one another of being in on Len's scheme. Soon they were mocking each other's interests. "You'd wake up early on a Sunday to listen to a lecture on haberdashery?" "At least I'm not an adult with a comic book collection!" Threats were made. Items were thrown at the mimes, both of whom were now cowering in the imaginary box. Catman walked to the stage, peeked into the empty trunk with more hope than reason, and returned to his seat forlorn. Frontier-Theory was nearing her boiling point. Ronnie was realizing he had a lot to learn about major press conferences.

At 6:59, Len, who'd been silently enjoying the furor, returned to the stage and asked the crowd to please calm down and listen to him for a moment. Several people swore and yelled that they would never listen to him again. Len apologized and admitted that he had, in fact, been stalling. There had been some logistical mix-ups, he explained, that had delayed the delivery of the event's key items and the arrival of the presenters. He had hired the mimes at the last moment to keep everyone entertained while things were sorted out. But now everything had been fixed, Len explained, so everyone should take a deep breath and take their seats. The real event was about to begin. The crowd decompressed. They wanted this event to happen.

"You have my *wahd*," Sir Len the Just announced, "everything needed to make this event a success is about to be *delivud* in a white van."

* * *

For nearly 40 years, the Grangerford firm Callahan & Ungrateful Son had specialized in the construction of tiki bars, garden arbors, backyard boardwalks, trellises, lattices, and other outdoor wooden projects that make sense in theory. The senior Callahan had been a good husband, donated to charitable causes, and dutifully attended weekly Mass. Years hence he'd tell people he deserved better than what happened that early morning at the McGregor Compound.

At first, he saw this shed job as a blessing from the Almighty: a high-dollar project that would allow him to strengthen his firm's rainy-day fund. And, as a complicated—if bizarre—design and engineering job, it would be the capstone of his career as a local craftsman. He was as excited as a staid, never-complain-never-explain War World II vet could get. At the end of this project, he would retire content and hand over his beloved company to his no-account boy who'd likely drive his life's work into the ground. Jimmy Callahan, his 20-year-old son, was just like his brother-in-law's kids—reprobate and lippy—so he knew his boy's faults were the consequence of his wife's genes (God rest her soul) not his bloodline or emotionally distant fathering.

Mr. Callahan selected an all-star crew, the most skilled and reliable he could gather. As with all jobs, he started this one by telling his team to work hard and smart, be kind, and see each day as a gift. Unlike other jobs, he also needed to remind them to avoid foul language and dairy products. He even created a laminated reference sheet for each crew member that had a list of all prohibited words and edibles—one side in English, the other in Latin (just in case). He also told the crew that if an older man in unusual clothes said anything to them, they should alert Mr. Callahan immediately. He also brought his family Bible with the Book of Leviticus dog-eared; he wanted to have a primary source handy should any fact-checking become necessary.

Jimmy—who, over the last year or so, had become increasingly irresponsible and prone to scratching his nose and disappearing into restrooms—said his father was being obsessive-compulsive. Mr. Callahan simply said, "Big job, son. We're on belt-and-suspenders behavior." Jimmy rolled his eyes; Mr. Callahan smiled on the inside knowing such advice was worth 100 hugs or other instances of affection.

Just imagine his crew's confusion that morning: They arrive at 7:00am on the nose, ready to begin work on a huge, customized shed commemorating the 1836 Battle at the Alamo. As if that's not strange enough, they exit their freshly washed white work van only to find an enraged crowd that ransacks their vehicle looking for, among other things, rare birds, Grateful Dead bootlegs, and the Archbishop of Canterbury.

Now imagine the three reporters. They'd been summoned to this out-of-the-way neighborhood with promises of cats, Cleveland-Capone capers, and a crypt's cache (respectively). But they end up being greeted by an old man dressed as a feudal lord of the manor, watching two mimes hide in an invisible box, and listening to a befuddled paperboy saying things like, "If this ain't an ungodly commotion, it'll serve the purpose 'til one arrives."

Then, when the reporters think things can't deteriorate any further, a white work van arrives, which is promptly searched and pillaged by scores of angry neighbors, and its senior-citizen driver leaps out, waving blueprints, yelling about learning Latin and giving up milk, and declaring that everyone within earshot is due for "a tail-whooping and biblical atonement."

* * *

As you might imagine, the following 15 minutes were not uneventful. Oaths were sworn, fistfights started, day-drinking commenced. Chairs thrown; noses bloodied. Utter chaos. Soon, others from across the neighborhood arrived, mostly attracted by the fireworks being shot off from behind Len's wall and a big-band recording of "God Bless America" blaring from the speakers. New arrivals decided to join the brawl, yelling and punching indiscriminately.

Even the journalists, those paragons of dispassion, shelved their bird's-eye view of events, tossing aside their notepads and taking part in the melee. Frontier-Theory was reported to have a savage left hook; Catman, they say, was adept at scratching. By all accounts, only the mimes held it together.

Everyone agrees that at one point McGregor climbed atop the wall, laughed uproariously, and shouted, "That's right, you selfish bastards! Fight it out! Bloody yourselves, you wretched curs! Justice is here! Justice is here!" After cheering on the melee, he raised his palms and face to the heavens and smiled.

Eventually, the bruised and battered neighbors started to file away. High schooler Ronnie saw McGregor walk up to Mr. Callahan and hand him an envelope. Already feeling concussed by the strangest morning of his career, Callahan turned pale after opening the envelope and looking inside. Eventually, Mr. Callahan gathered his thoughts and directed his crew back into their looted van.

As they pulled away, Len gave the paperboy the high sign.

As instructed, the dutiful squire handed each of the three reporters a gift bag. Inside was a promotional Visitor's Guide to Grangerford, a temporary tattoo of the word "Justice," an "I Love Buses" keychain, and a small envelope.

Catman refused to take the bag. He walked back to his beat-up Tercel—taking a quick detour to peek inside the empty trunk again—and glumly drove away. Frontier-Thesis threw the bag into the moat and spat on the ground. Ronnie had never felt so aroused. She stormed to her rented luxury sedan and burned rubber down the road.

Only Ronnie looked in the bag. He opened the envelope and found a note reading, "Proceed over the drawbridge and through the gate. You will find the vault, the artifacts, and the cats you were promised." Ronnie got the chills. Maybe the madness was just a test to see if he was worthy. By this time, he was alone. The neighbors and other reporters had decamped. When the fireworks and music stopped, the paperboy smiled and said, "That sure weren't on my day's agenda, but as the preacher says, 'We plan, God laughs.'" He then returned placidly to his paper route.

Ronnie saw that the drawbridge had been lowered. As he passed through the gate into the bowels of the Compound, he first noticed a relatively small two-story house. Ronnie expected a castle or temple of some sort. His disappointment quickly faded into shock. Surrounding the house were two acres of pavement. Every inch of land inside the wall was covered in asphalt. Not a blade of grass, tree, or bush in sight. Off to the side were a small bicycle with training wheels and a rusted swing set, both deteriorating from disuse but refusing to be forgotten.

Then Ronnie's shock turned into disbelief. Len and the two mimes appeared from behind the house. Each was pushing a giant hand cart. On one was an old, enormous safe. The second had a table, on which sat a small stereo and two cats in hats and boots. On the third, pushed by McGregor, was an Egyptian sarcophagus.

"Son, I might be a pinch unusual," Len said to Ronnie, "but I always keep my *wahd*." Ronnie, speechless, touched the ancient ornate coffin.

McGregor continued, first pointing toward the safe, "That *fiah-cracka* lady from Cleveland could've had all the evidence she needed, but she didn't have faith."

Then pointing to the cats, "Our round friend with the little mustache *coulda* seen the show of his life, but he didn't believe." Ronnie swelled with pride: He had kept the faith.

"Son, you have ambition and vision and courage. You will be *rewahded*." Len pointed to the sarcophagus. "It possesses more treasure than you could imagine." Ronnie trembled. He started planning his Pulitzer acceptance speech. He tried to decide how these antiquities should be divvied up among the world's great museums—and what kind of convertible he'd buy with the royalties of his memoir. He was having trouble even remembering what Kimmy looked like.

Len pointed to the sarcophagus lid and made a lifting motion. "Shall we?"

"Yes," replied Ronnie gravely, "we shall."

Len grabbed one end and Ronnie the other. McGregor nodded, and they heaved.

And out of the sarcophagus, of course, popped a third mime.

Chapter 45: Connections

At first, Ronnie was mystified. What. How. Why. Then he was livid. How dare you. Len began to snicker, tears of amusement welling up in the corners of his eyes. But that quickly gave way to raucous laughter with a pre-industrial Ohunka down his cheeks. This shattered, solitary man, holed up in a pseudo-citadel, was enjoying sincere, liberating, therapeutic laughter. Yes, Ronnie was apoplectic. But Len was happy, even if just for a moment.

The fallout from that Sunday morning's events would cascade over decades. Interestingly, little of it came from the neighbors in attendance. They were understandably mortified by their own behavior. They'd been hoodwinked by Len's implausible invitations, fought with their friends, and then raided a carpenter's work van. Not a great look. And they were not the type to publicly discuss disappointment and regret. The good thing about a lack of community is the easy avoidance of collective shame.

The HOA also wanted to expunge all evidence and memory of Len's hootenanny. Yes, the event had broken numerous neighborhood bylaws and county ordinances. But the community's lawyer was terrified to advance proceedings against McGregor.

It didn't take much research to understand that the neighborhood had incurred enormous liability by allowing a resident to maintain a moat, concrete wall, and two acres of paved earth. Worse, the HOA had, it could be argued, tacitly approved Len's event.

They had, in fact, received by certified mail but ignored McGregor's request for permits for the stage, mime show, sound system, fireworks, and seating for 300 guests. But as the HOA attorney explained in a confidential after-action report to the board, Len filed such insane requests nearly every month—his previous one sought permission for a blimp, boxing ring, mariachi band, and $600 in nickels—and nothing ever came of them. It had become standard operating procedure to photocopy each of his submissions, store it underground, and burn the original lest its spirit drive someone mad. How in the world were they to know that Len was serious about this event? In the end, the board voted, nearly unanimously, to pretend the "spectacle" at the Compound never occurred.

The only "no" vote came from Butch Tweed. He and the HOA had been thoroughly embarrassed by Len's "lawyer of international renown" at arbitration a few years earlier. After that fiasco, Tweed saw Len McGregor as his rival. The Compound Incident, however, made Tweed and the HOA seem laughably impotent. Tweed now saw McGregor as his nemesis. He vowed that McGregor would pay: He would destroy Len's beloved bus stop.

After her initial outburst, Frontier-Theory stewed. Obviously, there were no repercussions at work; her supervisors didn't have the nerve to point out that her exorbitant business expenses hadn't led to a news article, much less the splashy exposé she'd promised. She felt no remorse. The paper had gotten something out of her investigation: She had written a blistering review of the bed and breakfast she'd stayed in and a savage takedown of three restaurants in the county. She referred to

Grangerford as "Bumpkin Central," a slight that, as Len hoped, further distanced the town from the outside world.

Though the episode at the Compound had not gone as she'd expected—as a wise young man once said, "We plan, God laughs"—she had found the experience bracing. She now knew it was her calling to extend her special brand of justice-pursuing journalism far and wide. She became an adjunct professor at a local university, shaping the next generation of journalists, and wrote long-form pieces for national outlets, taking on the toughest stories and doggedly following them to wherever her personal sense of right and wrong led.

Catman licked his wounds on the return drive to magazine headquarters. Beyond the disillusionment caused by the event, he was left without a cover story for next month's edition. He thought his pit stop at the run-down filling station would only provide unleaded gasoline and Hostess cupcakes. But behind the counter was an enigmatic Abyssinian who hissed and swatted a small black-and-white television whenever someone changed the channel away from old cowboy movies. Catman was inspired.

He wrote a 10,000-word travelogue about his Tercel journey through rural America and what he learned about westward expansion and open horizons. He became a disciple of Frontier-Theory's teachings, even using her epithet "Bumpkin Central" in his unflattering description of Grangerford, solidifying its reputation as regional laughingstock. The trip was the pinnacle of Catman's career. Not only did he make that worthy Abyssinian a star; his essay was *Cat Fancy's* most-read article of the year. It even got blurbed in the next month's *Reader's Digest*.

The event's only real casualty was Ronnie. That morning sent him into a downward spiral; a spiral accelerated by completely unknown forces known widely to be Len. Had Ronnie been able to forgive and forget that day like everyone else, all probably would have been fine. Instead, he wrote the most incendiary editorial in the school newspaper's history, summoning the full force of a teenager's moral authority and demonstrating the wanting judgment associated with the incompletely matured male prefrontal cortex.

* * *

On Monday morning, the *Riverside Eagle Nest* published a special edition with Ronnie's scathing column. It opened with great style and fury:

> Local crackpot, Len McGregor, advancing in years and declining in cognitive function, orchestrated a sham of a farce of a circus at his knock-off Trojan-walled compound this weekend. Blowtorching community goodwill and his already meager reputation, McGregor selfishly endangered the health of sundry neighbors, mentally scarred a guileless paperboy, exploited no fewer than three hapless mimes, and revealed 130,000 square feet of illegal impervious surface that jeopardizes the health of the Ohunka and denigrates Mother Earth.

In the following 27 paragraphs, Ronnie vividly detailed the morning's events, launching a kindhearted paperboy on a lifelong mission to learn what "guileless" means and savaging the man thereafter known as "Blowtorch Len."

Ronnie's classmates couldn't believe that a sleepy monthly paper typically focused on school lunches and community-service projects suddenly included "cockamamie codger" and "only a city famed for its artistry and industry could produce an investigative reporter so beguiling and chic."

In a matter of hours, Ronnie's reputation grew beyond his wildest dreams. Other students, shocked by his chutzpah, began treating him like a brazen warlord, with equal parts admiration and fear. Kimmy, mortified by her poor appraisal of Ronnie's mettle, talked to him twice in the halls that day and told her friend to tell his friend that she was going to make him Rice Krispie Treats after school.

Ronnie's editorial-drafting process was fueled by Mountain Dew and egged on by the paper's young faculty advisor, the school's new English composition teacher. Michael Peace-Justice ("It's my *nom d'amour*" he told anyone who asked and many who hadn't) had spent a year at a Vermont Montessori school teaching elementary-aged kids how to battle oppression and make bespoke cheeses for the revolution. His school director had gently counseled him out: Peace-Justice's constant talk of the blood of workers oiling the capitalist machinery wasn't the right fit for that farm campus.

Peace-Justice faxed his résumé far and wide, happy to spread his gospel of liberation and state ownership wherever he'd be welcome. The Grangerford superintendent hadn't checked his references and hired him sight unseen: The district had been in desperate need of a literature teacher, and Peace-Justice's master's thesis ("Howard Zinn and Choose Your Own Adventure Books: A Critical Analysis") seemed smart.

Sadly, he hadn't had the smoothest transition to Riverside High. His new colleagues were of one mind that Michael Peace-Justice's long brown ponytail, lax supervision of his classroom, and accommodation of unruly hallway behavior undermined discipline. They also didn't like that he allowed students to call him "Mikey PJ."

The stern principal reminded him that, regardless of how things had been done at his previous school, Riverside teachers had a dress code. Men were to wear a dress shirt and a tie. Mikey PJ enjoyed his new position instructing these rural teens on writing poorly sourced but self-assured articles about the military industrial complex, historical materialism, and Beat Poets. So he acquiesced to The Man's demands. But he tie-dyed all his dress shirts and wore hemp ties with revolutionary slogans.

Regardless of the weather, he always rolled up his sleeves so students could see the "LOVE" tattoo on his left forearm and the "Justice Peace" tattoo on his right. Despite his submission to these ridiculous sartorial rules, Mikey PJ could still get no relief from the officious principal who continued to badger him about his wardrobe. But the new teacher was unfazed. He only wore his yellowed Walter Mondale campaign t-shirt on casual Fridays. Moreover, the teacher dress code said nothing about pants, and Mikey PJ thought he looked good in cut-off jeans.

He cheered Ronnie's initial draft for its doughty disregard for stuffy rules of punctuation and grammar and for its blasphemy of the false gods of respect for elders, civility, and fact-checking. He told Ronnie to stiffen his spine and go after McGregor personally; refraining from *ad hominem* attacks, lectured slaphappy Mikey PJ, was a luxury of the powerful. The oppressed had a duty to fight with all weapons available.

However, local teachers more familiar with the community than new-arrival Mikey PJ read Ronnie's polemic with dread. They understood that Len McGregor was not the kind of man to suffer such abuse quietly. The personal slights were one thing, but Ronnie's column noted that Len's neighborhood was "utterly forgettable apart from McGregor's stronghold-qua-insane asylum and a completely unnecessary and extravagant public bus line that ought to be eliminated immediately."

For the first 24 hours after the column's release, Ronnie was a local celebrity-outlaw. But then Blowtorch Len went to work in a way that only he could.

* * *

On Tuesday morning, the first vice president of the high

school's Dungeons and Dragons Club notified Ronnie that he'd been excommunicated and had to return the group's 10-sided die. "Transparent children. They're jealous of my new fame and coming fortune," Ronnie thought.

By the early afternoon, Ronnie had been impeached and convicted by the executive board of the Homecoming Committee for "sedition, vagrancy, and horse-thievery."

"Odd charges..." Ronnie thought.

In quick succession, his library card was revoked, all his coupons to local shops were deemed null and void, and he received a certified letter from the state's Roadside Safety Commission that he chose not to open. His early admission to Clemson was rescinded. And in a shock result on Wednesday afternoon, Ronnie, who'd been a shoo-in for Homecoming King, lost the vote to a sophomore third-string placekicker on the junior varsity football team.

Things continued heading south for Ronnie. He stopped going to classes, started drinking and smoking weed, got a redhead pregnant, dropped out of high school, and bounced around for a while until finally landing a steady job tending bar at the Dew Drop Inn. Some said that he still wrote anonymously from time to time about local events and the nature of suffering. They say he once had a very good blog. Sadly, though, he never lived up to all that early potential. As a grown-up paperboy once said, the great misfortune is when excellence peaks early and everything afterward savors of anticlimax.

There was, however, a sliver of a splinter of a silver lining to Ronnie's tragicomedy: He was a good kid, and he became a good man. He and the redhead built a life together. He made the drinks quietly; she delivered them with personality. Their boy went to college and was Navy ROTC.

The Compound Incident's ripples extended to Kimmy. She deserted Ronnie after his implosion and doubled down on basketball-betting, Fiero-driving Davey. He was the anti-Ronnie: Exciting persona, uncomplicated mind. It took years for Kimmy to realize—after Davey's gambling addiction and her son Matty's struggles—the good life she might've had with the earnest if moody Ronnie.

Her real life started to fray when Davey abandoned them, and it completely came apart during the animal-camp and county-commission sagas. It wasn't shredded so much as split in two. The priggish, earth-tone Kim hosted pleasant neighborhood parties and dusted her many clocks; the regal celebrity-martyr Kim held court at the Dew Drop and longingly watched bartending Ronnie from afar.

Teacher Mikey PJ was so furious about how he had been treated for his small role in these events that he committed to protecting other educators from the same. By the 1990s, he had changed his name to Michael Powers (a.k.a. Mikey P) and had his arm tattoos amended. He stepped up his role in the county's teachers' union and began his climb up the organization's ladder, ultimately becoming its president. Before long, the school board came to dread contract re-negotiations with the bellicose, ponytailed Mikey P and decided that everyone was better off if they just gave him everything he wanted.

Though everyone remembers Ronnie's editorial as the definitive account of the most extraordinary event in the county's recent history—well, up to that point at least—one of its long-forgotten details now reads as prophetic. In the final paragraph, Ronnie included the only on-the-record quote he was able to get from anyone at Len's Compound that morning. Everyone else was too ashamed to admit having been in attendance. Only Mr. Callahan talked.

Amazingly, Callahan bore no ill-will toward Blowtorch Len. "Unusual fellow, that McGregor. I sure hope our paths don't cross again. But there's a strange honor about him. He handed me an envelope that morning with a cashier's check for

$76,455.76—the full amount we agreed to in our contract. Len didn't get a shed. But I guess he was paying for something else."

* * *

Let's stop there. You need to rest up for tomorrow.

You're finally ready for Community Day.

RECORDING CONCLUDED: 2:24pm
Tuesday, January 12, 2021
Uncorrected transcript
Interview by Elizabeth Jones

Chapter 46: Recall

From: Dr. Jennifer Davis, MERCY STATE, COMS
Date: January 12, 2021 at 3:23 PM
Subject: coincidence
To: Elizabeth Jones, Esq. OFFICE OF THE PUBLIC DEFENDER

L—you won't believe this! I told our board of directors about the major donation from the odd old man, and when I mentioned the name "Leonard McGregor" and how he was dressed, one of my board members started laughing. He was crying he was laughing so hard!

The board member said that he's pretty sure that back when he was in high school in the 1980s, one of his classmates wrote a savage, hilarious column in their school newspaper about McGregor. It was about some event at McGregor's house —something to do with King Tut and mimes? I don't know. He swears that McGregor has a nickname like "Lenny Shotgun" or "Lightning Len." He also said the guy who wrote the column —he thinks his name might be Ronnie—works at that sketchy bar not far from your client's neighborhood, the one down in the Ohunka wastelands that became a casino during the pandemic.

I know this is completely unrelated to your client's case. But what a coincidence! And what a strange area!

--J

PS: Just FYI, the doctors thought they could bring the county executive out of the induced coma today, but he spiked a fever. They suspect it's another infection. They moved him back into intensive care. Simply a precaution. Don't worry, just a minor setback. With a little luck, before long he'll be awake and able to clear everything up about Community Day.

Part 5:

Community Day

Chapter 47: Overture

START: 11:12am
Wednesday, January 13, 2021
C.C.S.H.

Here we go!

After God-only-knows-how-long of public-health house arrest, a barbecue food truck was coming to the park. Everyone was emailing and texting one another. "I'm gonna crush some pulled pork!" "Lemme get at those burnt ends!" "Om nom nom nom!" Yeah, they were excited about the food, but I think, really, they just couldn't believe it was actually going to happen.

But the myth was true. While not an HOA-sanctioned gathering—a point made repeatedly through nasty distribution-list missives from the board secretary—Len's monkeyshines had gotten the job done. Ersatz Community Day was here. At noon sharp this heaven-sent mobile eatery was to begin selling smoked and slathered proteins to anyone possessing valid American currency and the pluck to congregate during a pandemic.

I stepped outside to our porch at 10:30am when I heard the truck arrive at the old bus stop. Halleluiah. The sun was out.

It was long-sleeve-t-shirt weather. The two young merchants staffing the truck anchored their mobile shop in the cleared gravel space by the bus stop sign. It made me smile to think that, very soon, happy-go-lucky neighbors, released from quarantine captivity, would be ordering chicken and brisket in the exact spot where years ago dour-faced early-morning commuters stood with travel mugs and, for that brief, peculiar period, tried to fend off Kim's furry, feral campers. I remember thinking that something magical must be buried under that gravel, some kind of magnet that attracts a spectacle. Imagine, I had that thought *before* the events of Community Day unfolded.

Soon I could smell the truck's unctuous wares. Around 11am, I started seeing families from across the neighborhood turning the corner and walking down our street toward the park. New moms pushing strollers; dads in roomy, untucked shirts carrying toddlers on their shoulders; retirees moving at a pace negotiated with their obstinate bodies; teenagers laughing too loudly and pushing each other for no reason apart from their being teenagers. Everyone was delighted by the prospect of once again sharing the company of the half-strangers we call neighbors.

The vendors had tacked a menu onto a post of the gazebo, actually right atop the county's health-and-wedding-fund notice—symbolically, perhaps; out of convenience, likely. They also placed, a few paces from the truck, a sign reading, "Line forms here." It all seemed so orderly.

And then I saw Blowtorch Len standing in the middle of the soccer pitch wearing a full tuxedo. Cummerbund, coat with tails, turquoise saddle shoes. He was holding a plastic box with a corsage. We made eye contact from 100 yards. He stiffened then bowed at the waist. I'll never know if he was asking me to dance or preparing to spar. He straightened himself, delicately wrapped the corsage around his own wrist, and then blushed. The flower matched neither his shoes nor his fez. "So a dance it is... a homecoming," I thought. Len walked toward the playground. He seemed loose as a goose, spry even, half his 126 years. He looked up to heaven and then began pushing an empty swing. I didn't know whether to laugh or cry.

* * *

As families arrived at the park, it seemed as though Len had vanished into thin air. I had committed to hawking him from our porch until the time came for my wife to shanghai me into joining the masses. But I was distracted from this surveillance by my civic duty to wave with great familiarity to people I had never met. I found myself cheerfully shouting, "So good seeing you again" to absolute strangers who seemed genuinely delighted to reciprocate the pretense.

Eventually Len reappeared, standing on a picnic table and scanning the forming crowd. He spied a group of wild preteens, swooped down from his perch, and plucked a girl about 11 years of age from her fluffle. He spoke to her for no more than 20 seconds. Eyes down, nose twitching, she nodded in ascent. He handed her a wad of cash from the ornate sporran he was wearing around his waist. She hustled to the gazebo, knelt near its steps, reached underneath, and unearthed a red wagon, which was empty apart from three bungee cords and a can of WD-40. She then got in line for the food truck, third customer from the front, and gave Len a thumbs-up. I could've spent all day trying to figure out what that exquisite absurdity was all about.

But those plans were hijacked by my better half. She came out of the house and brushed past me on her way over to the park. She was carrying a giant plate of homemade Rice Krispie Treats. The neighborhood moms had decided to potluck a big kids' meal instead of forcing pulled pork and collard greens on their adolescents. I understood from her silence that she expected me to join her. She'd been giving me the silent treatment lately. I had probably forgotten to unload the dishwasher or something. She'd also been making herself scarce and taking the kids to their friends' houses a lot, and I was still sleeping in the guest room. Like I told you, Covid had done a number on her. She was struggling.

Our little girl was already over at the playground with a couple of friends. Our son refused to come out of his room. He'd been moping around for a while now—sleeping a lot and always saying he wanted to be alone. I guess he was at that age. Or maybe the pandemic had affected him. Impossible to know.

As we made our way down the driveway, my wife and I saw that Nelly was standing in front of the bus stop sign. Her eyes were bloodshot and swollen. She looked at my wife and said meekly, "It's all my fault." She turned back to the sign, grabbed its post tight, and dropped her head in anguish.

You know, part of the American story is that people uproot themselves, explore, and resettle to find new opportunities. Greener pastures. Westward expansion. The frontier. That's a story of hope. But I think many of those people leave to get away from something. They're fleeing. It's a push from, not a pull toward. To stay where they are is to relive it all. They can't tolerate reminders of missed opportunities and mistakes. They know past and place are linked. The sufferers must move away from the latter if they are to move beyond the former. Unless.

Unless the sufferer needs to relive it all, has reason to be reminded. See, guilt and sorrow and shame serve a purpose. They don't let us forget about our unfinished business. They highlight and underline the items on the to-do list that haven't been crossed out. Some things can't just be left behind. At least not yet. They have to be confronted and overcome. Or expiated and forgiven. What I mean is: Nelly was still figuratively and literally clasping that bus stop sign because she couldn't yet allow herself to let go...

Chapter 48: Relapse

From: Dr. Jennifer Davis, MERCY STATE, COMS
Date: January 13, 2021 at 11:41 AM
Subject: surgery
To: Elizabeth Jones, Esq. OFFICE OF THE PUBLIC DEFENDER

Didn't want to text. I know you're interviewing your client again today. But the county executive was rushed into emergency surgery. Increased brain swelling again. They think it's related to the latest infection. Will let you know.

Praying,

Jen

Chapter 49: Confrontations

...I noticed Jimmy Callahan standing by the memorial garden alone and without tools. Maybe admiring his completed work. Maybe paying his respects. I walked over to introduce myself. He had a firm handshake and a still air about him. I asked why he took on this project.

"Many moons ago," he said, "my dad built all this latticework. And honestly, I'd forgotten all about it—hadn't seen it for 30 years. But this summer I got a late-night call from an anonymous British guy saying it had been torn up by vandals. I immediately knew I had to be the one to fix it."

I told him how much everyone appreciated his work and what a spectacular job he'd done. I said I'd ask the HOA to reimburse him for his time and supplies. He declined. "Wouldn't take a dime for it. It was an honor. Was my duty."

I joked that he must be busy if he feels obligated to patch up all his dad's decades-old projects. He smiled. "Nah, just this one. Pop served in the Pacific. Both of my older brothers died in Vietnam. Both. In the span of three weeks. This memorial was very special to Pop. Didn't take a dime for his work on it. In fact, he always said his two most memorable jobs were in this neighborhood." Jimmy laughed to himself. After a moment, I did too.

Len, I realized, was behind both: A garden dedicated to those who died in combat and a shed modeled on the Alamo. What was the link? Was grieving Len, who lost two parents, a wife, and a child all too early, memorializing lives cut short? Or was embittered Len, furious at his surroundings, celebrating those who go to war? I felt myself entering McGregor's house of mirrors in a wormhole. My mind wandered. I found myself thinking of goodly Mr. Callahan.

Eventually I said something about my dad and not seeing him since that Sunday night in my pajamas and the hard blue suitcase. Jimmy's handkerchief was monogrammed. He told me that his dad shut down emotionally after his brothers died. "Mom, before she passed, begged me to keep loving Pop no matter what. Work with him as much as possible—prepare to take over the family business." Jimmy sighed. "But I was a young punk. Didn't want any part of it. I resented everyone. Everything. Got into some real bad habits. Those habits were hard to break."

I said some other things for a little while. He said quietly, "Son, let me tell you what I needed to do. And, God knows, it took a whole lot of years to figure this out and a whole lot of help." He lifted his eyebrows and nodded his head. "I had to shake hands with all the ghosts around me. I lost my big brothers in that idiotic war. They were my idols. I screamed into my pillow for months. Pop just tried to get through each day. He wasn't perfect, but, bless his soul, he kept it together. Mom—imagine losing two boys in the prime of their lives. She did her best to keep our family intact. My parents were in agony. Stripped bare."

He stopped and looked at me for a while. Then he put his right hand on my left elbow. "Son, I couldn't get past all that without going through it first. Not something you can run away from. It'll always chase and catch you."

I think I told him how fortunate he was and about the two musketeers and some of my recent research and writing. Talking about what he'd gone through really affected him because he looked heartbroken and said abruptly that he needed to go. He gave me another firm handshake and said, "Son, take care of yourself."

But that seemed to make him disappointed in himself. I guess he needed more from me because he turned it into a hug. Then he said, "I self-medicated to get away from it. Built high walls. Some people lock themselves away or latch onto convenient explanations. Some disappear into vices. But that's just running away from the things that matter. Tears things apart. The only glue we got are the people around us."

* * *

I wandered around the park for a while. I had to cope with a few ignorant people giving me a little trouble about my writing. They could get overheated and threatening. Nothing too bad. But you never know. So I went home to get it, for self-protection, just in case. That's why I bought it. Best to have it just in case. I had the permits. Self-protection is legal. You know that.

At some point, I was standing by the road, not far from the food truck and gazebo, when Len himself tapped me on the shoulder. He was now wearing a long buckskin coat and a Davy Crockett coonskin cap. I guess this was the Alamo. Warrior Len's last stand. We just looked at each other. Neither willing to budge.

I squared my shoulders to him. "You're up to something, McGregor. Whatever it is, don't."

"I burrowed down for an eon. Now it's time, chief," he replied.

"People are here to relax and have fun. Let them be."

"This is sacred ground, Ace. They desecrated it. All of them. All of you. Reap *whacha* sow."

"Revenge won't make it better," I tried.

"They made a mockery of Community Day. To these wretched heathens, each and every day is Me Day. Well, it's time to pay the *pipah*."

"So they look out for themselves and don't think of others enough. That's humanity since the beginning of time. You're not going to change that."

"No, young man. Takin' *caih* of *yoahself* is one thing. *Shatterin'* lives is *anotha*. These people booze and lie. They gamble and cheat. Use *powa* for selfish gain. Ignore the needs of *othas*. They have *affaihs*, cook up shady deals and schemes. Only time they're not *caihless* is when they're being cruel. People can't live *togetha* that way."

"People have the right to do as they choose, McGregor."

"Ha! That's right, *ma* boy! What did ol' Johnny Milton say? 'Free they were made, and free they must remain.' But 'free to act' doesn't mean 'exempt from payback'." Len smiled at me, checking for understanding. "Ya *folla*, boy? The choice is free of charge; but the consequences of their choices have a big price tag."

"Price tag? Who are you to decide what's due? Are you setting the price, McGregor? Are you the collection agency?"

"I made a fine *livin'*, boy, and then I *retiahd*. Was ready to be put out to *passcha*. But the universe called me back to duty. It seems that justice had gone on an extended vacation. Date of return: unknown. All these people decided it was *betta* to reign in hell than serve in heaven. So I had to *staht* a second *careeah*. My new trade was comeuppance. And thanks to all the lowlifes, business has been *boomin'*."

"McGregor, you've got no right under heaven to punish a single soul."

"My lands, boy! I wouldn't dream of *punishin'* a one of '*em*!" Len pretended to be offended. Then he narrowed his eyes, "They'll take care of that themselves."

I didn't know what he meant. Only that he had declared himself judge, jury, and executioner. "You're just a self-righteous vigilante," I seethed.

"Sure, lad, I might quietly assist the cause of justice for time to time. But I wouldn't lay a hand on anyone. *Fah* be it from me to presume so much!" Again, he was playing the innocent. "But then again," he added with a doe-eyed shrug, "no one needs to force two rabid, *stahvin'* hyenas to fight. You just gotta give 'em the opportunity."

I was disgusted. "I want no part of your justice."

Len gave the heartiest laugh. "Of course you don't, boy! You're on trial, too!"

"What did you say to me?

"*Ya* heard me, kid. *Ya* no *betta* than the rest. Same *kinda* lowlife. Just a *bigga* disappointment."

I got a surge of adrenaline. I wanted to strangle him.

"Boy, we needed *moah* from you. This neighborhood, this county—we needed *ya* to be the glue. To help bind us up. But all your *writin'* and *protestin'* just helped rip us *apaht*."

I scoffed. "I did what I thought was right."

"Listen, kid. Every living *creacha* on this earth thinks it knows what's right. Anyone—hell, any animal—can pursue right and cause a *wah*. But *bein'* right and *doin'* right are two different things. Sometimes avoidin' the *wah* and takin' *caih* of your neighbor is *doin'* right."

"That's coward talk," I told him.

"Child, it takes a man's courage to deescalate the feud. No bravery left to be had when all the Hatfields and McCoys and all the Montagues and Capulets are dead."

McGregor was weak, I thought. With strength and pride, I replied, "*Fiat justitia ruat caelum*: Let justice be done though the heavens fall."

The look he gave me, I don't know if it was resignation or resolve. He said simply, "And justice you shall have."

Chapter 50: Superiors

More families mustered. Kids, sprung free from months of home-based juvenile detention and online learning, instinctively began romping about. Adults smiled and fist-bumped neighbors they hadn't seen in ages. Some gravitated to the now-snaking food-truck line. Others simply meandered about the fields, content to stretch their legs in a public place. Pith was on a bear-hug bender. Parents chatted amiably with one eye apiece on their contribution to the neighborhood's brood darting about the playground. Adults offhandedly careful-Michaeled and say-you're-sorry-Oliviaed while commiserating about overtaxed home Wi-Fi and old devices.

All the while, McGregor ninjaed about the multitudes. He sidled up to one neighbor after another. I probably saw 15 such dangerous liaisons. The encounters were nearly identical. He would whisper something, point to this or that, and then move to his next unwitting accomplice. He was either maneuvering chess pieces on a six-dimensional board or trying to make a game of solitaire look like Mouse Trap. The longest interaction was about 30 seconds, and that was only because Barb fainted when Len accosted her near the basketball courts. When she came to, he said but one sentence. She made it to her feet and—successfully inveigled to do God-knows-what—nodded vigorously and ran to her house.

Len's scheming lasted only 15 minutes. Then he flipped a switch from devious to avuncular and simply walked about the park enjoying the scenery and greeting neighbors. "How ya' doin'? Looking *fahwahd* to *bahbecue*?" "Good to see ya'. That meat smells divine, doesn't it?" Everyone was so happy. Excited. Content.

You know, I bet that's how it felt at Len's compound just before the mimes showed up.

* * *

"An assemblage of half-wits and slack-jaws." While I had been monitoring Len's engagement with the growing crowd, Masonry had lumbered up, surveyed the gathering, and delivered some of his signature good cheer. Again, after precisely articulating "slack-jaws," he stared at me for several moments longer than I thought appropriate. Eventually he looked away in exasperation. "They should all be sterilized," he concluded. I always struggle to find the right response when someone advocates neutering his neighbors.

My silence didn't matter. Masonry forgot all about me as he made eye contact with Len from afar. Both went still. This must've been their first encounter since the unlikely, torrid wooing of Gazebo Night. Masonry was the first to act. He batted his eyelashes. Len was unmoved. Masonry then smiled tenderly. Len did not reciprocate. Then in a final act of desperattention, Masonry formed a heart shape with his hands and held it over his chest. Len looked straight through him, unblinkingly, turned, and strutted away, thus coldly concluding the oddest of all May-December romances. Crestfallen, Masonry slunk away, presumably to join a convent. I wondered if his relocation costs could be covered by the proceeds of the

Nuptial Equity Fund.

Kim arrived at about the same time. She was wearing a sea-green velour tracksuit and had a silver alligator-skin clutch pressed between her left elbow and ribcage. With her right hand, she held the leashes of seven animals. Her squad comprised some kind of spaniel wearing a kerchief, an especially twitchy marmoset that obviously had plans, a baby yak who liked grass far more than running kids, and four weasels that resented having to sport matching hats.

It was entirely beyond me what convinced Kim to return to the scene of her crime, all these years later, again with four-legged weapons. But wild horses—which, thankfully, she seemed not to possess—could not have carried me away from whatever was about to happen.

I wanted to get close to her, but I was cut off by an agog gaggle of college girls all with puffy sleeves and water bottles. They were squealing various versions of, "That's Ms. Kim! I'm so dead! That's her! That's her."

Evidently, Kim's celebrity now extended beyond dramatists, pet lovers, and second-wave feminists into the broader collegiate community.

The gutsiest of the admiring lot eagerly stepped forward. She was impossibly slender, 19ish, and had wavy auburn hair parted perfectly down the middle with silver face-framing highlights. She had baby blue eyes and gold eyeshadow. She dug into her bag, thrust a Sharpie and notepad at Kim, and excitedly asked for an autograph, declaring. "Ms. Kim. I. Completely. Stan. You."

Kim didn't blink. Pith came up alongside of me and motioned to she-Stan with his chin. "That young lady's pants are so tight I can see her religion." Pith always had a sense for the divine.

"We're all KimGals," the young lady vocal-fried. "Ohmygod, did you even know that 'KimGals' was a thing? So cringe!"—theatrical eyeroll—"I'm the thirstiest! You just need to know right now that your performances at the county commission *were goals*." She sang "were goals" like she was auditioning for a musical.

Kim, seasoned at holding court in front of the younger generation, calmly said "Bet" and resumed her imperial silence.

She-Stan continued her praise. "I totally memorized your 11th appearance. I'm still shook. You tore off the bishop's miter and cassock and yelled, 'This is a smear-campaign crucifixion! The animal kingdom shall resurrect my reputation!' Ohmygod, Ms. Kim. You are the blueprint!"

This adulation perfectly corresponded with Kim's self-regard. She lifted her chin and extended a limp-wrist hand to be kissed. "What is your name, my child?" Kim asked the breeze.

"Ali, with an 'i'," the intrepid one replied, dazed with delight.

As Kim wrote a little note on the pad, Ali continued, "My older sister...she's over there..." Ali pointed to a late-20s woman texting robotically and studiously ignoring the live humans surrounding her. She had bleached white hair parted near her left ear and swept across her forehead.

Ali shouted, "Caitlan! Look who I'm with! I know! *I know*! Can you even?!" Turning back to Kim she continued, "My sister showed me your videos when I was in middle school, and we knew they were *everything*. That's Caitlan over there. She thinks she's adulting. By the way, she's not fat, she's pregnant."

I noticed that a group of young men, mostly in tank tops and brown sandals, were respectfully admiring the KimGals as they engaged in conversation with this local shero. Not wanting to interrupt that discussion, these budding gentlemen simply stared at the young women and quietly talked among themselves, occasionally nodding at one lady or another, likely praising her poise. It was wonderful to see in these young men the fruits of our social progress.

As Kim finished jotting down a purposely impersonal inscription, she coolly replied, "In the future, you needn't treat me like divinity, Ali-With-An-I. Believe it or not, I'm flesh and blood, similar in some ways to you and the others. I'm merely a conduit between Yahweh and the animal kingdom."

Ali got the shivers. Kim almost smiled at her youthful admirer as she returned the marker and notepad. "But next time," Kim whispered with more than a little annoyance, "do remember to avert your eyes when you approach me."

Meanwhile, Blowtorch Len walked up and down the food-truck line, asking if everyone was excited about the barbecue. All said yes; many thanked him for making the arrangements. A few even applauded. With a glassy stare, he repeated, "It's my *plezsha*."

I was so caught up in this majestic moment that I didn't take much notice of Matty who was silently attending his mother. He hadn't tried to chat up any of the KimGals or join the spectating boys. He'd kept his distance. But when Ali's audience with Kim had concluded, Matty pushed past me without even looking my way. In the moment, I interpreted the adrenaline rush I felt as a response to his shove. I should've keyed in to his black oversized jacket and his dead-eyed expression.

* * *

I noticed a statuesque woman in a perfectly tailored red pantsuit standing by the gazebo trying to get everyone's attention. I recognized her as the overdressed and tone-deaf karaoke singer at the Dew Drop. She removed one of her red-bottomed peep-toe pumps and tapped a gazebo post as though she could control the companionship- and meat-hungry crowd with Robert's Rules and a Louboutin.

She had the polished, confident cluelessness of an Ivy-League grad working in management consulting. "Pardon me, friends, pardon me, I'm the esteemed director of county health, medical, safety, and justice issues, Scarlett Bennet, master of public health," she began with a television anchor's smile. "I'd like to call this meeting to order."

Everyone looked around in confusion, not knowing much about this person with the expansive title and power to chair a meeting they didn't know they were attending. Blowtorch Len sat on a bench, smiling broadly.

"I appreciate your inviting me here today to receive the proceeds of your community's collection for my—I mean, *the county's*—Nuptial Equity Fund." She beamed with pride and a great sense of deserving. As I scanned the crowd's reaction, I surmised that she had misread the room.

"Wait up! Wait up!" shouted Pith, leaving my side and loping toward the gazebo while affectedly adjusting his privy parts. "Let me get at that box real quick. Imma give it a blessing—the holiest of waters, I'll tell you what." The crowd guffawed, admiring Pith's piety.

Bennet beamed obliviously, replying, "Thank you, thank you, common citizen! This county's select enjoy your primitive religious traditions!" I so appreciate when our betters are gracious toward us.

She continued, "During these challenging times, it is essential to prioritize fairness and justice, mkay? With so many of you enjoying so much unearned advantage..."

"I haven't been allowed to work in six months," someone said flatly.

"...it is only right that you pay your fair share as our county government looks out for all of its citizens—and when we say 'all,' we mean *all*!" She raised both hands, which had been recently manicured.

"My business closed because of your rules," someone else replied with a louder voice.

She continued unfazed. "I had dinner at *Maison du Pouvoir* last night with the county executive and some of our supporters—you really must try their foie gras, I don't know how they force-feed those geese, *but God I'm glad they do, mkay*—and we committed over our digestifs to a new initiative called 'A Fearsome Equity of Authority.' We are sure that once you understand it and come to see how it has forced you to change for the better, you'll thank us..."

"I haven't seen my grand-daughter in person yet, and she was born seven months ago," someone said selfishly, evidently not understanding "equity" as it was discussed by Director Bennet and her colleagues at the county's most expensive restaurant.

"So let me close by recognizing your contributions—not by *thanking* you but *recognizing* your fealty to our leadership. The dollars that you might have spent on your own selfish concerns but have instead properly returned to the common good..."

"I'm not sure we can pay our mortgage this month," shouted someone.

"...have not only stemmed the tide of this terrible illness. They have also ensured wedding justice! I will now accept your gratitude! Who's first?"

* * *

I felt another tap on my shoulder. I turned to see, of all people, the bartender from the Dew Drop Inn. He was with the red-headed waitress. He grabbed my elbow and gently turned me toward the road. He pointed to the old, faded bus-stop sign and murmured, "This is where it all started for me... *aherrm*...and ended."

From the middle of the four-square court, Len was staring at us with a Cheshire-Cat grin.

Ronnie and I stood silently. I imagined him standing in that exact spot exactly 33 years earlier: An earnest 17-year-old with a blonde leonine mullet flowing behind him and promise stretching out ahead. Hopping off that early-morning bus, dreaming of recovering Egyptian artifacts and impressing his crush, Kim. All that talent and potential.

Eventually, he said, "I can't chronicle today. I wish I could. But I can't."

I kept looking forward and mouthed, "I know."

"Once bitten, twice shy. I can't do it. I paid the price for reporting on Len McGregor in 1987."

I mouthed, "I know."

Some time passed.

"When the truth is crazy, people don't know what to make of the truly crazy around them," he whispered, rationally explaining the irrational.

I didn't have anything to say.

"Maybe the craziness is true. Or maybe it's just crazy. How can you tell?"

"I know," I think I said.

Chapter 51: Justice

And then everything started happening so fast. I focused on the question-and-answer session with the county's health/medical-safety/justice/lack-of-self-awareness officer. There was a great deal of, shall we say, feedback on her policies.

She did, however, handle the back-and-forth in a stately fashion. At one point, she climbed to the top step of the gazebo and, using a long stick like a scepter, pointed at various vocal members of the crowd. As she trained her gaze on one constituent after another, she announced, "I hereby cancel you in the spirit of justice!" and "By the power vested in me, I suppress your opposition to me in the name of democracy!" and "I rescind your right to dissent in the name of free speech!"

A few neighbors had been so moved by her presentation that they joined her at the gazebo, yelling at the indignant crowd, "In the name of inclusion, I expel you from this park" and "Diversity of opinion does not give you the right to disagree!"

My attention was redirected toward some bickering by the baseball backstop. An older woman in a Patagonia fleece was lecturing three or four couples about the socialist implications of the Little Free Library outside the gazebo. I knew our unfriendly neighborhood prig from church. She liked to get to

Mass early to keep a list of who was running late. Her parish-flex superpower was saying the prayers faster than everyone else. Once I saw her walk up to the balcony and start playing the organ just to drown out a kids' choir that wasn't up to snuff. A real peach, this lady.

Anyway, she had somehow identified those responsible for building, placing, and stocking the threatening box of mostly sci-fi paperbacks and how-to gardening guides. She could not comprehend their refusal to admit that this sinister box was obviously home to listening devices monitored by God-knows-who. She conceded that she was glad it had six copies of *The REAL Story of the U.S.S. Joe McCarthy* (authored by her husband, treasurer of the Elks). But she needed these neighborhood villains to acknowledge that their civic project was an affront to capitalism, government-funded libraries, and the Lamb of God.

Most of the accused stood in silence, either shocked by her lunacy or hoping she'd eventually tucker herself out. But several refused to go down without a fight. It was hard to make out all the venomous dialogue, but I distinctly heard "Jesus invented libraries!", "You're on the payroll of Big Tech and the Illuminati!", and "What about my mother's Nicholas Sparks collection?!?" Though unquestionably the instigator, Helen the Scold was wounded to the core by others' unwillingness to accept her browbeating. She tore off her wig, threw it to the ground, and then sought refuge behind a man in dungarees and a "Korean War Veteran" hat.

Her protector began screaming "Communists!" while swinging his cane with such agility that one really did have to wonder if he carried the cane for steadying or martial purposes. Pith walked over to the wig lying in the sand and said, "That there is a high-quality wefted cap, bet your life. Shame to see it disrespected."

Nelly was overwhelmed by the arguments rippling across the

park. She let go of the bus-stop sign and screamed, "This is all my fault! I have to make amends!" As she sprinted away from the park, I think I heard her yelling, "Why didn't my dog warn me about the dangers of the Little Free Library!"

* * *

Two uniformed Grangerford police officers and a plain-clothes detective arrived on the scene. I assumed they were there to make us all disperse. But they had other business. They scanned the crowd and lit upon three teenaged boys sitting on a picnic table. These were the hooligans who'd set off fireworks on the gazebo's roof ages back. I guess the fuzz finally decided to haul them in. I'd been the one who called the cops on them that night, so, in the spirit of full-circle-ness and neighborly nosiness, I followed the law-enforcement team so I could witness the confrontation.

"Young men, let me cut to the chase," said the detective as the two uniformed officers got their handcuffs warmed up. "We'd like to have a conversation about a property crime that took place here at the park."

All three teens snickered. "Officers, thank you for protecting our community, but we have no idea what you're talking about," said the smart-aleck-est of the crew, knowing the incident took place late at night and that there are no security cameras around the gazebo. "I was studying at home the night the gazebo's shingles caught fire. My two associates were volunteering at the food bank. We're not the culprits, but we'll be sure to alert you should we learn of anything that might be of service to your investigation." The two associates tried to stifle their laughter.

The detective smiled appreciatively. "I'm grateful for your willingness to help with that case. You and your associates are fine citizens." The detective's eyes then narrowed. "But we're here to talk about the vandalism of the memorial garden."

Suddenly, something in the air, perhaps barbecue smoke, caused the teen's smart-aleck-ness to dissipate.

"An anonymous source," continued the detective, "had installed security cameras around the garden years ago and sent us some revealing footage. Three young men who were evidently perfectly impersonating the three of you—from your hats all the way down to your shoes—seemed to have done the deed. Once we get down to the station, maybe you can give us some insight into who those mimics might be."

Who knew the miraculous powers of barbecue smoke! In an instant, it had somehow transferred smart-aleck-ness from the teen to a law-enforcement official.

The uniformed officers handcuffed the three, and the detective patiently twirled a fourth set of handcuffs around his fingers. The county's leader of health and haughtiness, Scarlett Bennet, MPH, who was still engaged in "community discourse" near the gazebo, saw this event unfolding and ran to the scene. Her sense of justice would not tolerate the detention of three victims of impersonation.

She yelled, "What is the meaning of this! Unhand these young men immediately, *mkay*! Do you have any idea who I am?" The detective apparently didn't know that she in charge of nuptial equity funds, medicine, safety, justice, and interfering with arrests.

The detective continued to spin the handcuffs. "Director Bennet, so nice to see you. I do, indeed, know who you are. What a pleasure." He smiled sincerely. "We were just taking in these young men for suspicion of destroying the memorial garden."

"If you know who I am, you must know I emailed the entire county declaring that it would be immoral to investigate that incident since those responsible were pursuing justice. They were rebelling against the toxic culture that erects monuments to our wars of genocide and empire."

"Oops," said the detective. "That email must've gone to my spam folder." Now the barbecue smoke was *increasing* the ambient smart-aleck-ness! Wonders never cease.

Director Bennet couldn't handle another second of this man's impudence. "Let these young men go immediately, and I will consider not reporting you to your supervisor. This is a question of justice, and I have expertise."

The detective stopped spinning the handcuffs. "Speaking of questions, I have a few for you." Bennet then auditioned for county director of taking umbrage. The detective continued, "Did you know someone found the hatchet, spray-paint can, and sledgehammer used in the incident?"

"Of course I didn't know that, *mkay*. If I had, I would've fined such a person for violating my directive against investigating this heroic act!"

"So you didn't know that the someone who sent us the video of the vandals' act also used the serial numbers on those items to figure out where they were purchased?" Over by the tetherball pole, Len was the picture of schadenfreude.

"I...ummmm...didn't know...uhhh, *mkay*...that is... ummmm... quite something..." stammered Bennet. Evidently, barbecue smoke also dissipates haughtiness.

"And did you know that your credit card was used to purchase those items at the hardware store?"

"...uhhh...*mkay*...justice...*mkay*...truth...ummmm..."

"And it was also used at the sporting goods store to purchase three hats and three pairs of shoes that look exactly like those worn by the three freedom fighters we're taking to the station! What a mystery! How in the world did your credit card purchase items used in vandalism *and* items to reward the vandals?"

"...uhhh...equity...mkay...umm..."

"Even stranger—get this!—we have video of you talking to these three young men outside of *Maison du Pouvoir* the night of the crime. Too many coincidences to count!"

Scarlett Bennet was then promoted to county director of the right to remain silent.

* * *

I then noticed six or seven scowling people storming toward Kim who was tending her flock of park-unfriendly animals. The leader, a man of about 45, who always listens to big band music on his porch while the sun sets, got within an inch of Kim and extended a rigid, trembling finger toward the tip of her nose. He growled, "I can't believe you would show your face at *this park...*" and then he redirected his finger toward her leashed companions "*...with them.*"

One of his compatriots yelled, "My aunt got bit by one of your otters! She needed stitches!" Another screamed, "My dad got scratched up by your emu!"

The initial group was quickly joined by others. The grievances against Kim's homebrew animal-daycare operation were many and durable. The swarm was looking for a fight to the finish, but if the uproar bothered Kim, she didn't let on. As she once told me in a very different setting—though also with smoked meats and differences of opinion—she was accustomed to impudence, and it only made her stronger.

Deep down, I thought she was getting condign punishment, and it seemed cathartic to the rabble, so I was inclined to let it play. But I just can't stand mob justice. And, dang it, our purpose today was to eat barbecue, not strengthen the case for the beatification of our resident martyr. After allowing a reasonable amount of persecution, I decided to mediate.

But before I could act, a phalanx of KimGals rushed to the scene to protect their icon, screaming and threatening the posse like only privileged college students in a safe environment can. They didn't care about Kim's bite victims or her neglect of Matty; they didn't care that Kim's selfishness had contributed to the end of the bus stop or that her performances in front of the commissioners had unnerved the entire county. What mattered was that Kim was famous and that she was the leader of their tribe. To Kim they would forever be loyal, right or wrong.

A young lady with long, straight black hair, Doc Martens, and high-waisted jean shorts took the lead. She faced off with Kim's prosecutors, put her fingers in her ears, bent at the waist so her torso was parallel to the ground, and shouted on repeat, "You are problematic! I feel unsafe! I will find a knife and cut you without remorse!" Fierce finger snaps from her clan.

An old man with a volunteer fire company t-shirt tucked into pleated slacks got in Rapunzel's face and shouted, "My generation believes in manners and chivalry! I will shiv you with relish!" Chants of "USA! USA! USA!" from his clan.

The warring sides volleyed curses and insults with an intensity fueled by months of benevolent forced exile.

Bartender Ronnie, who'd been staring at the bus-stop sign, eventually noticed the near-brawl taking place behind him. He had no emotional investment in that drama. But then it registered with him that Kim was at its center. He was cast back to 1987 and devolved into simp mode. He took two quick steps in her direction like he could chase down all those lost opportunities—Rice Krispie Treats never made, Fuddruckers meals never shared, romantic lines practiced in front of a mirror but never delivered.

But just as quickly, he stopped and watched those taillights disappear. He turned back to the bus-stop sign where the red-headed waitress was standing alone and trying not to cry.

Ronnie cocked his head and looked at her without saying a word. Between them passed actual memories of an unplanned pregnancy embraced, diapers changed, cancer-scares weathered, and bills that couldn't be paid. She couldn't stop the tears now. He walked back to her, hugged her with all his might, and then gave her a long, closed-eyed kiss on the cheek. He whispered something in her ear, both laugh-cried, and then they hugged again for a very long time...

Chapter 52: Reveal

From: Dr. Jennifer Davis, MERCY STATE, COMS
Date: January 13, 2021 at 2:03 PM
Subject: county exec
To: Elizabeth Jones, Esq. OFFICE OF THE PUBLIC DEFENDER

The county executive just passed away. There was a hemorrhage during surgery.

Call when your interview is over.

—J

Chapter 53: Ego

...It was a bit after noon now, and the food truck's growing line had yet to make any forward progress. The natives were growing restless. A nervous young man with low-top Chucks and a vintage Genesis concert t-shirt stepped out of the truck. He girded himself and announced in a quavering voice, "Errr... we're going to be delayed in...ummm...serving you?" His up-speak spoke volumes. "See...errr...none of the food's ready yet? Someone...uh...someone unplugged all our equipment from the generator?"

There were groans from the hoard. An exasperated voice called out, "This is how they get ya!" Another, slightly angrier, yelled, "Classic bait-and-switch! Watch them try to upsell us now." Someone else chimed in, "I've been saying this for years. Give them an inch, they take a mile."

"Just like the Compound Incident," I thought to myself, "a delaying tactic to bring the crowd to a boil."

And, indeed, anger coursed through the crowd. Faces scrunched and fists clenched. They came here for a purpose, and they wanted satisfaction. But Len, of all people, was the calming force. He walked up and down the line, saying cheerfully, "I'm sure it'll be ready soon" and "Good things come to those who wait" and "That *bahbecue* will really hit the spot!"

They were pacified. A few happily replied with, "Almost time to meat-gorge!" and "Get those ribs in my belly!" Everyone thanked McGregor for making the day possible.

Over by the tennis court, a fresh melee had broken out. A group of residents, long fuming about the neighborhood's new swing set, slides, and monkey bars finally erupted. They had *somehow* identified the community members who had served on the Playground Improvement Workgroup of the Procurement Committee. They cornered the spendthrifts responsible for this gaudy purchase and demanded apologies and refunds.

Workgroup members—who were prevented by the terms of the donation from revealing that a local philanthropist had provided the funds—ferociously defended their purchase by citing survey results of residents' opinions, the dilapidated condition of the old equipment, and Science.

I couldn't make out all the arguments because the opponents' grand inquisitor was praying loudly, alternating between seeking wisdom and appealing to God to afflict her profligate neighbors with boils and sores. I heard one of her compatriots claim children who spend time on metal seesaws get scurvy. A double-chinned guy wearing suspenders over a white undershirt pointed to a bunch of seven-year-olds and said it was "high time these loafers graduate out of schoolyard grab-ass and into welding."

One of the accused, a 30-something guy wearing the jersey of his favorite basketball player, screamed back, "You don't want to tangle with me! I'm a lethal soldier! I play first-person shooter video games in my mom's basement."

* * *

Just as things seemed to be spiraling out of control, a semblance of order was restored. The food truck window slid open, and the young man announced that they were ready to serve.

The crowd cheered. Spirits were lifted.

The first customer stepped up, and the young woman inside asked happily, "What can we get you, ma'am?"

This first patron had had an hour and a half to consider her order, and she knew there was a long, hungry line behind her, so she replied, "Everything looks so good, I'm just not sure what to get. Let me see here. Maybe I'll get the pulled pork sandwich, but, you know, I should stay away from the carbs, that's what my girls have been telling me, I need to watch my blood sugar, I'm pre-diabetic you know, so I have to be careful..."

The young server, experienced with such situations, smiled and nodded to acknowledge the impossible choice and then repeated "What can we get you, ma'am?"

The customer continued vocalizing her deliberations. "...I should be good now so I can be bad tonight. Maybe I'll get some soft serve later, that's a good idea, that's exactly what I'll do. So maybe the smoked chicken platter. Oh, I don't know, I just can't decide, how's your brisket, is your brisket good?"

The crowd groaned. Someone shouted, "Sweet baby Jesus! Let's get this train moving." Someone else yelled, "Just order some ribs and move your keister to the side. Daylight is burning!" Another voice, "I've been saying this for years. This is how they get ya. This is why the Chinese are eating our lunch. Mark my words—our taxes are going up."

* * *

Barb returned from her house with a cardboard box. She stood next to the food truck and shouted, "Hello, neighbors. Hello. Hmmp! Pardon me. Everyone! Hello? Ahem! One-two-three, all eyes on me." The crowd's general reaction was the inability to even with this. But Barb was on a mission. She would force them to even, come hell or high water.

"*A-a-ahem*! I must have your attention for an important announcement. Neighbors, I need you to raise your left hand if you can hear me. Show me you've turned on your listening ears by lifting your left hand. Good. Alright now, everyone please clap twice if you are tracking me..."

In the good-news department, I can report that, at that moment, the dilatory lady who was first in line to order was no longer the most unpopular person at the park.

A little bit of handclapping and a whole bunch of razzing convinced Barb that she had enough of the crowd's attention. "I couldn't help but notice that many of you are failing to keep six feet of distance from one another. And most of you are not wearing mandatory face coverings. So..."

Barb reached into her box and pulled out a medical-grade mask and held it aloft. "Ta-da! I need each of you to wear one. I'll charge only $3 apiece. I plan to be reimbursed by the HOA for my hard costs and time, but I don't expect payment for my leadership..." Barb paused. I imagined her thinking to herself, "Hold for applause." But based on the crowd's reaction, Godot would've arrived before cheering. So she concluded, "Exhibiting leadership in crisis situations is the cross you bear when you earn a master's degree in public health."

This was the moment Barb had been waiting for. She longed to be appreciated. By her family for all she tried to do for them. By her friends for her loyalty. By her community for her commitment to others' health. She hadn't been given anything in life. But she worked, and she gave. She just wanted a little recognition and gratitude.

"You can wipe my ass with that mask, Barb!" someone yelled. Peals of laughter across the crowd.

Another voice: "Masks were invented by the Kremlin! Stalin's estate gets all the proceeds. I read that on Patriot America Truth News. It's on the internet. Do your own research, sheeple!"

Another voice: "We fought the Cold War so we wouldn't need to put up with little libraries and those hammer-and-sickle masks!"

A group of older men started singing, "The Battle Hymn of the Republic."

A portion of the crowd, however, was having none of this ignorant, fascist mask-opposition. Their brand of patriotism was of the loving, paternalistic variety. Each took a handful of masks and distributed them across the park with heavy sighs of disappointment in their neighbors. They also dispensed unrelated, unsolicited advice (on diets, parenting, lawn care, etc.) as an extra indication of their altruism. Needless to say, the park's ambient rancor intensified.

I saw Blowtorch Len, pleased as punch, standing by an oak tree. He was using a stick as a baton and conducting an imaginary orchestra.

* * *

Finally, the woman at the front of the line got her order (jambalaya and cornbread) and the second guest stepped up. He had the superb posture, slight frame, and neatly trimmed mustache of a corporate compliance officer. He seemed the type of a man who, on Saturday mornings, would don a casual blazer and quirky socks, drive an hour to a café, and read poetry, tracking each line with the eraser end of a pencil, imagining that someone was admiring him from afar.

He adjusted his shell-rimmed glasses, shot his predecessor in line a withering look, and snootily announced, "I know *my* order. *I* came prepared." A few snickers from the crowd. "I shall have the catfish fingers and the sweet potato fries."

Several people cheered his swift, certain order. "Now we're cooking with gas!" someone shouted.

But the food-truck attendant replied sheepishly, "Sir, I'm so sorry. Those items are on the menu of our brick-and-mortar location, not this food truck. We have limited options here. We don't have either of those."

Flustered and humiliated—the public esteem he had generated by needlessly abusing his neighbor was forever erased—he looked at the giant menu hanging on the gazebo. "Well, uhhh, everything looks so good, ummmm, I'm just not sure what to get. Let me see here. How's your brisket, is your brisket good?"

Someone yelled, "Sweet Jesus, will I die before I get some ribs!"

At that moment, a white Buick Lucerne with a flashing yellow light attached to the dashboard screeched to a halt in front of the park. An ample man of about 75 with immaculately coifed white hair slowly opened the door and winched himself out of his seat. He strode imposingly toward the gazebo. His monogramed canvas belt was doing Atlas-like work under his globular midriff. He smelled like Aqua Velva and sulfur. This was the kind of man who would laugh at his own joke and then repeat it since those not laughing certainly hadn't heard it.

Several people grimaced. Poser Poet, hemming and hawing at the front of the food-truck line, caught a glimpse of the new arrival (who was now ostentatiously clearing his throat in front of the giant menu) and suddenly looked like he expected to be clapped in irons. He grabbed a handful of Saltines from the food-truck counter, handed the attendant a $10 bill, and got out of Dodge. The young woman with Len's wagon sprayed each axle generously with the WD-40 and then stepped to the front of the line...

Chapter 54: Response

From: Dr. Jennifer Davis, MERCY STATE, COMS
Date: January 13, 2021 at 2:52 PM
Subject: governor statement
To: Elizabeth Jones, Esq. OFFICE OF THE PUBLIC DEFENDER

The governor is going to make a public statement at 3:00. It has something to do with your client and the death of the county executive.

If you take a break and see this, please give me a call.

Chapter 55: Simmer

...From the steps of the gazebo, King Rotundity announced, "As you know, I'm Butch Tweed, the 13-time president of your homeowner's association. I speak with the voice of the people."

"The 'people' are half-wits and slack-jaws!" shouted Masonry who was especially frisky on the rebound.

Someone else piped up: "You still skimming money from the HOA budget? Or you get that fancy-ass Buick just by making fishy deals on road projects?" Lots of knowing nods from the crowd.

"Those were trumped up charges! That story was a hoax!" yelled someone with a t-shirt reading "Re-elect Tweed: The Generally Trustworthy Leader We Deserve."

Someone else yelled, "I graduated near the top half of my class when I got my master's degree in public health!"

Over at the food truck, both employees were now loading stacks and stacks and stacks of Styrofoam containers bursting with smoked meats into the young woman's wagon.

Butch Tweed continued. "I'm not here to collect the community dues so many of you owe. I'll deal with you miscreants later." Poser Poet was now hiding under a picnic table and praying a rosary. Tweed went on. "I've got a strong jaw..." – more like beefy jowls, I thought— "...and the HOA did not approve this event." Half of the crowd rolled their eyes, the other half gulped.

He continued, "I'm a generous man, and I was willing to look the other way. But you have abused my charity. According to Community Crisis Ordinance 94a-3b passed to combat the pandemic, this gathering exceeds the maximum allowable occupancy of an outdoor space." Gasps and unintelligible shouts from the crowd.

"As such," Tweed intoned, "clothed in immense power, I am hereby shutting it down. All of you must hit the bricks. This is the U. S. of A. This is still the land of liberty and righteous emergency authority."

The crowd was now at its boiling point. The handful of fights about inconsequential neighborhood matters served as just the opening act. Pompadour Butch's edict was the headliner.

In the face of the public fury, Tweed was placid. He allowed the hysterics to continue for about 10 seconds before raising both arms high in the air and making a "simmer down" motion, repeatedly pushing everyone's feelings to the earth.

"Hear me, people," counseled Tweed. "Despite your moral failings and illicit conduct, I am a reasonable man and a great leader. Thanks to my grace, you are eligible for redemption. Even you, Jasper Alden-Branigan. I see you hiding under that table with your Saltines, and I'll get those dues from you or I'll repo your recycling bins and rescind the variance for your solar panels."

Jasper was now trying to use a plastic spork to give himself hand stigmata. Such was his mortification and need for a literary element to his public suffering.

The crowd hushed. "Because of my mercy," Butch continued

slowly, building the suspense so all those within earshot could linger on his benevolence, "all of you have the opportunity to stay here and eat your barbecue."

The crowd collectively breathed a sigh of relief.

"But to ensure this event does not spread the virus and to guarantee we are taking care of our community, I simply need," Tweed said, raising a clipboard over his head, "each of you to sign this contract promising you will vote for me as a write-in candidate for the state legislature on Tuesday."

The crowd fulminated. This was too much. Tweed was using the pandemic, using the needs of his neighbors, using the draw and the legacy of this gathering for his own selfish purposes. Another violation of community. Another brick in the wall. Like killing a community bus stop to help your struggling business. Like stopping friends from sitting together in a community gazebo unless they pay for your daughter's wedding. Like defacing a community garden to advance your political beliefs. Like fighting over a community playground or a community book box, like shutting down schools, churches, and the Ohunka walking loop.

The screaming and fighting across the park had reached a fever pitch. Physical altercations seemed imminent. Pith was right. This was Reckoning Day.

And then the county executive showed up.

Chapter 56: Attention

It was unbelievable. He decided our Community Day was his campaign event. He shows up just to get votes. Brought his wife and an assistant so he looks like a big deal, like a big, important man. And can you believe this, he brought a security guy? A mountain with sunglasses and a sidearm. Like the county executive is so important. Like he deserves special protection. Big man. Big, fancy, important man. What a weakling. Needs hired muscle. So he starts walking around the park with that shiny, fake smile and greasy hair. Shaking hands. Patting backs. "Get over here, you!" "There he is!" "Here comes trouble!" Laughing it up. Playing the perfect family man. His happy wife and her make-up and hair. Everyone loves him. Everyone loves the big man. I'm a man, too. I'm important. People finally started paying attention to me again. My research and writing were special. Everyone was talking about it. I'm the one who won the Rhodes Scholarship. I was the youngest cabinet secretary in the state's history. I'm the one who everyone said would be a county executive or governor someday. Go ahead, big, important man. Walk around the park. Get all those hugs...

Chapter 57: Remit

From: Dr. Jennifer Davis, MERCY STATE, COMS
Date: January 13, 2021 at 3:17 PM
Subject: gov speech
To: Elizabeth Jones, Esq. OFFICE OF THE PUBLIC DEFENDER

Liz—governor's speech about to happen. All the outlets are streaming it.

She's coming into the room with her staff now.

She's starting. Looks somber.

-says she's known your client for 20 years

-gave him his first government job, he was her aide when she was state senate prez

-jokes she was the matchmaker between your client and his future wife

-your client could be at ease with royalty but stuttered when that cute girl was around

-says she cried at their wedding and was honored to be godmother to their son

-your client was most talented 25yo she'd met, smart, persistent, funny, cares about less fortunate

-creative mind, saw and solved problems faster than anyone

-when she became state attorney general in 2009, she told the governor to hire him immediately

-that governor made him one of youngest cabinet secretaries in state history

-he also became one of the most successful, led groundbreaking transportation project

-says she almost chose him as her running mate as lieutenant gov when she ran for governor in 2012

-was loss for state but good for him and family when he left public life to focus on his health

-she considers his wife one of her dearest friends, loves their kids like her own

-says events of Community Day were devastating, tragic, such loss of life, senseless

Gov pausing to compose herself.

She's taking a break.

Her staff are moving things around behind her podium.

Hold on. Staff bringing some people into the room.

Will write again when she continues.

Chapter 58: Triumph

...But the adulation didn't last long. The crowd suddenly had a more pressing concern than feeding the ego of a crooked, two-bit politician: The attendants of the food truck had gingerly stepped forward. The park went memorial-garden silent. The two were holding hands and trembling. They debated in hushed tones and intense gestures who would speak. The young lady summoned the courage.

I suddenly realized the girl with Len's wagon was sprinting down the road away from the park. Her red cart was stacked four feet high with dozens and dozens of Styrofoam containers overflowing with barbecue and held in place by the bungee cords. She ran as if chased by fiends. Truly a dramatic smoked-meats exit for the ages—made Kim's summer-sausage exit look amateurish. The young lady never looked back.

The food-truck worker gathered herself up, lifted her chin, pulled back her shoulders, and headed into the storm.

"I'm sorry, everyone," she announced. "But we're all sold out of meat. We have no more ribs, chicken, brisket, pulled pork, turkey, sausage..." she trailed off, looking cold and confused. She snapped out of it and tried to make lemonade. She announced with synthetic pep, "But we'd be more than happy to serve you beans, okra, or our signature bok-choy coleslaw."

The park detonated. Bedlam. After months of quarantine, the people had been promised barbecue and friendship, but they'd be given side orders and warfare. They couldn't take it. Hell was emptied, and all the devils were here.

As per usual, Pith had nailed it. Len had gathered people up, but it wasn't for a sense of community.

* * *

Punches were thrown, aimlessly but ardently. Primal screams. The Little Free Library was toppled, and several people kicked its remains. A handful of neighbors were trying to dismantle the swing set with their bare hands. I saw that poor Pith was inside the gazebo, pounding a picnic table and repeating the Serenity Prayer. Occasionally, he'd un-serenely scream something about slow-cooked beef.

His four-year old daughter was now riding a vintage Harley chopper and doing doughnuts in the middle of the baseball diamond.

The Communist-baiting old man banged the side of the food truck with his cane, yelling, "China put you up to this? You on the take? A vinegar-based side-dish is no substitute for pork and liberty!"

Barb was lying on her back, eyes closed, under an oak tree mumbling, "I floss. I always wash my hands for at least 30 seconds. I have a master's degree in public health."

Moving far faster than I thought possible, Masonry was bringing wheelbarrow after wheelbarrow of bricks from his backyard. He started erecting a structure around the food truck. In a loud, monotone voice, he vowed, "I was guaranteed barbecue. I was defrauded. I will entomb you in a sarcophagus of your lies. As the King Tut of mendacity, you will spend eternity in a crypt of coleslaw."

The labor leader I'd met at the Dew Drop, Mikey P (née Mikey PJ), hustled over to the two frightened food-truck operators. I could hear him trying to unionize them, telling them that his organization would always look after the interests of the young and vulnerable. I saw that Ronnie too was watching this exchange, but his eyes were wider and his jaw tighter than mine.

Thirty-three years ago, when Ronnie needed a grown-up to settle him down, Mikey PJ had egged him on. Mikey PJ prioritized his own political agenda above a high schooler's best interest. So when Mikey P ended his sales pitch to the food-truck workers with, "I always know what's best for the youth of our community," Ronnie coolly walked over and walloped him in the nose. "No justice, no peace," I thought.

To that point in my life, I'd never been witness to a wilder scene. Screaming and fighting across the entire park. Battles old and new, trivial and grave. Doing unto others however they saw fit. Selfishness unleashed. Community lost.

And there, standing on top of the gazebo's roof, was Blowtorch Len McGregor, triumphant. His face and palms were raised to the sky. His revenge was complete. He was at peace.

And then the most unbelievable thing happened...

Chapter 59: Recourse

From: Dr. Jennifer Davis, MERCY STATE, COMS
Date: January 13, 2021 at 3:37 PM
Subject: more speech
To: Elizabeth Jones, Esq. OFFICE OF THE PUBLIC DEFENDER

Governor about to speak again.

A bunch of people entered the room. Maybe 15 of them, they're now standing behind the governor.

-gov says Nov 1 was among darkest days in state's history

-6 lives lost, many families shattered, community will never be the same

-says only one person is to blame, no amount of sympathy or loyalty should distract us from that

-we can't blame society or circumstances, responsibility belongs to individual who made the choice

-we should be willing to forgive but justice does not forget

-everyone affected by that day deserves closure

the people standing behind the gov are holding photos. I can't tell what of.

a few are crying, governor stops speaking, she is hugging them and talking to them softly

looks like gov is taking another break

governor's staff bringing a desk and chair into the room

staff arranging papers on the desk

not sure what's happening, will write again when it restarts

Chapter 60: Rapture

...In an instant, all the commotion across the park stopped. Everyone and everything went still. All heads turned to the road. A 1982 Winnebago motorhome pulled up to what had once been the bus stop. A posterboard was affixed to the passenger side window. It read "Blue Line."

Nelly cheerfully hopped out of the driver's seat. Her inventory and the bus stop were no longer at war.

Using two large binder clips, she attached a single piece of loose-leaf paper to the faded bus-stop sign. On the page was written "The Francisca and Molly McGregor Memorial Bus Terminal." From her bag she pulled a mallet and two small, white wooden crosses that I recognized from the makeshift memorial on the side of Central Union Highway near the Ohunka walking loop. She gently pounded them into the ground next to the bus-stop sign's post. At long last, the community had properly commemorated this spot.

Then with sublime confidence, Nelly announced, "All aboard, friends and neighbors. I've got a schedule to keep."

The crowd was transfixed. Several people sleepwalked toward her. Each handed her something—a few dollars, a dandelion, a mint from the bottom of a purse—as payment and then stepped inside. A line formed, and no one spoke. The new Wayfarers.

By the flagpole, Barb and Kim hugged silently after a 17-year estrangement. Barb looked like the weight of the world had been lifted from her broad shoulders. Over and over, Kim repeated, "I'm sorry." In her own way, Barb cared about this community. She was like connective tissue, binding neighbors together. I hoped her hug would reassemble Kim, reintegrating the personalities divided by crises years ago.

Blowtorch Len climbed down from his perch and reached into a bush near the gazebo's entrance, pulling out an envelope. He walked up to Pith, whispered in his ear, and handed him the gift. Pith tried to decline. McGregor smiled and cradled the back of Pith's head in the most loving, paternal way. He then leaned forward so they could touch foreheads. Len whispered to Pith one last time and then made his way to Nelly. I saw Pith open the envelope and then fall to his knees laughing and crying in turns.

Nelly met Len at the bollards that separated the bus stop from the park. She immediately wrapped him in a Pith-hug. When she finally let go, she grasped both of his hands, holding them between their waists as though they were to be wed, and looked at him unflinchingly.

"Please, please forgive me, Mr. McGregor. You deserved so much better."

He was shaken by Nelly's apology. He sucked his lips over his teeth. His chin quivered. He tried to look away.

But Nelly, reconciled and reborn in a public confessional, moved her torso to maintain eye contact. "I did you wrong. We all did you wrong. When I was scheming, I didn't even think to think of you. You didn't cross my mind. I was so selfish. So sinful. I'm sorry."

Len regripped Nelly's hands and mustered a quiet, "I know, my *deah*, I know."

She wasn't finished. "You cared about this place. You cared about these people. But I was too wrapped up in myself to appreciate any of that. And I hurt you along the way. But I want to live in the kind of community that you were trying to build. I'm going to do better. I promise. Someday, I'll deserve this place."

Len smiled with closed lips and filled eyes. He placed his right hand on her left cheek and said gently, "You already do, my *deah*."

Nelly wiped the corners of her eyes, exhaled, and hugged Len again. She said, "We'll save you a seat" and then walked back to the Winnebago.

McGregor came up alongside me as the silent line for the makeshift bus grew. They didn't know where they were going. Or exactly why. But for Wayfarers, it's the traveling that matters. For a minute Len and I were statues. I noticed rust on the front fender of the Winnebago.

Finally, Len whispered, "Is this the Ark?"

"No," I replied.

"The *Raptcha*?"

"Nope."

"Exodus?" he asked.

"No, damnit, Len, no. It's just a used recreational vehicle with expired plates," I explained.

He started to laugh, quietly at first and then with full voice. "Is there a difference?" he asked.

I had nothing to offer. Still smiling, he began to weep. He tussled my hair and looked at the Winnebago. Through a window we could see Nelly waving him to come aboard. He thought for a moment and said, "Think I'll take a ride. We won't be gone for long. A dove with an olive branch will be pecking at the windshield before we know it."

I had no idea what he meant. But as Pith once told me, it's best to let such statements pass by. Contemplating Lenny's adages is like analyzing a house of mirrors. Or deciphering an oracle. Or decoding the "Waste Land." I just smiled at him.

But he wasn't finished with me. He grabbed me by my shoulders and looked at me earnestly. His face changed. It was serious but not stern. This wasn't a lecture. It was counsel. He rubbed his hands up and down on my upper arms twice and said, "Everyone deserves a shot at redemption. Even you, *Mista* Secretary. You didn't care enough about this community. But you still could."

I wasn't sure what to say. He looked different. Before this moment, he always seemed to be calculating. Always sizing people up. But now, I think I saw hope in him.

"Son, it's too late *fah* me. I'm too old and too broken. This Moses won't see that Promised Land. But you can. *Ya* just need to be Joshua. *Gatha* them up. Finish the *joyney*."

I told him I didn't have it in me. That I was empty.

Len wouldn't accept that. "Son, this world gave you *nuthin'*. Then it tried its damndest to keep you down. After you earned *somethin'*, it took all that away. That's how this world treats people like us. People like Nelly. But the world can't take all of it. You have *moah* deep inside you, my boy. Find it. But don't use it *fa yaself*. Give it to this *neighbahood*."

No matter how angry Len had been at this community, no matter how long he'd been bitter, he couldn't help himself. He wanted to protect this place and these people. He'd failed to bring them together. But maybe someone else could. Maybe that's why he'd had eyes for me from the start. He was passing the torch. The flame was faint but still burning.

He cut to the front of the Winnebago's line and boarded. No one seemed to mind. Nelly grinned and let go, her redemption complete. She announced to those still waiting, "Sorry, folks. We're all filled up now. Another will be along in time."

No one complained. She told her passengers to buckle up, honked the horn twice, and pulled away.

* * *

I was amazed at how quickly the park emptied. Without any direction, the entire crowd dispersed, intuiting that their work there was done. They'd played their part in Len's—hopefully—last production. The curtain had been lowered.

A handful of neighbors had joined Nelly and Len on the Winnebago, heading who knows where. The two young food-truck workers pulled up stakes, steered around Masonry's abandoned project, and drove away. Just about everyone else departed without a word. Pith sauntered away, head down, charting the terrain with the envelope in his back pocket, leaving his daughter to play with her friends. Barb and Kim, holding hands, walked back to Kim's house, taking the path through the woods to the east. Even Butch Tweed retired silently. Just like at Len's compound 33 years earlier, after madness and brawls, people decamped to return to their normal lives.

Within a few minutes the park was all but empty. The county executive and his crew still stood in disbelief by their car on the southwest end of the park. He thought he'd come to a peaceful community event to rustle up votes but found it ignited and then vacated. Matty sat alone, trembling, on a bench.

Barb's husband—of course—stayed to pick up trash. The only sounds came from the gaggle of kids still running about the playground, blessedly oblivious to their adults' drama.

It was strangely peaceful. Maybe we'd all be OK, I thought. Maybe the occasional outburst is healthy. A pressure valve. The only way to cope with the insanity. If everyone forgives and forgets, we can move on, return to normal. No lasting damage; no harm, no foul. I smiled.

I watched Barb's husband walk about the park, cleaning up the mess left by others. A good man. I always admired him. There should be more of him. I stood up. It was time for me to join him. The two musketeers on a clean-up adventure. I relaxed. We'd all be OK. Everyone was healed, I thought.

But then Matty began to bleat and jogged toward the middle of the park.

Chapter 61: No More

Matty's voice grew louder and his pace faster as he made his way to where the sundial once stood. Soon he was at full caterwaul and throttle. Pain-rage uncorked.

When he reached the dying grass between the flagpole and memorial garden, he jolted to a stop. He moved both hands toward his chest. I remembered that picture of him on Kim's wall, that angelic little boy with a gun bigger than he was. My body wanted to pace and drink little cups of water.

He tore open his oversized jacket. I hoped dozens of aluminum pinwheels would fall out. But it was a semiautomatic rifle. Oily, metallic, ruby-black testosterone. He moaned and thrust it into the air. He began by shooting straight at the sky, like he was trying to wound God.

I don't know what he had had planned. Who or what he had targeted in his addled mind. But his eyes eventually, maybe accidentally, fell on the memorial garden.

He went still. Seemed to stiffen. Then he yelled. Roared. Until he ran out of breath. Then again. Ferocious. Heaving and listing in exertion. Throat- and gut-ripping fury.

It had never occurred to me before that moment how the sight alone of the garden must have torn him to shreds.

Matty—a fatherless son—galled by a project crafted and repaired by loving Father and loving Son Callahan.

Matty, the abandoned child, mocked by a public shrine to those who left too soon.

Still wailing, he marched toward the garden, firing at its trellis, benches, fountain, and plaque, trying to raze or erase it all.

Part of me thinks, or wants to think, it could've ended right there, with Matty exorcising his demons alone against the wood and stone. But Barb's husband, that holy man, couldn't bear the thought of Matty's solitary suffering. And, of course, he showed no fear. He dropped the garbage bag he'd been holding, a bag full of items carelessly discarded by others, and jogged toward Matty. I could hear him pleading "please," "son," "honey," and "dear child," along the way. Matty heard his voice and stopped shooting. He turned and saw Barb's husband, the gentle, generous man who would never, ever get out of his life.

At first, Matty tried to steel himself, tried to harden his own heart, probably thinking it manly to continue his wrath. But it couldn't hold. This godly man softened the young man's heart. Barb's husband dropped to his knees in front of Matty. Maybe begging him to stop. Maybe praying for the aid of the heavenly Father since Matty's earthly father had failed. I heard him say to Matty, "Son, you deserved better."

Those were the last words Barb's husband ever spoke. His position of supplication happened to be directly between Matty and the incoming gunfire of the county executive's security guard. Barb's husband was martyred on the ground between the barren flagpole and lifeless garden.

* * *

It's hard for me to remember the exact order of events. Two shots hit Barb's husband in the back. I saw the puffs of blood. He slumped forward, his head coming to its final rest near Matty's feet. At first, I didn't understand what had happened. It didn't compute. I got my wits back as Matty shouted and tried to revive the corpse. I realized that I'd heard a couple of shots before the fateful two, but my brain hadn't processed them. They'd just been ambient noise. I suspect that the security detail began shooting as Matty was annihilating the garden. He probably didn't see Barb's husband running toward Matty until it was too late.

I suddenly realized there was yelling. I don't know why, but instead of turning to my right to see where the shots came from, I turned backward and to my left toward the yelling. The kids from the playground—scared by the sound of gunfire, I guess—were screaming and crying. They were all sprinting in my direction. Again I got confused. It was too much all at once. Then I saw that they were all running to hide under the gazebo. A nine- or ten-year old had found an opening on the east side and had crawled underneath. The others were following him.

It didn't take long for Matty to understand that Barb's husband was gone. It also didn't take him long to understand who'd killed him. He lifted his eyes to the street and saw the security guard standing, gun in hand, in front of the county executive, the county executive's wife, and the young aide. A minute earlier, Matty had shot furiously, indiscriminately into the sky to injure God for the loss of his first father. Now he shot furiously, indiscriminately into the county executive's team for the loss of his second.

The security guard's gun was down, by his side, when he fell. As far as I could tell, he'd stopped shooting once he accidentally struck Barb's husband; I don't know if he was in shock, guilt-ridden, or out of rounds. I was near the south end of the gazebo, so I had to have been in Matty's peripheral vision as he marched westward from the garden to the street, shooting incessantly along the way. But he must've had tunnel vision because he gave no indication of noticing me. He kept shooting and shooting. Spraying all four of them as they stood there. Then spraying their limp bodies, too. Spraying the car, the ground, the street.

Somehow, the county executive had survived the initial burst. He made it to his knees and started crawling toward the gazebo. He was wheezing. I could hear gurgling blood. Matty just stood there, laughing with his head cocked. He let the county executive crawl five or ten yards before he started taunting the wounded man and shooting at his feet, telling him he needed to speed up if he was going to get away. Matty must've hit him again, I don't know how many times, because the county executive collapsed and didn't get up. I'm sure Matty would've finished him had his magazine not gone empty. He calmly dropped the weapon and removed his coat and backpack. He knelt down and emptied its content. Magazines, clips, zip ties, two handguns. He loaded up.

The county executive was playing possum. His insides were torn up, but somehow none of the shots had been fatal. They say the others died on the spot. Matty either assumed he was dead or got distracted by the commotion. The last of the playground kids were still screaming and scurrying under the gazebo. Matty raised his eyes in that direction. I was in his line of sight.

I wasn't going to stand on the lake's shore and wait for someone else to come to the rescue. I looked straight at him. I didn't flinch. It felt good. I said, "No more," without the muffle of the crook of my elbow.

Matty squinted like I didn't compute. I said it again, louder. "No more." It felt like testosterone.

This time Matty grunted and smiled. He raised his gun with

just his right arm but only level to his hip. Like I wasn't even worth the effort of a proper aim. He shot a few times. I heard one or two hit the gazebo. I don't know if he hit me before or after I dove to the ground. I just know that I felt it enter my upper leg and that I heard my femur break.

The pain didn't come immediately. First, I saw blood spreading across the thigh of my cringe khaki shorts. I was on my back. I reached down to my leg with both hands as though I could fuse it back together. Matty was 10 or 15 yards away. He could've ended me. But he must've decided I wasn't worth the time he'd need to finish the job. He had a different priority. He went after the kids.

He unloaded on the sky again; warning shots, I suppose, across God's bow. He was still on the south end of the park, and he saw that the kids were disappearing as they ran from the playground toward the gazebo. He took a few steps to his right and said, "Where are you going?" When he made it around to the east side of the gazebo, Matty saw that the kids had found an opening and were hiding underneath. He laughed and walked toward their bunker.

"Come out, come out, wherever you are," he shouted in a singsong voice. He then started shooting the ground around the edges of the gazebo. "Don't you want to play?" More shots into the earth. "Marco! Marco! You're supposed to say 'Polo'." More shots. "Come out, come out, wherever you are!"

Seventeen years earlier, innocent little Matty tried to save the lives of scared animals cowering under the gazebo. Now, broken Matty was about to take the lives of scared children cowering in the very same place. He stood by the opening and announced, "You have three seconds to come out, or else you're in big trouble. You better not wet yourselves, you little babies."

No noise. No movement.

"Come out now!" he yelled at the top of his lungs. Shots into the earth. Kids screaming in terror.

"One!" he screamed. Shots into the sky. Crying.

His magazine was empty again. He threw the rifle to the ground and grabbed for the two automatic handguns in the holsters attached to his chest rig.

"Two!"

And that's when I shot Matty twice in his back.

* * *

I'd brought the gun to the park to protect myself. In case anyone tried to start trouble with me about my writing and stuff. It was in my waistband, along my back. It was covered by my shirt and pullover, so no one would've known. Matty had left me on the southwest side of the gazebo. Just left me laying there. Forgot all about me. When I realized what was about to happen, I crawled eastward along the south end of the gazebo. I got behind him. He had no idea I was there. I was able to hoist myself up and stand by leaning my left shoulder against the gazebo. I was afraid to put any weight on my right leg. I thought it would snap in two. Everything was easy from there. It was a pleasure, actually.

Those kids deserved better. They just needed someone to take care of them. Me. It felt so good. Pop, pop. Matty dropped to the ground and rolled over on his back. Two blood stains were forming on his shirt. He brought both hands to his chest as though covering them would make them disappear. He was gasping for air. Snarling. I made my way to him. I picked up his discarded rifle and threw it as far away from him as I could. I didn't want to take any chances.

Using the gazebo as support, I stood above him for a little while, watching. Thinking. Then thinking some more. Len was right: I wasn't empty. I had more inside. I'd give it to the neighborhood. It was time. One more to the forehead finished Matty. And that was that.

The God's-honest truth is I can't remember ever feeling better than I did in that moment. No pain in my leg. No worries. Nothing. Total peace. My only regret is that I didn't get to kill him twice.

RECORDING CONCLUDED: 4:42pm
Wednesday, January 13, 2021
Uncorrected transcript
Interview by Elizabeth Jones

Chapter 62: Resurrect

From: Dr. Jennifer Davis, MERCY STATE, COMS
Date: January 13, 2021 at 4:46 PM
Subject: miracle
To: Elizabeth Jones, Esq. OFFICE OF THE PUBLIC DEFENDER

Governor speaking again

-says that even in this tragedy we can see the loving hand of God

-we must remember that while 6 lives were lost that day, all 9 children were saved

my god, the people standing behind the gov are parents of the children, they're holding photos of their kids

-gov says that your client was an angel sent from heaven that day

-he was the hero these kids, their parents, and that community needed

-with today's passing of the county exec, your client is only surviving adult eyewitness

-says while we can't rely solely on your client's account, it does largely match the evidence

-your client used excessive force but he stopped a murderer who would've murdered more

-justice demands that your client be recognized as hero not villain

MY GOD she's pardoning your client for any crimes he may have committed related to Nov 1

-says she is proud this pardon will be her last major act before her term ends in two days

-parents behind gov are hugging and cheering

-says your client was unquestionably unwell in weeks, maybe months before Nov 1

-many of his actions were unacceptable—letters, articles, behavior at work, threats, a protest

-says your client is an imperfect hero but says emphasis needs to be on "hero" not "imperfect"

-his case should now be understood as medical, not criminal

-he'll remain hospitalized until doctors and judge decide he's not a danger to himself or others

-she's aware that pre-conviction pardons are rare and that trials are usually key to justice

-but says she can't be sure he'd receive justice in future

-a future prosecutor could pursue your client for political reasons

-conspiracy theories already swirling about that day, could make a fair trial impossible

she's asking her staff if documents are ready, they say yes

she's now seated at the desk

-says last few years have been unreal, mentions fake news, unprecedented isolation, fear, restrictions

-it's been difficult for everyone, says it's time for communities to come together

-says we begin today by ending this tragic chapter and starting to write a new one

Oh god, I just noticed your client's wife is one of the parents standing behind the gov

She's also holding a picture

My lord I didn't know your client's daughter was one of the kids under gazebo

-governor says she's signing two orders, first is full pardon for your client

She signs document and hands it to staffer behind her, says "that's that"

-governor says second is executive order declaring Jan 13 to be state's annual Community Day

She signs document, says we are responsible for one another, says take care of your neighbors

Governor stands, applause

Gov hugs your client's wife. Both crying.

Gov pulls back, put her hands on sides of wife's head, says, "I know, I know"

Wife hugs a very tall man. He also has a picture. Shaved head.

Gov hugs him too, says "you're a good man"

Everyone smiling and crying I can't believe this. Miraculous. Call when you can.

Chapter 63: Authored

START: 12:33pm
Thursday, January 14, 2021
C.C.S.H.

Pith came to visit this morning. He said yesterday was eventful. Said he went to a boring press conference but then had all sorts of fine ladies huggin' up on him. I laughed and told him we gotta take the good with the bad.

He said he didn't mind the hugging so much, but the governor got a little fresh. Grabbed his backside. I told him that was unlikely. He said that he was planning to tell the media about how she got handsy and that a respectable gentleman like himself couldn't tolerate that. But then the governor said she'd take care of some of his parking tickets and overdue books, so he was willing to call it even. When I laughed and told him that none of that was true, he said that *some* of it was true, and the rest *should've* been true. Good dude, that Pith. He also got weepy about my saving his daughter. I told him it was nothing. Just Golden Rulin'.

Speaking of which, I asked him about the envelope from Len. He tried to brush it off. But I pressed. Told him he at least owed me that story, you know, *for saving the life of his daughter*. He laughed and reluctantly agreed. But then he announced that now we're even. My boy Pith sure knows how to bargain.

After Len got down off the gazebo roof, he whispered to Pith that he would've given up on community if it hadn't been for Pith. Len said that Pith treated people right and had kept the neighborhood together for a generation. Pith tried to tell him that he was just trying to take care of his people. Len replied, "That's why I'm giving you these—I know you'll do right." The envelope had two documents. A copy of Len's will: He's leaving everything to Pith. And a signed blank check—a signed blank check!-- with "down payment" written in the memo line.

I was flabbergasted. I asked Pith if that story was true. He said, "It shouldn't be, bro, but it is."

You know, when the governor hired me more than 20 years ago, back when she was in the state legislature, I came clean to her. Before she gave me the job, I said she deserved to know about my past. I told her about my mom, the foster homes, my sister's troubles with the law, what happened in England, the hospitalization. I told her she had a bright political future and might not want to get mixed up with a problem like me. She said that we can't turn back the clock. What's passed is past. She said she didn't care who I was but who I had become. And *would* become. She said hiring me wasn't charity; it was an investment, and from that day on I had to give dividends to others. God, I'd forgotten about that conversation until just now. I guess for too long I just reinvested in myself.

Anyway, Pith got me up to speed on developments in the community. Masonry and his family moved out. That didn't surprise me. Now's a time for recommitting to neighbors, and that's not exactly Masonry's style. I guess I used to have sympathy for that guy because I understood him. It's easier to keep people at a distance when you look down on them. Contempt as self-protection. But that's no way to live. No more insularity.

We need to stay glued to our neighbors. So good riddance to Masonry. Or as Pith put it, "Sometimes parting is all sweet and no sorrow."

Butch Tweed finally stepped down. Nelly's now president of the HOA. I knew great things were in her future. I knew it. But Pith said it's already gone to her head. Claims she's making Pith exotic-dance at HOA meetings until his back neighborhood dues are paid off. I told him I found it hard to fault her: He does have rhythm and curves that won't quit. He conceded the point. But I also told him that if he wants to sue Nelly or the HOA, I know a lawyer who's about to have some free time on her hands. I can put you two in touch. Good dude, that Pith.

Oh, and he actually said that he's thinking about running for the county commission. He wants to fix the Ohunka. Do something about the dams and irrigation projects and fertilizer. Also said that maybe they could figure out a ride-sharing operation at the old bus stop. Some way for folks to get together. Good dude, that Pith.

Barb and Kim aren't doing so hot. You can imagine. But Pith says folks are rallying around them. There was even a fundraiser down at the Dew Drop. And the HOA is planning to name the memorial garden after Barb's husband in a ceremony this spring. After Jimmy Callahan fixes it up again. He's doing a full remodel. The HOA already put up a special plaque honoring that day's victims. Supposedly they're considering some kind of recognition for me, like putting my name somewhere on the gazebo, once things are cleared up. I asked Pith if "once things are cleared up" is a euphemism for "if I'm ever declared not crazy and released from captivity." He laughed and said, "To-*may*-to, to-*mah*-to, bro." Good dude.

But I doubt that will ever happen. I'm resigned to my fate. Since they arrested me that night, everyone's just wanted a simple answer for what happened on Community Day. Heck, when you and I first met, I could tell that's what you wanted, too. You thought I was taking you on a wild goose chase with this story. From the start, I tried telling them that Community Day wasn't a happening, it wasn't an event. It was a culmination. An outcome decades in the making.

But when you connect dots, people say you're a conspiracy theorist. I tried to tell them it's not crazy to believe things are related; it's crazy to believe they're *not*. As though you could have understood Matty without understanding his deadbeat dad and Kim and Barb's husband and the foxes and a cappella! Like you could understand the park without understanding Len and the bus stop and Nelly and the animal camp. Like you could understand our county without understanding the Dew Drop and the consignment shops and the Ohunka. Like you could even begin to understand Community Day without understanding our neighborhood and the pandemic! This isn't some fevered hodgepodge. It's a story begging to be authored.

People need stories. Stories help us understand and get through. And, sure, they might not always be perfectly accurate. But they have truth. There's a difference. We don't need to fact-check *Romeo and Juliet* or "love thy neighbor" or Thanksgiving, you know? When you lose a job, do you want an economics lecture? When a friend dies of cancer, do you want a biology textbook?

I couldn't explain our county and its history using spreadsheets. What charts and graphs would do justice to these people and what they've gone through? And what about the pandemic? God almighty. People were terrified. Out of work. Sick. Confused. Furious. Depressed. Lonely. What cold, hard facts and figures could possibly explain that? None. None. Only art could explain it. Sure, I took some liberties with a few names and events. Of course, I added a little spackling to fill in some holes. Forget "literally." I gave you something you could take seriously. I gave you truth. *Truth.*

But none of that matters. I understand. They can keep me here under these fluorescent lights on their ludicrous pretext. I'm content. I brought justice to the neighborhood, and I did justice to the community's story.

The doctors said I could probably get out of this wheelchair in about a week. The bone is healing up. They want to start me on physical therapy. The nurse said I'll probably have a permanent limp because of the muscle damage. But it'll be something I die with, not die from. I'll be like Len, limping around into my golden years. Remember how my wife once said that unless I was careful, Len McGregor would be my future? Prescient, huh?

It's amazing: Ever since Community Day, I've had no desire to go on my long, solitary evening walks. That need completely disappeared. I do wonder if Len still walks the neighborhood. I wonder if Nelly still scurries away from her demons with her dog. I wonder if the Wayfarers have come to a rest.

Maybe Community Day cured all of the palliative peripatetics. No more ache to walk off.

Maybe the era of being alone alone is over.

Well, it was nice getting to know you.

Don't be a stranger.

FINAL RECORDING CONCLUDED: 12:54pm
Thursday, January 14, 2021
Uncorrected transcript
Interview by Elizabeth Jones

The End

Epilogue

From: Harvey Bennet, OFFICE OF STATE ATTORNEY
Date: January 14, 2021 at 1:06 PM
Subject: Charges
To: Elizabeth Jones, Esq. OFFICE OF THE PUBLIC DEFENDER

Ms. Jones:

This morning, we received the paperwork from the Office of the Governor regarding your client's executive pardon. The Attorney General has certified the order. Once your client accepts the pardon, my office will permanently suspend the manslaughter, reckless endangerment, threatening a public official, conspiracy, and weapons charges pending against him. The governor's decision is final and non-reviewable. We will consider the matter closed.

The timing of the governor's announcement was fortunate for your client. I'm obliged to tell you that, last night, we received new evidence in his case. An anonymous source provided to our office the previously missing video of Nov. 1 ("Community Day") taken by the security cameras around the memorial garden. Though the cameras cover only a portion of the park and, therefore, the recording only captured a portion of the events, this new evidence contradicts key parts of your client's story, including why his fingerprints were on the rifle and why the county executive suffered several gunshots from short range..

But with this case now concluded, we will likely never know if your client's account is the truth, on the outskirts, or in a different world altogether.

www.ingramcontent.com/pod-product-compliance
Lightning Source LLC
LaVergne TN
LVHW100511110826
845146LV00002B/600

* 9 7 9 8 9 9 5 7 7 1 8 1 4 *